A man, a hemp rope ~~...~~ *though in a gentle breeze, his neck* ~~...~~ *angle. Heavyset, about fifty-five or sixty, and naked. Rolls of fat hung like melted wax around his middle.*

"That's him!"

"Who?" Richard asked.

"The man I saw hanging."

"You said it was a deer."

"No, I just saw him!"

"You had a vision, just now?"

I nodded. A vision. Much more acceptable than the product of a tumor, a nightmare or a hallucination.

Brenda settled the paper on the table between us and started reading aloud. "Local businessman Matthew J. Sumner was found hanged in his garage. The grisly scene…"

My fears about tumors instantly vanished. The murder had taken place somewhere else. In a field. I knew it had. I'd seen it. The deer must have represented this guy. My mind had given me a vision of something I could understand.

★

MURDER
ON THE
MIND

L. L. Bartlett

W☉RLDWIDE®

TORONTO • NEW YORK • LONDON
AMSTERDAM • PARIS • SYDNEY • HAMBURG
STOCKHOLM • ATHENS • TOKYO • MILAN
MADRID • WARSAW • BUDAPEST • AUCKLAND

If you purchased this book without a cover you should be aware that this book is stolen property. It was reported as "unsold and destroyed" to the publisher, and neither the author nor the publisher has received any payment for this "stripped book."

For Ian,
the best brother in the world.

MURDER ON THE MIND

A Worldwide Mystery/October 2007

First published by Five Star Publishing.

ISBN-13: 978-0-373-26615-9
ISBN-10:   0-373-26615-4

Copyright © 2005 by L. L. Bartlett.
All rights reserved. No part of this book may be reproduced or transmitted in any form or by any means, electronic or mechanical, including photocopying, recording or by any information storage and retrieval system, without permission in writing from the publisher. For information, contact: Five Star Publishing, 295 Kennedy Memorial Drive, Waterville, Maine 04901 U.S.A.

This is a work of fiction. Names, characters, places and incidents are either the product of the author's imagination or are used fictitiously, and any resemblance to actual persons, living or dead, business establishments, events or locales is entirely coincidental.

® and TM are trademarks of Harlequin Enterprises Limited. Trademarks indicated with ® are registered in the United States Patent and Trademark Office, the Canadian Trade Marks Office and in other countries.

Printed in U.S.A.

Acknowledgments

Over the years many people have read and commented on *Murder on the Mind*. Thanking them all would probably be impossible; however, several of my first readers immediately come to mind. Ed Whitmore, Alison Steinmiller and Vivian Vande Velde gave me my first effective feedback, and for that I am truly grateful. For several years my critique partner, Liz Voll, had an opportunity to comment on my work. Guppy Marjorie Merithew was instrumental in editing the draft that snagged the attention of my wonderful agent. And my staunchest cheerleaders are my current critique partners, Gwen Nelson and Liz Eng. I'd like to give a broad thank-you to my Sisters in Crime chapter, The Guppies: The Great Unpublished, although that name is a misnomer as many of its members have achieved their dreams of publication. Thank you all for encouraging me in mine.

I also wish to thank my agent, Lynn Whittaker, who had unswerving belief in the book, and my editor, Hugh Abramson, for shepherding the book to publication.

ONE

SOMETHING WALLOPED ME in the gut. A hit without substance—without pain. It sucked me from the here and now to a vacant place where a hollow wind brushed my ears.

I waited.

There. In my peripheral vision: *Coming out of the mist. An animal. A deer. A buck.*

I blinked and was back in the bar, bending over the felt-lined table.

"You gonna shoot or not?" Marty growled.

My fingers tightened around the cue, which stopped their sudden trembling. I held my breath as I made the shot. The cue ball kissed the six and sent it into the left corner pocket. I straightened, trying to hide the unexpected panic churning my insides. "That's another five bucks you owe me."

Marty chewed the unlit stub of his cigar, fumbled with his wallet, and dug out a crisp five-dollar bill, slapping it onto the table. "Double or nothing."

Uh-uh. I needed to get out of there. Think about what had just happened to me.

"I'd love to, but I start a new job first thing in the morning." I snatched up my winnings and replaced the cue stick on the wall rack. O'Shea's smoky, blue-collar friendliness had been a haven from boredom and loneliness, reminding me of the taverns back home in Buffalo, only it was pool, not darts, that drew the Sunday night crowd.

"Go ahead, leave," Marty grumbled, gazing down the length of his cue. "But be back here—same time next week. Me and

the boys are gonna win back everything you've taken from us."
His break shot went wild. He should've stuck with darts.

"In your dreams," I said, and shrugged into my leather
bomber jacket.

"Are y'leaving so soon, Jeffrey?" Pretty Annie McBride,
an Irish lass of about twenty-five with a killer smile, hefted a
tray of drinks as she served a couple at a nearby table.

"Have to, darlin'."

"An' when are y'going ta ask me out? I'm not getting any
younger, y'know."

I eyed her appreciatively but considered my thin wallet.
"Soon."

"I'll be collecting Social Security at this rate."

"Forget him, Annie," said Ian from behind the bar. "Find
yourself a nice Irish boy." He winked at her.

"I'm half Irish," I countered to a round of laughter from
Ian and the regulars. "My mother was an O'Connor—you
can't get much more Irish than that."

"Never you mind them, Jeffrey," Annie said. "But don't
wait too long, or I will find me some nice Irish lad." Annie
smiled kindly and headed for the kitchen. I watched the door
swing shut behind her.

Marty and another patron were already engrossed in a new
game as I headed for the exit. "G'night, all."

A chorus of goodbyes followed as I left the pub.

I set off at a brisk pace, heading for my apartment three
blocks away. A March thaw had melted the snow, but the
temperature had plunged back to freezing and the bracing air
soon cleared my head. The pub had been overheated and
reeked of stale beer and sweat. No wonder I'd zoned out.

I thought of the cash in my wallet. Maybe my good luck at
pool would stay with me when I started the job at Metropolitan Life. My unemployment benefits were about to end, so I'd
been desperate to take the entry-level insurance claims job.

Hands stuffed in my pockets, I watched my feet as I

walked. After I got that first paycheck, I'd ask Annie out. It had been months since I'd had any feminine companionship, and celibacy is highly overrated. I just hoped Annie's friendliness wasn't a put-on to get a good tip.

Traffic was sparse as I crossed Third, the sidewalk empty as I headed past the caged-in businesses that lined the street. I was usually cautious, but thoughts of the new job and what had happened at the bar distracted me as I dodged the miniature skating rinks on the cracked pavement. The next day would be nerve-racking. New names, new faces. Probably a backlog of case files, too.

"Hey, dude, got some spare change?"

A large, silhouetted figure blocked the sidewalk.

Aw, shit.

A gust of frigid wind grazed my cheek. I jammed my hands deeper into my jacket pockets, tried to get past him.

"Hey, asshole, I'm talkin' to you!" The hefty teenager stepped into the lamplight, grabbed my jacket. Another figure emerged from the darkened doorway of a closed deli. Though shorter, the other kid brandished a worn baseball bat, looking just as threatening. I avoided his glare and the challenge in it.

In spite of the freezing cold, I broke into a sweat as I pulled away from the kid's grasp. "Hey, guys, I don't want any trouble."

"Then give us your money."

Damn. I'd just won fifty bucks at the bar and now a couple of two-bit punks were going to shake me down for it. But I'm not stupid.

I thumbed through my wallet. "You can have what I got."

"Is that all?" the shorter kid asked, slamming the bat into his palm. "You got a ATM card? We gonna go visit your bank."

"I've been out of work for months. There's no money left."

The big guy grabbed my left arm in a vise-grip. "Lester, why don't you introduce our friend here to Reggie?"

Lester flaunted the wooden bat so that the logo burned into

it was visible in the lamplight. A Reggie Jackson special, decades old but just as lethal as the day it was made.

"C'mon, guys, I gave you everything I had."

"Reggie wants to teach you a lesson," Lester said.

I took a step back, yanking my arm from the linebacker.

Across the street, a hooker ducked into one of the doorways. Distracted, I almost didn't react as Lester swung the bat. I dodged, catching him with a satisfying kick to the groin. The bat went flying and he sank like the *Titanic*.

His friend snatched the bat, heading for me like a killing machine. I stepped back, raised my left arm to fend off the blow, but he caught me. The audible crack of bone sent me staggering. Skyrockets of pain shot up my arm.

The bat came down again, slamming into my shoulder, knocking me to my knees.

Icy water soaked through my jeans.

The bat came at me from the left, crashed into my temple, and my head hit the pavement. My vision doubled. Stupidly, I tried to raise myself as the bat connected with my skull once more.

Damn, I thought just before losing consciousness. I wasn't going to make it to my new job in the morning.

I DRIFTED FROM PAINFUL REALITY, lost in some misty wilderness. I'd escaped one nightmare…but escaped to where?

Tangled sensations enveloped me—rising dread, irrational fear. The mist began to evaporate, and I focused all my senses on the emotion.

From out of the void, a figure approached, surrounded by an aura of smothering emotions. Hatred, revenge—it spewed these and more. Unable to bear the torrent, I tried to turn away. The figure—a hunter—stalked its prey, but instinct told me I was not the quarry.

It paused in its search. The intensity of its rage choked me— kept me from taking a decent breath. I thought I'd pass out when the stalker moved away. Horrified, yet fascinated, I couldn't tear my gaze from the dark, retreating figure. What was being hunted? Why couldn't I see it, warn it?

The danger lingered.

I shuddered, afraid of the bizarre, gruesome death I knew was to come.

The figure faded into the surrounding emptiness, and I began to relax.

I was only dreaming, after all.

TWO

"HE'S DIFFERENT," RICHARD SAID.

Hidden behind the butler's pantry door, my head half-shaved like a punk rocker, eavesdropping on a private conversation…yeah, I'd say I was different.

"Of course he is," Brenda said. "After what happened, I'd be surprised if he wasn't."

Broken arm, fractured skull. Emotional wreck. Working on paranoid, too. I leaned in closer, straining to hear.

"He's keeping something from me."

Richard didn't know the half of it.

"What?" Brenda asked, over the clatter of silverware dropping into a kitchen drawer.

"He mentioned nightmares back at the hospital. I should've pressed him on it, but I don't want to push him too hard. He still doesn't trust me." He fell quiet for a moment. "Something strange happened at the airport. I was looking for the claim checks. He knew they were in my wallet, but he hadn't seen me put them there."

"A logical place for them. Or maybe he's psychic," she offered offhand. The top dishwasher rack rolled out, glasses clinking.

Silence. I could imagine Richard's stony glare.

"I'll call UB Medical Center tomorrow," Richard said. "See if I can find a doctor to treat him."

"Then what will you do with him?"

"Nothing. He's here to recover."

"What if he wants to go back to New York?"

"Then he can go."

The dishwasher door closed.

"Bull," Brenda said. "You want him here. You want to turn his life around, remake him in your own image. But he's your brother, not you. For years he's made his own life without you. He'll need to make his own life again. Don't be disappointed when he no longer needs you."

Trust Brenda to be pragmatic.

"Want sausage or linguine for dinner?" she asked.

Tiptoeing back to my room, I closed the door. I leaned against it, closed my eyes, unsure what I was feeling. Panic came close.

Yeah, I was different.

I stretched out on the single bed in that shabby little room and thought about what happened.

After six months of unemployment due to downsizing, I'd been about to resume my career as an insurance claims investigator. Until the mugging.

Ten days later, I was four hundred miles away, in Buffalo, New York, moving in with my older half-brother and his live-in-lover. Broke and dependent on their kindness, I was lucky to have somewhere to go.

Dr. Richard Alpert hadn't changed much over the years. Silver now mixed with the dark brown hair around his temples, and in his full mustache. New lines creased his face, but along with the brains, Richard had the looks and, as sole heir, he now possessed the Alpert family fortune.

The flight from LaGuardia to the Buffalo-Niagara International Airport had taken fifty-seven minutes. With my skull-pounding headache, it felt like fifty-seven hours. Brenda Stanley, the pretty black woman behind the security barrier, waited for us. At thirty-four, a year younger than me, Brenda's an old soul whose eyes reflected the depth of her compassion. After a quick kiss and embrace with Richard, she turned to me.

"Jeffy Resnick, you look like shit. You need to gain ten pounds, and I'm just the one to fatten you up."

She was right about the weight loss. Ordinarily I'm just an average guy. Brown hair, brown eyes, and a respectable five-eight in height. More comfortable in denim than a suit and tie. Now my jeans hung from my hips. A sling hid the lightweight summer jacket—the only one Richard could find back at my apartment. A knit cap covered my partially shaved head.

Brenda frowned and, careful not to press against my broken arm, gently hugged me. She stepped back. "You two aren't fighting, are you?"

"Brenda," Richard admonished.

"Well, I know how it is when the old man and the kid get together."

Because of a twelve-year age difference, Richard and I had never been close. Our reunion in the hospital in New York days before had been rocky. We'd called a truce. Now to see if we could live with it.

"We're not fighting," I assured her.

"Good. You two get the luggage," Brenda said. "I'll bring the car around. Those parking lot thieves are gonna hit me up for five bucks. Highway robbery," she muttered, already walking away.

"Come on," Richard said, and started off, following the overhead signs to the baggage carousel.

"Why don't you marry Brenda and make an honest woman of her?" I asked, struggling to keep up.

"I've been trying to for years. She says it would break her mother's heart."

"Marrying a rich, white doctor?"

"It's the white part that's the problem."

Richard had filled me in on the most recent details of their lives. I'd met Brenda only once several years before, when they'd come to Manhattan on business. I liked her right away. They had been colleagues at The American Patient Safety Foundation, a think tank outside of Los Angeles, where

Richard evaluated new medical equipment. Brenda was a reg-istered nurse and his assistant, although neither she nor Richard had worked much with patients.

Budget cuts ended both their jobs, and they moved back to the old homestead in Buffalo. With the inheritance, Richard didn't need to work and he wasn't sure what he wanted to do next. He seemed quieter, more introspective—if that was possible. I'd have to ask Brenda later.

We arrived at U.S. Airway's baggage carousel, already in motion. Suitcases, boxes, golf clubs, and skis slid past the already thinning crowd. Richard patted his pockets.

"They're in your wallet."

"What are?"

"The claim tickets."

A quick look in his wallet revealed the missing claim checks. Richard eyed me suspiciously. "Jeff, you were inside the terminal when the skycap gave them to me."

Was I? I shrugged. "Lucky guess. But you don't need them in the Buffalo airport. C'mon, let's go home. I'd rather barf in familiar surroundings."

"AND ON YOUR RIGHT IS THE Vietnamese grocery store," Richard announced, sounding like a tour guide. He'd been giving a running commentary since we'd pulled out of the airport, while Brenda drove the streets like a native.

"Where's the snow?" I asked. It was, after all, March, and Buffalo is famous for chin-high drifts.

"It melted," Brenda said. "But it'll be back."

Shrunken, dirty mounds of the stuff still littered the edges of parking lots and streets. I took in the seemingly endless ribbon of strip malls. "Video stores, head shops. Looks a lot shabbier than I remember."

"That'll change in a heartbeat," Brenda said. Sure enough, we approached the Grover Cleveland Golf Course, crossing the city line into Amherst, the suburb where Richard lived.

The neighborhood dated back to the twenties, the houses built and maintained by old money.

Brenda turned right into LeBrun Road, driving slowly, letting me digest the neighborhood changes. As she pulled into the driveway and parked the car, I got a good look at the house. The three-story brick Tudor looked the epitome of good taste. A gray slate roof and leaded bay windows overlooked the winter-matted carpet of lawn and the privet hedges bordering the sidewalk.

Richard retrieved the luggage from the trunk, letting me soak in the house. My nails dug into my palms.

"Come on inside," he called, sounding jovial.

"Can we go around front for a grand entrance?" I asked, taking my duffel from him.

"Sure." Brenda took out her key, leading the way.

I'd lived in that house during my teens and had never been through the front entrance, always using the back door, feeling like the unwanted guest that I was.

Inside the great oak door, the freshly waxed marble foyer shone, reminding me of a mausoleum. Brenda didn't like housework. They must've engaged a cleaning service. The house had been empty for years since Richard's grandmother's death. And though they'd been there for three months, the furniture in the living room was still shrouded in sheets.

I set the battered duffel on the polished floor and looked up the grand staircase. "Where am I bunking?"

"Grandfather's room," Richard answered.

Tension knotted my gut. "Your grandmother's probably turning over in her grave since Brenda moved in. You put me in the shrine, she'll positively spin."

"It's not a shrine," Brenda said. "I've been redecorating."

"Well, plant me somewhere before I keel over. Those pills don't put much of a dent in these headaches."

I picked up my duffel, forcing myself to follow Brenda up the stairs. Richard brought up the rear. With each step, a weird heaviness expanded through my chest. It was dread, wasn't it? Or maybe I was having a heart attack.

I paused near the top, dizziness sweeping through me. I leaned heavily against the banister.

Richard took the duffel from me. "You okay?"

I gave the barest of nods, forcing myself up the last step. My vision dappled, nausea churning inside me.

Brenda stood by the open door, like grande dame Leona Helmsley in one of her old Queen of New York ads.

I paused at the threshold.

Déjà vu.

I'd been there before.

But of course I'd been there. I'd lived in a room down the hall for four years.

Anger boiled out of the room before me. A vivid memory struck: Mrs. Alpert's blue eyes blazing, her lips clamped into a thin, purple line.

It was her anger.

Panic gripped me. I backed away, nearly crashing into Brenda.

"Jeffy, what's wrong?"

"I can't go in there."

"Jeff?" Richard said.

"I can't stay in there."

Although she'd been dead for years, Old Lady Alpert's lingering presence was attached to her dead husband's bedroom. I tried to step forward, but my legs wouldn't move. A wall of betrayal stopped me.

"Jeff?" Richard repeated, his voice sounding wobbly.

I ignored him. "What about my old room?" I asked Brenda.

"There's no furniture—"

"Curtis's room?" Curtis Johnson, Mrs. Alpert's chauffeur, had lived in a room off the butler's pantry.

"We don't have sheets for a single bed," she said.

Hardly able to breathe, I stumbled away, groped for the

banister, and smacked into the wall, setting off explosions in my broken arm. I nearly tumbled down the stairs, collapsing on the bottom step.

Hunched over, I cradled my arm to my chest, rocking in rhythm with waves of pain. Tears of frustration, anger, and shame burned my eyes.

Richard brushed past me, crouched before me. "Jeff, what's wrong?"

I couldn't look him in the eye.

Brenda sat beside me, her hand resting on my shoulder. "You don't have to go in there, Jeffy."

Couldn't catch my breath—couldn't face her. "Sorry, Brenda. You went to a lot of trouble—"

"We'll fix you up with something. I'll hop over to Kaufmann's and get you some sheets and a lamp. They'll be yours—nobody else's—and no bad vibes attached to them, either," she said, as though reading my mind. "Come on. You'll feel better after a nap." She pulled me to my feet.

I couldn't look at Richard—not yet. Brenda took my hand and led me through the house, winding through the kitchen and butler's pantry.

The door to Curtis's room squeaked open, a friendly, welcoming sound. Curtis taught me to play gin rummy and poker. He'd been a good friend to a lonely teenaged boy. The walls of his room were beige, in need of fresh paint. An old, iron single bed with a white chenille spread was pushed against one wall. A battered maple dresser sat next to the empty closet. The bathroom housed a narrow shower, toilet, and a small sink. Though it resembled a cheap hotel room, the place embraced me.

I sat on the bed and shrugged out of my sling. Brenda took my jacket, hung it in the closet. I avoided Richard's physician's gaze.

"I don't know what came over me back there. I'm okay, Rich. Really. And the room is fine."

Richard set my duffel down. "You sure—?"

"Yes," I said, forcing a smile. "This'll do fine. Besides, you said my stuff will be here tomorrow. Bug off, will you, before I fall on my head and you make me go back to a hospital."

Richard looked ready to do just that, but then dutifully backed away.

Brenda stepped closer, squeezing my hand. "Welcome home." She kissed my cheek, closing the door behind them.

Silence.

My chest ached from the strain of suppressing so many emotions—fear topping the list. I kicked off my shoes and stretched out on the bed, covering my eyes with my good arm.

Richard's ancient, nasty grandmother was dead. She couldn't reach out and grab me from the grave. I squeezed my eyes shut to blot out the memory of her hateful glare.

And then there was the dream....

THREE

THE DARK FIGURE WAS BACK, STALKING ITS prey with a calculated viciousness. Terrified, the white-tailed buck ran blindly across a field of short-cropped hay.

I watched the hunter pull the cross-bow's trigger, let the arrow fly. It hit with a smart thwack, ripping through the deer's heart. The buck ran ten yards before dropping in the snow.

Confident, the hunter strode to the kill, hauled the animal onto its back, crouched down. The wicked knife flashed in the waning light as the hunter gutted the carcass.

Sensations pummeled me. Startled fear, helplessness, and an overwhelming sense of victory. But the mix of emotions didn't gibe; the deer was goodness crushed, while the stalker radiated a sense of triumph, as though evil had been destroyed, instead of the destroyer snuffing out an innocent life.

I KILLED TIME PUTTING AWAY the clothes and toilet articles Richard had packed for me. Running out of things to do, I headed for the kitchen.

Brenda was alone at the counter. I took a breath to steady myself before entering.

She looked up from the sausage she tended on the stove. "Feeling better?"

I pulled out a chair at the table. "Maybe a little shaky. I could sure go for a sugar fix."

In seconds a glass of milk and a plate of chocolate chip cookies materialized before me. I ate three, feeling better with every bite. When I finished, I took the dishes to the dish-washer. Leaning against the counter, I dipped my right hand into my sling, scratching the skin around the top of the cast.

"Itches, huh?"

"I was gonna bend a coat hanger to scratch way down, but figured I'd end up a bloody mess."

She leaned across the counter to a ceramic crock filled with kitchen utensils and grabbed a chopstick. "Try this."

The stick reached my elbow from the top of the cast, and nearly as far from inside my wrist.

"Keep it," she said when I offered it back. "Just don't tell Richard where you got it. He'd tell you horror stories on infection and stuff. Doctors don't understand a patient's needs at all."

"So says the nurse."

"You got it, baby."

"Where is Rich, anyway?"

"In his study, where else?" Was there resignation in her voice?

I tucked the chopstick into my sling and glanced around the kitchen. "It's weird being here again."

"I can imagine." She adjusted the flame under the skillet.

"Looks pretty much the same."

She glanced around the old-fashioned kitchen. "Sort of like living in a museum. Still, maybe we can make it homey. If we decide to stay."

If? That wasn't the impression Richard had given me.

"I was surprised you guys had moved back."

She covered the sausage and moved to the counter to chop celery for the salad. "No more surprised than me. Richard sold the condo and here we are. Most of our stuff is in storage."

I wasn't about to press her on what was obviously a sore subject.

"Rich's grandmother had a housekeeper and other help around the house. You do everything yourself?"

"No. A cleaning service comes in once a week. Cooking's fun, but even that's starting to wear thin." She sliced a tomato.

"I've heard a few stories about Mrs. Alpert from Richard. I'll bet you could tell some, too." She looked up from her work, a mischievous glint in her eyes.

I took the bait. "Old Mrs. Alpert hated me. I was a constant reminder that Rich's mother was…" I considered my words carefully "…not her choice of maternal material for her only grandson. The fact that I looked like our mother didn't help."

"So I heard."

"One Halloween a friend in the school's drama club loaned me the lead's costume from *The Headless Horseman*. I got a flashlight, and the tall ladder from the garage…."

"You didn't—"

I grinned. "Around midnight I climbed outside her window and tapped on the glass until she woke up."

Brenda laughed. "God, you were a rotten kid."

"She screamed, woke up the whole house. She threatened me with reform school—made Rich come straight home from work at the hospital. I thought he'd kill me."

"What did he do?"

"Lectured me about the old lady's bad heart, but I always thought he was secretly proud of that stunt. Poor Rich, he always had to behave."

She smiled. "It means a lot to him that you're here, you know."

I fell silent, feeling awkward again. Why was it so easy to talk to her and so hard to relate to my own brother?

"Brenda, is something bothering Rich?"

"You catch on fast." She looked thoughtful. "It was harder for him to lose his job than it was for me. He'd worked at the Foundation almost eighteen years."

"I can identify with losing a job."

Her frown deepened. "It's more than just that." She was quiet for a long moment, then forced a smile. "Now that you're here, maybe we'll have some fun."

Did that mean there'd been a distinct lack of fun in their

lives? It never occurred to me that Richard could have problems. Or was he living proof that money can't buy happiness?

I glanced down at the counter, noticing a large manila envelope with my name on it. "What's this?"

"I called the local brain injury association. Probably none of the info will apply to you, but it might give you some answers."

Back in my hospital room in New York, I'd been impatient with Dr. Klehr's explanations. The stocky man smelled of stale cigarette smoke, and looked like he over-indulged on cheeseburgers and fries. We hadn't built a trusting doctor/patient relationship in the short time I'd known him. He and Richard had been exchanging professional pleasantries when I'd interrupted them.

"Can you just give me the bottom-line diagnosis?"

Nonplused, Klehr turned. "Mr. Resnick, you suffered a classic coup-contrecoup injury."

"Which means?"

"The injury occurred in a part of the brain opposite the point of impact. The injured tissue resulted from changes in pressure which traveled through your brain. Very simply, you've suffered some brain damage."

Klehr kept talking, but I didn't hear a word.

Brain damage? How could something like that have happened to me—be that wrong with me?

Dr. Klehr paused; I picked up the sudden silence.

"It sounds a lot more ominous than it really is," Richard said. I'd looked at him in disbelief.

"You were lucky," Klehr continued. "The swelling was minimal. You haven't suffered seizures."

Yeah, that made me feel lots better. I couldn't get past that phrase "brain damage." Did that mean I'd never balance a checkbook again, or was I likely to go out and kill for kicks?

"What does that mean?"

"Memory loss, as you've already experienced. And you

might notice a loss of emotional control. One of my patients cries at McDonald's commercials. You might get angry easily."

"Is this permanent?"

"Perhaps, but not necessarily."

"When will I know? How can I tell? When can I go back to work?"

He shrugged. "I wouldn't push it. An injury like yours takes time to heal."

"Weeks? Months?"

"We'll talk later. You've got enough to think about for now."

With a few parting words, Klehr left us alone. Richard chattered on, refusing to even consider worst-case scenarios.

I'd eyed him with distrust. He'd already known. Klehr explaining the extent of my injuries to me had been just an afterthought.

Was paranoia a side effect of a bruised brain?

I fingered the envelope, hefting its bulk. "Thanks, Brenda. I'll look it over later."

Much later.

AFTER DINNER, BRENDA PLAYED barber, trying to even out my hair. It would do until it grew back in.

Later, with Richard safely holed up in his study and Brenda off to her meditation class, I sat alone in the spacious, well-lit dining room. The large manila envelope Brenda had given me sat before me on the polished oak table. The return address read: Brain Injury Association of Buffalo. That in itself sounded life-altering. Swallowing my fear, I tore open the flap, spilling the contents across the table.

Most of the brochures heralded the virtues of long-term care for family members suffering severe head injuries or strokes. Only a family with Richard's financial resources or fantastic insurance could afford those medical wonder-palaces.

Was Brenda trying to shame me into counting my blessings? No, she wasn't petty. Besides, thoughts like that painted me as a prime example of the self-centered personality changes indicated in one of the booklets.

After skimming the material, I was grateful I'd emerged from the mugging mostly intact. Still, two punks had taken my life—maybe my independence—from me. So what if it wasn't much of a life. It was a comfortable rut that, with the new job, just might've gotten better. The possibility that I might never again work in any kind of meaningful profession terrified me.

A little blue booklet caught my eye: a "How-to-Handle" manual for families of the brain injured. As I skimmed it, the things that seemed to apply to me practically jumped off the page. Yes, I was irritable and overly emotional, as proved by my refusal to stay in the room Brenda had fixed for me. I was afraid of being permanently dependent on Richard. What if he tired of me? Where else could I go? How would I live until I could work again?

Sorting the pamphlets according to size, I set them in orderly piles and deposited them back in the envelope.

Aha, denial! Just as the manual predicted.

No, damn it. I had a choice—to just sit back and let life happen to me, or take my best shot at rebuilding a life. It would never be the same, but maybe that was for the best. The past five years held few memories worth taking out and polishing fondly anyway.

I stood too quickly, my vision suddenly dimming.

A spiraling abyss sucked me in—sickening me, shattering my new-found resolve.

The deer hung before my wide-awake eyes, swaying slightly in some unfelt breeze, its tawny hair catching the incandescent light from the lone bulb that lit the room. The cloying smell of sweet blood filled my nostrils. Then a voice in slow-mo repeated like a mantra, "Youprickyouprickyouprick—"

THE CHANDELIER'S BRIGHT LIGHT WAS BACK.

I swallowed, nearly falling into my chair again. The muscles in my arms quivered in reaction. Moon-shaped grooves marred my palms where my fingernails had dug in.

If the dream could overtake me during my waking hours, I could be doomed to a life in the places described in the pamphlets I'd so cavalierly discarded only moments before.

FOUR

A WHITE BEKINS TRUCK pulled up in front of the house at ten the next morning—a bright moment on an overcast day in mid-March. Before we left Manhattan, Richard had arranged for everything I owned to be packed and delivered. The arrival of my personal possessions was a tangible connection to my former life. A life where I'd been in control, responsible.

Brenda and I watched from inside the house as Richard directed the men to unload the cartons in the sun porch.

"I'll make coffee," Brenda offered, as Richard handed me the inventory.

I rested the pages on my cast, flipping through them with my good hand. Clothes, books, dishes, linens, various pieces of furniture. Obviously missing were items of quick cash value: my stereo equipment, binoculars, TV, personal computer, Nikon—and my gun. The guys who'd mugged me had taken my wallet and keys, then ransacked my place. The cops found fingerprints, but nothing would come of it in a city where scores of muggings or robberies happened daily.

My excitement vanished as I, a former insurance investigator, remembered I'd stupidly let my renter's insurance lapse. I'd had to let a lot lapse during six months of unemployment. Goddamn downsizing.

Richard watched me carefully, his eyes filled with pity. "Why don't we get that coffee?"

He clapped me on the shoulder and headed for the kitchen. I didn't follow. Instead, I waited until the last of the cartons were off the truck and the men started unloading the furniture.

My stomach lurched as two men in overalls struggled down the ramp with the shabby couch. Spray-painted Day-Glo orange stripes crisscrossed the back and cushions. The dressers, end tables, and every other piece of furniture were likewise marked. The movers stacked it all in the garage, save for the bed. I had that moved to Curtis's—my—room. Maybe steel wool and elbow grease would remove the paint.

The movers finished in record time. Richard appeared at the appropriate moment, opened his wallet, and gave them a generous tip; then the big empty truck lumbered back toward Main Street.

"You want help unpacking?"

"Uh…maybe Brenda could give me a hand." I didn't want Richard to see all my crap—and that's just what it was—in the glaring light of day.

"You sure you won't have some lunch?" Brenda asked as she approached.

I shook my head, trying to pull loose the tape on the top of a box of underwear. Her fingernails were longer than mine and she easily worked one underneath, pulling the tape off. I opened the top, looked inside, and closed it again.

"What do you want me to do?" she asked.

"Restacking the boxes would be a big help. A lot of this should go right into the garage. The kitchen stuff—things like that. Maybe Rich can help us with those."

She reached for another carton and started working on the tape. "I think we have some box cutters in the kitchen junk drawer."

"Don't bother with that. It goes outside."

Brenda examined the unmarked sides of the box.

"It's the silverware," I explained.

She shook the box and was rewarded with the faint clink of knives, forks, and spoons. "How'd you know?"

I shrugged, distracted, and attacked the tape on a box from the next stack. It came off, the top lifted—good, my bathroom stuff. The disposable razor from the hospital cost me a pint of blood each morning.

Despite her size, Brenda had the strength of a longshoreman. She opened a box filled with towels. Wrapped amongst them were several framed photos, slightly bent and scratched, the glass missing, presumably smashed. One of them bore a trace of orange paint—Shelley, in happier times. I hadn't seen the photos in two years. Why had I held onto so many of my dead wife's possessions—still unable to part with them?

Brenda and I didn't talk much during the sorting ordeal. She'd hold up an item and I'd give her a yea or a nay. It wasn't long before the nay pile stretched three times higher than the yea pile. Luckily the garbage men would be around the next day.

Later, feeling weak and sick, I watched Brenda make my bed before she retreated. Napping on my own comfortable mattress gave me my first taste of security since the mugging.

When Brenda woke me for dinner, I staggered from my room like a drunk. Red wine accompanied the entree—corned beef and cabbage.

"What's the occasion?" I asked, stifling a yawn.

"St. Patrick's Day. Besides, it beats burgers any day," Brenda said, placing a huge helping on my plate. "I bought Irish soda bread to go with it. Dig in."

She served Richard and herself and they started eating. I poked at the cabbage with my fork.

Richard swallowed. "Something wrong?"

"The night I got mugged, I'd been with friends at a pub." I pushed a potato around. "Nobody came to the hospital. Nobody called."

They stopped in mid-bite, glancing at each other. "Maybe they didn't know." Brenda reached over, clasped my hand. "You'll make new friends, hon."

They spent the rest of the evening cooking up plans to

paint my room, trying to cheer me. I should've felt flattered, but the attention only depressed me. I wanted to be left alone.

By the time I said good-night, they looked more exhausted than I felt.

Darkness shrouded the cold, dank room, the atmosphere charged with dread. Fatigue weighed me down so I could hardly stand. Something nudged me from the side. I turned, hands outstretched to stop its gentle swaying motion. My fingers probed the softness, tried to curl into the lingering warmth, but the hairs were too short.

Hairs?

I fumbled in the darkness until encountering a sticky warmth—blood? Its sickly sweetness turned my stomach. Startled, I backed away until I could make out the still form in the shadowy room. A ten-point buck, dressed out—its genitals and internal organs discarded—and hanging to bleed. Its lifeless, glassy eyes bored into my own.

The back of my throat closed. I couldn't breathe, couldn't scream, as a wave of horror and triumph engulfed me, obliterating all rationality and what was left of my sense of self.

I awoke, nausea nearly choking me, stumbled to the bathroom, and vomited. I sat, heaving, my head threatening to explode. Spent, I collapsed onto the cold linoleum. This had been no dream. This time I had stood alongside the dead buck, felt and smelled its death tang.

I couldn't stop trembling. I couldn't tell Richard something was terribly wrong. Not yet. Not when I had no understanding of what was happening to me.

FRIDAY MORNING THE THREE of us drove to one of those big franchise hardware stores to choose paint, and buy brushes and drop cloths.

It felt good to be out among normal people, people who

weren't sick—who hadn't had their brains bruised. There seemed to be a lot of them out and about. Retired men, women with small children, young adults choosing wallpaper, paint, vacuum cleaners…. Didn't any of these people work?

While Richard and Brenda debated the merits of natural versus synthetic paintbrush bristles, I strolled down aisles filled with build-it-yourself furniture, nails, screws, garden tools, and everything in between, until I landed in front of the rope and chain display. Synthetic and natural fibers came in various lengths and widths, prepackaged or ready to cut on large spools.

I crouched by a spool of Manila rope, half-inch width, by twelve hundred feet. The hemp felt splintery between my fingers. So…familiar. When I pressed it to my nose, the image of an old, dank, wooden shed or garage filled my mind.

In my dream the hanging deer had swung in a gentle, easy arc, but the light had come from a different angle….

I turned the rope over and over in my hand.

"Can I help you, sir?" asked an acne-scarred young man.

I dropped the rope and straightened. "No. Just looking, thanks."

As he walked away, I turned my attention back to the spool. The rope meant something, but I wasn't sure what.

"Oh, there you are!" Brenda said, coming up behind me. "Which one of these color chips do you like?"

We started painting after lunch, though my broken arm kept me from doing much. After several hours of bad jokes and insults, the room looked better. The paint fumes aggravated my headache, so I ended up sleeping on the living room couch.

My mind stayed on a circular track. What the hell was happening inside my head? The dreams and hallucinations were too real.

Then it came to me. A brain tumor. Caused by the severe blow to my skull.

What else could it be?

I stole into Richard's study, flipped through his medical

texts until I found the symptoms. Yes, I suffered from drowsiness, lethargy, personality changes, impaired mental faculties.

I was going to die.

Awake half the night with worry, I wondered if I should draw up a will…then I remembered I had nothing of value to leave to anyone.

Richard and Brenda slept late. Brenda later told me it was a Saturday morning tradition for them to have a huge breakfast and skip lunch. Richard and I sat at the kitchen table while she made toast, then chopped vegetables and grated cheese for omelets. I waited for a conversational opening, but Richard buried his nose in the newspaper.

"Uh, Rich. I—I haven't been sleeping well."

He barely looked up from the sports section. "You're in a new place. Give yourself a few days." He continued reading an article on the Buffalo Sabres, absently grabbing a slice of toast from his plate.

"No…I mean, not since the mugging."

Richard looked up again, swallowing. "I can't prescribe something to help you sleep. I won't."

"That's not what I mean. What could make a person not sleep?"

He shrugged. "Anything weighing on your mind."

"Could someone with this kind of brain injury get a…a tumor?"

He folded the newspaper, setting it aside. "First of all, it would take months before you'd even notice symptoms. I looked at your x-rays and, believe me, I called in the best for consultation. It's my professional opinion that you're going to be just fine. What you need now is rest, time to recover."

I took a deep breath. Richard was a good doctor. But…

"Then I don't understand it, because I don't feel the same any more. I'm…different."

"Of course you are; you suffered a trauma—" Brenda piped in.

I shook my head. "No. I don't mean the mugging. I mean I'm different."

Hadn't Richard said the same thing?

He pushed the paper aside, eyes narrowing. "How?"

"I've been having these weird dreams."

Brenda looked up from her cutting board, but said nothing.

"The nightmare you mentioned in the hospital?" Richard asked.

"Yeah, that's when it started. I keep dreaming about a deer."

"A deer?"

I forced myself to continue. "It's a bow kill, and it's hanging in a garage to bleed. But there're all these weird emotions tied to it: triumph, horror. Every time I dream about it, the emotions get stronger. One time it'll be a perverse sense of satisfaction, then it'll be absolute terror."

Richard frowned. "I'm not a psychiatrist, but it could just be a reaction to being mugged. You were a victim, like the deer. You could've died."

"But that's not the worst of it. It's not just a dream any more. I've been having—" God. No going back once I said the word: "Hallucinations. When I'm wide awake."

Richard's stare went right through me.

"I might see it, feel it, smell it," I continued. "I live it. This thing—this deer—is hanging. In a garage. It's slit from stem to stern. And its eyes—"

I closed my own, remembering that nauseating, oppressive dread. "They're open and they're glassy and they're just so...dead. And whoever killed the buck feels tremendous triumph."

Richard's eyes were wide. Definitely no turning back now.

"I hear these words, over and over: 'You prick, you goddamn prick,' and...." I let the words trail off.

"My God," Brenda muttered, dropping her paring knife into the sink.

Richard squirmed. Maybe the thought of a brain tumor

wasn't so farfetched after all. "I don't have any pull at UB Med Center, but I have a few friends here in town I can call. If it'll make you feel better, we could—"

"No!" Brenda cried, diving for the newspaper. She thumbed through the thick pile, searching. "Didn't you see the headline? Weren't you listening to the news?" she said, her eyes wild. She spread the front page of *The Buffalo News* out across the kitchen table before us. The banner screamed: Businessman Found Dead in Bizarre Ritual Killing.

"What about it?" Richard asked.

"I heard it on the radio earlier. This guy was found in his own garage—eviscerated, hanging like a deer to bleed!"

Anxiety churned my gut.

"They've got no clues—nothing to go on," she said.

"What's that got to do with—?"

"Don't you think it's the least bit unusual that Jeffy has a dream—?"

"Don't start with that psychic stuff again," Richard warned her. "He just said it was a deer."

I wasn't listening.

Psychic?

Pure, blind panic hit me.

I wanted to puke.

The image was back.

I rested my head in my good hand, covering my eyes.

A man, a hemp rope cutting into his throat, swayed as though in a gentle breeze, his neck twisted at an odd angle. Heavyset, about fifty-five or sixty, and naked. Rolls of fat hung like melted wax around his middle.

The rustle of paper stopped. "Jeffy?" Brenda pointed to a coarse-screened, head-and-shoulders photo of a man dressed in a business suit.

"That's him!"

"Who?" Richard asked.

"The man I saw hanging."

"You said it was a deer."

"No, I just saw him!"

"You had a vision, just now?" Brenda asked, excited.

I nodded. A vision. Much more acceptable than the product of a tumor, a nightmare, or a hallucination.

Brenda settled the paper on the table between us and started reading aloud. "Local businessman Matthew J. Sumner was found hanged Friday in his garage. The grisly scene…"

My fears about tumors instantly vanished. The murder took place somewhere else. In a field. I knew it had. I'd seen it. The deer must have represented this guy. My mind had given me a vision of something I could understand.

How the hell did it do that?

Why the hell did it do that?

And why had it started more than a week before the murder took place—when I was in a city more than four hundred miles away?

I skimmed through the story, desperate to find out the facts. But the police were giving out few details.

According to the M.E., the Bison Bank vice president had been slain sometime late Thursday afternoon or early evening. Sumner was found hanging from a rafter in his own garage; his Cadillac Seville was missing. He'd been killed somewhere else, as evidenced by the marks on the body and lack of blood at the scene. His wife found him late Friday afternoon. She'd been visiting friends in Palm Beach the previous week. Funeral services were to be announced later.

I looked up. Richard's grim gaze remained fixed on me.

"This explains everything!"

"Calm down," he said.

"But I've got to do something about this."

"What?" He exploded from his chair to pace the floor. "What do you think you could possibly do?"

"I...don't know. But don't you see, it means I'm not crazy. I'm not—"

It didn't mean I wasn't crazy. I sounded crazy even to myself. Smoothing the newsprint, I stared at the photo of the dead man. He looked familiar.

Richard took his seat, his right hand methodically massaging his clenched left fist. "Jeff," he began, his tone reasonable— his physician's voice. "A head injury like yours can cause all kinds of problems. Make you believe all kinds of things."

"You mean I can't trust what I think? What I know?"

"It's something you should consider."

I continued to stare at the news story, read it over and over again, my conviction growing deeper with each new reading.

The tension in that kitchen was nearly unbearable. Finally Richard headed for the door.

"Where are you going?" Brenda asked.

"For a walk, before I say something we'll all regret."

Brenda watched him go, looked after him for a long moment. Then she took out the plastic wrap and started putting away the chopped vegetables.

"You believe me, don't you, Brenda?"

She nodded solemnly.

"What the hell is wrong with him? Does he think I want to know this stuff?"

She didn't answer.

"He's my brother—not my keeper."

"I think he's trying to be your friend." She sat down across the table from me, reached for my hand. "He's worried about you. He'll tell me I'm encouraging you in a fantasy."

"It's not a fantasy."

I looked down at the damnably familiar, yet unfamiliar, face of the murder victim. I considered asking her to help me, but what could she do? And I couldn't put her in a position where she'd have to choose sides.

And what if Richard was right? Was my willingness to

accept the possibility of possessing psychic abilities proof that my thinking was skewed?

At that moment, I didn't know what to believe.

When Richard returned an hour later, his cheeks pink from the cold, Brenda and I sat at the kitchen table, listening to the radio's hourly newscast.

"Any new developments?" he asked.

I shook my head, wanting nothing more than to escape his scrutiny, yet defiant enough to stay. Ignoring us, he poured himself a cup of coffee, then disappeared into another part of the house.

The day dragged.

As Buffalo had no all-news TV station, I didn't miss a single radio news broadcast, obsessed with finding out more details on the murder, yet little was forthcoming.

Richard kept circling back to the kitchen, watching me. Did he think he'd made a mistake bringing me home to Buffalo instead of committing me to a mental institution?

It was almost four when, despite the strain between us, Richard suggested we take a walk and I accepted. I needed to think, plan. Walking would also help me rebuild my strength, something I'd need if I was going to be involved in this thing—this investigation. As far as I was concerned, it was a done deal. Now, how to do it.

We started out at a leisurely pace, heading south. The trees were stark silhouettes against the white, late afternoon sky. Despite its proximity to Main Street, the neighborhood was quiet. Hard to believe the student ghetto around the University's South Campus was only a mile away.

Eventually Richard broke the silence.

"How're you feeling?"

Not the question I'd expected. "So far, so good."

"You've only been out of the hospital three days. You need time to heal."

I met his hard, blue eyes. "I'm okay, Rich."

He paused, his gaze piercing me. "No, you're not. You've had a serious injury. Don't push yourself too hard."

The set of his mouth gave away the depth of his concern. He exhaled a puff of breath. "Come on. Let's go home."

We didn't talk about the murder any more that day.

I hit the rack early but stared at the ceiling for hours. The visions had stopped, replaced by unanswerable questions that circled my head, keeping me from sleep. The biggest one was: why?

Why was this happening to me?

FIVE

THE SUN HADN'T come up yet, but I'd already showered and dressed by the time the Sunday morning paper was delivered. I spread it across the kitchen table, grateful to study it in solitude. As I'd hoped, the top story was still the Sumner killing. Sumner was survived by his wife, Claudia, and three grown children, Rob, Diane, and Michael. There'd be no public viewing. Private interment would take place Monday morning.

Noises from another part of the house caught my attention. I decided to make myself scarce while Richard and Brenda breakfasted.

Back in my room, I sat on the edge of my bed. With eyes closed, I cleared my mind. The man in the newspaper picture was older than the face imprinted on my brain. Could I have met him? It seemed likely. But not in New York. It had to be years ago, when I still lived in Buffalo.

The newspaper said he'd worked for Bison Bank over twenty-five years. Did I meet him at an early point in his career? I'd never had a bank account until I'd joined the Army. Maybe it had nothing to do with banking.

I thought back to my first summer job at Benson's car wash. I'd wipe down sleek Corvettes and angular Cadillacs, wishing for a junker of my own. Was Sumner a customer? I remembered the job, but not the people associated with it.

Damned frustrating, those holes in my memory.

Another summer I'd flipped burgers at some fast-food joint—anything to keep me out of the house and away from the crotchety old Alperts.

I let it go. Eventually it would come to me.

Despite my faulty memory, the bright morning invigorated me. On a whim, I decided to reconnect with the rest of the house, avoiding the kitchen and Richard and Brenda. It was soon obvious that only three rooms were in use: the kitchen, the study, and—I assumed—the master bedroom suite upstairs. Like the living room, much of the furniture in the other rooms was still shrouded in sheets.

Slipping into Richard's study gave me my first feeling of homecoming. The old, leather-bound books had always attracted me. The dark-paneled walls lent a feeling of security. Years ago, Richard's wizened grandfather used to live behind the big mahogany desk. Sometimes we'd sit at opposite ends of the room and read the old man's books. He'd smoke his pipe, the sweet tang of tobacco filling my nostrils. The grandfather clock ticked loudly in the empty silence. Mr. Alpert and I weren't friends, but we weren't exactly enemies, either. I couldn't imagine Richard taking his place in the oversized, burgundy leather chair.

A set of the *Encyclopedia Britannica* filled the shelves behind the desk—recent, by their copyright date. Richard must've brought them from California. I pulled out a volume, intending to look up psychic phenomena, and quickly decided against it, shoving the heavy book back into the slot from where I'd plucked it. It might be better to bungle my way through the discovery process with no preconceived expectations—or limitations.

Could I make it work for me? I picked up objects in the room, trying to zero in on previous owners, previous history.

A heavy glass paperweight was cold in my palm. The delicate wings of the butterfly encased inside seemed poised for flight, but I felt nothing odd or sinister. Likewise with the dust-free pipes and stand on the polished desk, sitting there as though waiting for old Mr. Alpert to strike a match.

But something had happened to me when I'd first entered

the house. Cold dread…horror. Melodramatic, maybe, but that's what I'd felt. It was time to make another visit to the upstairs bedroom.

My sneakered feet squeaked on the polished floor as I rounded the corner. The hallway seemed to extend miles ahead of me, like a camera trick in an old Hitchcock film. The staircase, when I reached it, also seemed to have telescoped in length.

I swallowed, took a step. Okay. Fine. On the second step, the sensation of alarm hit me. Something waited for me in Mr. Alpert's room. I forced myself to continue upward, tried to be logical. Could the house be haunted? Oh yeah, the skeptic in me taunted, that made a lot of sense. Just as reasonable as visions of dead men and deer.

My legs were lead by the time I topped the stairs. The closed bedroom door taunted me. Come on, chicken boy, face the worst.

Panic made me turn, nearly stumble in my haste to get the hell away. I wasn't up to facing whatever lingered in that room.

Not yet.

I grabbed my jacket from the hall closet. Outside, the air was cold, the blue sky clear and incredibly normal. I felt calmer as I poked at the matted leaves around the shrubbery. Tulip spikes protruded through the crusty dirt. The remnants of a hibernating garden lined the property. I followed it around to the side of the house and the driveway, facing the garage. Only drilled holes remained where a backboard had once been. When I was a kid, Richard and I had sometimes played one-on-one. Maybe it was still in the garage.

I went inside the large, three-car structure, what had once been a carriage house, rediscovering the apartment above. The door opened with a painful creak. I tramped through the dusty galley kitchen, dining area, two bedrooms, living room, and small bath. I vaguely remembered a married couple—the housekeeper and gardener—living there when I was a teenager. My nose wrinkled in the musty, cobwebbed rooms.

Old furniture, cartons of dusty books, gardening equipment, and other junk were still stored there.

A smile tugged at my lips, the seed of an idea forming, but it was too soon to hit Richard with any new requests.

Downstairs in the garage's empty bay, I studied the clutter of my own furniture and boxes. Some kind of organization was definitely needed. I pawed through the cartons. My old business cards surfaced first. I'd kept two sets, one with the company address, fax and phone numbers, and e-mail address, the other a calling card. Figuring I could still use those, I stuffed them into my coat pocket, along with a tape measure and a couple of half-used spiral notepads.

My next find was my old analog watch, with one of those Twist-O-Flex bands. I slipped it onto my right wrist, since the cast covered my left and ended at the knuckle line. I'd reset it once I got inside. I also found my out-of-date passport, grabbed an old pay stub, a canceled check, a bank state-ment—anything with my name and address on it, in case I needed to prove who I was.

I'd once considered being a private eye, investigating the field after my four-year hitch in the service—had even earned an associate degree in criminal justice. But New York's man-datory three-year apprenticeship had been a major turnoff. I'd had enough of being someone's lackey in the Army. Plus private investigators' lives are damned boring. I couldn't see myself on endless stakeouts, spying on adulterous spouses, looking for runaway kids, or repossessing cars from people down on their luck.

The insurance field is boring, too, and guarantees mountains of paperwork. But the pay and the hours are definitely better, the income reliable, and the work inherently safer. Too many people own guns these days—and use them. Through my work in insurance, I'd known a couple of freelance P.I.s in the city. Quarterly taxes left them cash-starved, with no benefits.

No, thank you.

I foraged until I came across my good suit, a shirt, and my lined raincoat—enough for me to get started. Closing the side door behind me, I headed for the house. Inside, I found my family tucked away in Richard's study.

"Uh, Brenda, where's the iron?"

She looked up from her book. "In the laundry room. You need help?"

"No, thanks."

The dungeon laundry room was in the same place as in years before, although the appliances were brand new and top of the line. I tossed the clothes on the washer and awkwardly set up the ironing board. Trying my best to iron out the wrinkles, I scorched my pants cuff. Moments later, I looked up to find Brenda standing in the doorway.

"I can do it."

"Oh, I know you can—when you have two good hands. But right now, you've only got one."

I let her take over. Now that my investigator's training was coming back, I wanted to look my best—trustworthy—when I interviewed witnesses. Having that goal made me feel whole again.

Richard showed up as Brenda handed me the freshly ironed dress shirt. I eased it onto a hanger, catching sight of his disapproving stare.

"Why don't you just say it?" I challenged.

"Oh, now you're reading my mind, too?"

"It doesn't take a mind reader to tell what you're thinking," Brenda muttered. She turned off the iron, set it on the washer to cool, stowed the ironing board, and stole out of the basement, leaving me alone with a man itching for a fight.

"Jeff, you're not well."

"I'm not sick, either."

"No, but you are recovering from a serious head injury. I think you should just slow down."

"I'm not exactly running around."

He eyed the suit. "No, but you can't just show up at the church and—"

"Now who's a mind reader?"

"I read the newspaper, too. You plan to go to the funeral."

"If I can get in. How else can I meet Sumner's family and friends?"

"Jeff, you can't just barge in, interfere with people's lives—"

"And I just can't sit around contemplating my navel twenty-four hours a day, either."

He followed me upstairs and into the kitchen. I laid the suit and shirt across one of the chairs, and sat down, not daring to look him in the eye.

"You don't believe me," I said.

Richard took the chair across from me. "I don't know what to believe."

"I don't know how to make you understand. It's like a nightmare, only it doesn't stop when I wake. I have no proof, just a strong feeling that what I know is true."

"Jeff, is it possible you're twisting the facts to support a delusion?"

"I knew that man was dead. I felt his death. Now I've got to prove to myself I'm not some kind of lunatic. But I can't. Not until I see the place. Not until I talk with the people who knew him. Not until I can put all the pieces together."

Richard stared at the table. "Okay. Then let's prove—or disprove—it together. Let me help."

I considered his offer. Was he only placating me? It didn't matter.

"Okay."

"Where do we start?" he asked.

"Tomorrow. At the funeral."

SIX

RICHARD AND I SHOWED up at Christ the King Roman Catholic Church half an hour before the funeral Mass was due to start. We had to park on a side street three blocks away.

Days earlier, I had realized I was picking up the feelings of my fellow passengers on the plane. Yet, even with that experience under my belt, I wasn't prepared for the prickling sensations that radiated from the mob outside the church.

The murmur of voices vibrated through me like the buzz of a hive. The press of close-packed bodies seethed with a myriad of emotions. I penetrated the gathering, swallowing down sudden panic. Fists clenched, I gulped deep breaths of air so cold it scorched my lungs. Richard's eyes bore into mine. Was he waiting for me to freak?

I wouldn't give him the satisfaction.

Two policemen stood atop the church steps, keeping the horde of newsmen, photographers, and rubberneckers at bay. Private security had been hired, too. A man in a black overcoat checked names of mourners against a list on a clipboard. We didn't bother to check in with him—he wasn't about to let us in. With nothing much to see, I wandered through the crowd, eavesdropping.

Refused entry, a man spoke to a woman in low tones. "Matt and I were friends for over twenty years."

"There's no point hanging around," she said. "Maybe United Way will have a memorial service for him." She took the man's hand and led him away.

I scanned the crowd, seemed to recognize one of the reporters, who stood with a still photographer, but I couldn't place the face. I turned aside—didn't want him to see me in case he recognized me, knowing I'd feel foolish when I couldn't come up with his name.

Behind me a clique of young people stood huddled in a knot. "Think Diane even knows we're here?" someone asked.

"I've never been turned away from a funeral before."

"Like you've been to a million funerals," her friend said.

A white hearse turned the corner, waiting for the crowd to part so it could stop by the church's side entrance. I had to stand on tiptoe to watch as the funeral director and his associates escorted the bronze casket into the church. Where were the official pallbearers? This wasn't like any funeral I'd ever seen or been part of.

Richard glanced at his watch. "Mass will be at least an hour long. You don't want to wait until it's over, do you?"

"I don't know yet."

I should've done something. Asked people questions, but I didn't know who to single out—or what to ask. If the people standing outside the church weren't on the official attendees list, were they close enough to the victim to have known anything that would help me?

Richard stuffed his hands into his pockets. "Jeff, your cheeks are getting chapped. Your lips are practically blue. If I didn't know better, I'd diagnose you as cyanotic."

"Don't you mean hypothermic?"

"Come on, let's go home."

I looked back at the crowd. He was right. Coming to the church had been a complete waste of time. Besides, Richard looked frozen.

"You win, old man. We may as well go before the cold settles in those arthritic bones of yours." Truth was, I felt lousy, but I wasn't about to admit it to him.

As we neared the edge of the crowd, I broke through a ribbon of triumph—the same as I'd felt in the dreams.

I whirled, scanned the blur of faces around me.

The killer was there. Somewhere.

I shouldered my way through the mourners, heading for the barred oak doors, but my inner radar had already switched off.

Organ music blared from loudspeakers mounted on the side of the building. Pain lanced my brain as I rushed forward, searching for someone I couldn't even recognize.

The big doors banged shut behind a dark-coated figure. I dove for the brass handles, and a thick hand grabbed my wrist.

"Hold it, pal," the officer said sharply. "Unless your name's on the list—"

"I've got to get in there! It's an emergency!"

"What kind of emergency?"

I stared into the cop's skeptical face. "Who just went in?"

He glared at me.

"Please! It's important."

A hand grasped my shoulder. I spun around.

Richard. His eyes mirrored mine—an unspoken panic. "What is it?" he shouted over the music.

"The killer's inside."

He stared at me in disbelief. "Who?"

"I don't know."

I'd felt that presence, that gloating sense of triumph. Then the contact was gone—camouflaged by the mass of people still assembled on the steps, the trampled grass, and sidewalk.

BACK IN MY ROOM, I downed a couple of the little pink tablets and crawled onto my bed. My plan for the rest of the day was to keep a low profile. Richard hadn't said a word to me on the short ride home. Maybe that was good. Then again, I didn't like being condescended to either.

I closed my eyes and prayed for sleep, but my mind refused to rest. I couldn't stop thinking about what I'd experienced at the church.

If I was going to work on this case—and that's just what

it had become to me—I'd have to approach it like one of my insurance investigations.

I got up, found a sheet of paper, and filled both sides, writing down everything I knew. Then, armed with a pair of scissors, I trucked out to the garage and the recycling bin to retrieve every newspaper article on the murder. I dumped the brain injury pamphlets in the trash, stashed the articles in the big manila envelope, and deposited it in my bottom dresser drawer.

A fat phone book sat on the kitchen counter. I grabbed it and settled at the table to make a list of numbers. First up was the public library. Richard hadn't offered me the use of his computer, and the Internet, and I wasn't about to ask. I'd never been a sportsman, so I knew next to nothing about deer hunting. I figured I'd better educate myself on the subject with some good old-fashioned books.

I called the Department of Motor Vehicles about a replacement copy of my driver's license. With no ID, I was a nonperson. I waded through the recording for what seemed like forever before speaking to a human being. Contrary to DMV lore, she was courteous and helpful. Good thing I'd gathered up so much potential ID. I'd need it to get a duplicate of my license.

Next on the agenda, I had to get started on the legwork before the trail got too cold. Time to face the enemy.

Richard was in his study, parked behind the big desk, reading. He'd changed out of his mourning attire to yet another cashmere sweater and dark slacks, every inch the man of leisure.

I cleared my throat, feeling like a sixteen-year-old with a hot date and no wheels. "I need to borrow your car."

"Are you crazy? You've admitted having hallucinations, your arm is in a cast, making you a danger on the road, and you want to borrow *my* car?"

"How else can I get around?"

"Don't you think you've had enough excitement for one day?"

"Come on, Rich. I'm a good driver."

"I'll take you wherever you want to go." His expression darkened in irritation. "And where would that be?"

"The cemetery. Then Orchard Park."

"To do what?"

I shifted my weight from one foot to the other. "To talk to people?"

"About Sumner? Why?"

"To find out who killed him, of course."

"How're you going to pass yourself off?"

"What's wrong with saying what I am—an insurance investigator." This was beginning to feel like an interrogation.

"Because you're not working for anyone at the moment. And misrepresenting yourself will cause trouble with the law."

I stepped closer to his desk. "What do you suggest I do? I know things about this case."

"It's not your case!"

"What if the police never find who killed Sumner? Look, I have to do something. I know things about the situation— things I can't explain knowing. Am I just supposed to sit around and do nothing while a murderer runs free?"

Richard's voice possessed that deadly, practiced calm so characteristic of the medical profession. "Tomorrow we'll go to UB and we'll—"

"No, damn it. And stop patronizing me. I don't need a psychiatrist and I resent the implication. I just need—"

Need what? It sounded crazy even to me.

"Just let me borrow the car."

"No."

"Then tell me how to get to Forest Lawn Cemetery from here and I'll walk."

Richard sighed. "I told you, I will drive you anywhere you want to go."

I grabbed him by the arm. "Then let's go."

SOMETIMES IT SEEMS LIKE just about everything in the city of
Buffalo is either directly on or just off of Main Street, and
Forest Lawn was no exception. We didn't talk much during
the ride. I wasn't yet adept at judging my brother's moods.
Was he truly angry or just annoyed?

We drove through the cemetery's back gate, and Richard
slowed the car to the posted ten miles per hour down the
narrow roadway. The tombstones stood stoically against the
brisk March wind.

"Where to?"

I had no idea, hoping the funny feeling inside would guide
me. "Take the next left," I bluffed.

Richard complied, and we meandered down the single lane
of asphalt, following the twists and turns through the older, more
historical sections and then into the newer parts of the cemetery.

"This is hopeless, Jeff. How're you ever going to find
Sumner's grave among all the thousands here?"

"Well, for one thing it's fresh."

Richard glared at me.

We came to another crossroad and I pointed to the right.
Richard slowed the car as a lone woman dressed in dark
sweats jogged toward us. Solidly built, with pink cheeks, she
looked like she'd been out in the cold for some time. Richard
muttered something under his breath, and I kept a sharp
lookout, hoping I'd know Sumner's grave when I saw it.
Instead, that weird feeling vibrated through my gut.

"There!"

A mound of freshly-dug earth marred a snowy hillock.
The crowds had gone. No headstone marked the grave, just
the disturbed ground and several sprays of frozen roses and
carnations. Richard stopped the car and I got out. I walked up
the slight hill, looked around, saw no one. Good. I bowed my
head and closed my eyes, concentrating—waiting for that
funny feeling that had been guiding me, for some fragment
of intuition to drift into my consciousness.

Nothing.

I frowned. The niggling feeling that had drawn me here was still strong, but whatever compelled me to come had not been the victim.

I heard the hum of a power window. "Well?" Richard yelled. "I don't know."

The window went back up and Richard revved the engine.

I ignored him and walked around the grave. Many sets of footprints marred the light dusting of snow, but only one stood out in the freshly smoothed-over dirt. I stared at the prints. Someone had stood here for several minutes, judging from the depth of the prints. Someone in jogging shoes. I compared the print to my own foot and frowned. About the same size. Lots of people jogged through the cemetery, so who would've noticed if one of them stopped at one particular grave for an inordinate period of time on a cold, wintry day? It was probably one of the mourners—maybe even the one I'd tried to follow into the church. Too bad we hadn't hung around until after the Mass. But then how would I have known what to look for?

I closed my eyes, concentrating again, hoping to suck up some residual…feeling, sensation—*something*.

Nothing.

I looked down at the prints and placed my own feet on either side of them. I closed my eyes, my right hand balling into a fist. Yeah. Now I was getting something. Triumph? Yes, the person who'd stood here felt triumph over the dead man— the same emotion I'd experienced in the dream. Already I trusted these feelings…hunches?…as real.

And there was more.

Dread.

But dread didn't adequately describe it. Overwhelming despair made my eyes tear. The quack in New York had said a head injury fucked with your mind, and now I couldn't tell if the emotions bombarding me were my own or the dead guy's.

Suddenly something I'd felt so sure about only seconds before seemed insubstantial when I tried to analyze it rationally.

None of this was rational.

But that didn't mean it wasn't real. I took a breath and gathered my resolve. Okay, so what was I experiencing? I closed my eyes—thought. Cold, calculating, bean-counter mentality at work.

Thoughts that were not my own crept into my mind, lingering like a fog: *Youprickyouprickyouprickyouprickyouprick.*

Nothing new in that.

Try again.

Eyes closed, breathing steady, sensations seeped into me. My fists clenched in righteous indignation. *That fucking prick had it coming to him.*

Images.

Twilight.
Sumner's eyes bugged in terror.
Heart pounding.
A heavy object—a brick?—slammed into his temple. He went down.
Darkness.
The scene shifted. A baseball bat came at me—split my skull.
I staggered, nearly fell.

"Jeff!" Richard's voice shattered the spell. "Are you okay?"

My hands shook. I stared at a trampled pink carnation. I'd learn nothing more here.

"Yeah."

Shoving my right hand in my coat pocket, I started for the car, grateful to get back to its warmth.

Richard studied me, waiting. "Well?"

"Well, what? I don't know anything I didn't know before. Being here's just convinced me that I need to look further."

"And where's that, Orchard Park?"

I flexed the fingers on my left hand as far as the cast allowed, desperate to warm them. "I have to start somewhere. Maybe his neighbors can tell me something."

Richard put the car in gear and headed for the exit. "I should've brought a book."

"You could just loan me the car."

"No, next time I'll bring a book."

THE TEMPERATURE HAD dropped ten degrees and dusk had fallen by the time I finished canvassing Sumner's upper middle-class neighborhood on Forest Drive, right in the Village of Orchard Park. No one answered my knock at quite a few of the houses. I didn't bother with Sumner's own house, which looked forlorn, although there were lights on inside the gray clapboard colonial.

Flashing my old ID had done the trick. None of the neighbors questioned my being there, but I learned virtually nothing. Sumner may have been gregarious in his public life, but the family didn't mix with the neighbors. They'd lived in the house for six years and kept to themselves. Sumner's children were grown, and no one paid much attention to the middle-aged couple's comings and goings. And besides, I was informed on more than one occasion, my potential witnesses had already spoken with the police and had told them everything they did—or didn't—know.

Though I'd given my card—with Richard's phone number scribbled on the back—to a few of the neighbors, I didn't expect to get any calls.

I opened the car door, climbed in, fumbled with the seat belt. Richard squinted at me. "Any luck?"

"Looks like I froze my balls off for nothing." I glanced at the fuel gauge. "And you wasted a tank of gas."

Richard stared at me. "You look like shit. How do you feel?"

"Like shit."

Richard shook his head and put the car in gear as I sank back into the leather seat. The pounding in my head left me feeling vaguely nauseated.

"When did you start swearing? I don't remember you swearing so much," I said.

"You drove me to it. Now what?"

"I'll have to rethink my approach." Sumner was a business-man…a banker. "I'll have to talk to the people he worked with. But I can't use my insurance ID there, in case someone decides to check up on me." I glanced at my brother. "Where do you bank?"

He turned the corner. "All over. Grandmother didn't believe in keeping all her money in one bank—in case it failed. She got burned during the Depression. I never bothered to consoli-date her holdings."

"Then you must have accounts at Bison Bank, right?"

"Yes," he answered warily, giving me a sidelong glance.

"How much—if you don't mind my asking."

Richard shrugged, his eyes on the road. "A couple million."

"Million? You inherited millions?"

Richard nodded, his eyes still intent on the road. "Of course."

I should've remembered that little fact. That I didn't was another example of my faulty memory. "How many?"

"Last year I paid taxes on the income from fifty-five million." He tore his gaze from the road. "Anything else you want to know?"

"If you've got that kind of money, what the hell are you doing living in Buffalo?"

"Because L.A. wasn't working out any more."

I sank back into the leather seat, ignoring the edge that had crept into his voice. "I guess someone with a few million on deposit wouldn't have any trouble getting me inside the bank. I mean behind the scenes, where Sumner worked. Right?"

"I can try," he said, resigned. He glanced at the dashboard clock. "I'll make some calls in the morning."

"Thanks. Could we hit the Amherst library on the way home? I kind of reserved some books in your name. Which reminds me, I need to go to the DMV and get an official ID. Then maybe the library will let me take out my own books."

He sighed. "No problem."

Meanwhile, dollar signs danced through my mind. I considered the hospital bill, the plane fare, the movers. Richard could well afford to help me. So far there'd been no strings attached to the money he'd spent bailing me out, but how the hell would I ever repay him?

AFTER DINNER, I ESCAPED to my room for a little research. Despite the lingering headache, I forced myself to study the library books, and it wasn't long before I knew more than I cared to about bow hunting and field dressing game. From the description in the newspaper, that's exactly what had happened to Matthew J. Sumner.

The body had been shot through the back with an arrow. I didn't have to imagine the consequences of such an injury. My scrambled brains served me a graphic display of frothy blood spraying across stark, white snow. And the photos of gutted deer helped harden me to the vision of Sumner swinging from the rafter, his body looking more like a slab of meat than a human being.

While the newspapers hadn't mentioned mutilation—the severed and missing genitalia—it would be consistent with what I'd read about butchering Bambi. A bullet in the back of the skull would've been a quicker, neater death.

Settling back on the mattress, I did a little educated guesswork. Sumner was probably shot with a three-blade razor-sharp broadhead, carbon-shaft arrow from a compound bow. At least that's what the book's author recommended for greatest efficiency, speed, and accuracy.

I could get a look at the autopsy report at the medical examiner's office. In the case of violent deaths, such records are usually made public. The death certificate was also public record, but I didn't need to see that either.

I spread the clippings across the floor and bed and read and reread them all. The newspaper's speculation that the killer was some kind of crazed woodsman seriously differed from my own impression.

Most of the articles had been written by a Samuel Nielsen. Was he the familiar-looking guy at the church? I'd known a Sam Nielsen in high school. Could he be the same person? If so, it might be worth making his acquaintance again.

I picked up all the clippings and put them back in the envelope, then attacked the stack of parapsychology books. They weren't enlightening. Most of the information seemed anecdotal, rather than scientific. No wonder Richard remained skeptical. Besides, nothing seemed to apply to me.

All this investigating exhausted me. Would Richard be secretly pleased if I pushed myself beyond my physical limits and ended up back in the hospital?

To forestall that, I hit the sack early, but even after I'd turned out the light my mind continued working. I kept thinking about the weapon. I could call or visit all the archery supply stores and ranges listed in the phone book, but who said the killer had to buy locally?

I fell asleep to images of gutted deer and men, their dead, glassy stares focused on nothing.

SEVEN

THE DMV WAS CROWDED when we arrived the next morning. Richard handed over the California title to register his car in New York State, and got his picture taken for a driver's license. After we filled out our respective paperwork, Richard flashed his identification and the poor patient—me—was given preferential treatment and escorted directly to the cashier. Did the good doctor get the same treatment in five-star restaurants?

They promised the licenses would arrive in about a month. Good old New York State bureaucracy. In the meantime, we were both given temporary paper licenses; mine looked lonely in my empty new wallet. According to the law I could drive again. Now if only I had a car.

Next step, the bank.

Being a large depositor had its benefits. Once inside Bison Bank, we sailed past security and headed for the executive offices. We stepped off the elevator on the tenth floor and Richard led the way to the reception desk. I followed, soaking up the layout as I went. Richard was learning. He'd made the appointment for lunchtime so I could snoop.

We paused in front of the receptionist, a skinny young woman with brassy blonde hair and a winning smile.

"Good morning. I'm Richard Alpert. I have a twelve-thirty appointment with Ron Myers."

The receptionist rose from her desk. "Right this way."

"Is there a drinking fountain around here?" I asked.

"Just down the hall, to the left."

"Thanks. I'll catch up with you, Rich." She nodded at me and led Richard away; I headed in the opposite direction.

Being lunchtime, the place was relatively empty. It didn't take long to find Sumner's old office. I could see by the frosted glass flanking the door that the light was on inside. I tested the handle. Unlocked. A quick glance around proved no one was in sight. I stepped inside.

The blinds were raised, giving a panoramic view of the city—not that Buffalo in March is all that attractive. Craning my neck, I could see the ice on Lake Erie shining in the distance. The peons in the tellers' cubes on the main floor would covet such an office. Cherry hardwood furniture buffed to perfection. Someone had already started packing Sumner's personal items into a sturdy cardboard carton.

I sat in the plush swivel chair, settling my good arm along the armrest, closed my eyes, and breathed deeply. I'd hoped to glean some insight into the man, but instead a memory from long ago surfaced, and I suddenly realized where I'd met Matthew John Sumner.

It was my mother's birthday, and the blue pressed-glass bud vase was the most beautiful thing my ten-year-old eyes had ever seen. I must've stood in Woolworth's gift section, staring at it, for more than five minutes, my attention completely focused on the $3.95 price tag. I had precisely $1.14 in my jeans pocket. I looked around. No one nearby. Slipping the vase under my jacket, I headed for the exit.

"I saw what you did."

My heart froze as I looked up into the stern face of the tall, hefty man above me. I'd never stolen anything in my life and now, on my first foray into crime, I'd been caught.

The man crouched down to my level, holding out his hand. Without a word, I handed over the vase.

"Why would a boy like you want something like this?"

I couldn't look him in the eye. "It's…it's my mother's birthday tomorrow. I don't have enough money."

"I see." He straightened. "Wait for me outside."

Being a frightened child, I did just what the adult told me to do. Minutes later, he came out of the store.

"Young man, you know it's wrong to steal."

Hot tears of shame stung my eyes as I nodded solemnly.

He handed me a paper sack. "Here. You give this to your mother on her birthday. But you have to promise me you'll never steal again."

Gaze focused on my feet, I nodded. He patted my shoulder. Without a word, I turned and ran all the way back to our apartment.

I NEVER STOLE AGAIN.

My mother had cherished that cheap piece of glass, but I couldn't look at it without feeling shame over how I'd obtained it.

Sitting in Sumner's chair, I pondered my debt to him. Our fleeting encounter some twenty-six years before had made one hell of an impression on my psyche. What else could explain the visions of his murder?

I left the whys for another time and forced my thoughts back to the present, studying Sumner's desk.

His Rolodex was fat and well worn. Taking out my little spiral notebook, I jotted down any phone number that looked promising, including those of his children. The desk itself was already pretty much cleared, and the computer was switched off. Aside from the fact it was illegal, it was also unlikely I could tap into the bank's databases to check Sumner's files. I thumbed through a diskette box next to the terminal. Nothing looked to be personal.

Several photos decorated the walls behind the couch: Sumner's wife, children, him receiving an award.

I sat back in the comfortable chair, grasping the arms, waiting for that funny feeling to come over me.

Nothing.

The file cabinets were locked, but the desk drawers weren't. I sifted through them and found the requisite pens, pencils, and other office supplies, along with a battery-operated razor, a toothbrush, and a tube of minty-fresh toothpaste.

The credenza's cabinets housed an assortment of trophies, paperweights, and award placards. Buried in back was a framed drawing of rainbows and colored balloons, crudely done in marking pens, like something a child might do.

I grasped the frame with my good hand, studied it. Nothing special about it or the drawing, which looked to be done on heavy card stock. On impulse, I fumbled to remove it from the frame and found that it wasn't just a drawing, but a folded, handmade, one-of-a-kind invitation.

Come to a first birthday party for Jackie, January tenth, seven o'clock, three years before.

No address listed, so whoever sent it assumed Sumner knew where the party was to be held. But who was Jackie? It wouldn't be too hard to check the birth records for that date. I hoped the child had been born in the Buffalo area. I jotted down the date.

I slid the invitation back behind the glass, turned it over, and continued to study it. It must've meant a lot to Sumner, or why would he have framed it? Then again, why wasn't it on display any more? Why was it hidden?

Suddenly that queasy, unsettling feeling coursed through me. My fingers convulsed around the wooden frame as intuition flashed:

Nightfall.
Chest constricted. Throat closed on stifled sobs.
No!No!No!No!No!No!
A venom-filled voice—slow, draggy: "Get back in the car."

Rising panic.
Closed in. Dark. An unspeakable horror—

I dropped the frame as though burned, shattering the vision. Gasping for breath, I pulled at my suddenly too-tight collar. I sat back, wiped my damp palms on my pants, willing myself to relax.

Fear. Got that in spades.

Raw terror. The world destroyed in a way that nothing could ever make right.

I frowned. These little nuggets of psychic insight were graphic, but not particularly helpful. At least not yet.

Unwilling to touch the frame again, I used a ruler to push it back into the cabinet, slamming the door.

"Can I help you?" An attractive redhead stood in the open doorway, her mouth pursed in annoyance. "This is Mr. Sumner's office. Unless you have a damn good reason to be here, I'm calling security."

"Sorry. I—" My mind raced, and in an instant I decided to tell the truth. "I'm waiting for my brother. He's meeting with Ron Myers. I didn't feel well, and the door was open, so I ducked in."

She looked at me with suspicion. Okay, so it wasn't the whole truth.

"I'll leave." I quickly rose and the room suddenly lurched around me. I grabbed at the file cabinet for balance, and the woman hurried to my side, grasping my elbow to steady me.

"Are you okay?"

"I need to sit." She led me over to the low couch. "This is embarrassing. I thought I was better, and now...."

She took in my lopsided haircut. "Were you in an accident?"

"Mugged. In New York."

"That happened to my sister a couple of years ago."

Now that I had her sympathy, I might just get some information out of her. "My name's Jeff. Jeff Resnick."

"Maggie Brennan," she said, and offered her hand.

My fingers clasped hers, my gaze captivated by her deep blue eyes.

She wasn't what you'd call beautiful. Fine lines around her eyes hinted at years of smiles. The color of her eyebrows didn't match her auburn hair, cut in an out-of-date Dorothy Hamill wedge, but the style suited her. Her dark business suit made her look confident and competent.

"Umm. My hand?" she prompted.

Like a fool, I still clasped it.

"Oh, sorry." I pulled back my hand; the palm had gone moist again. "Did you say this was Mr. Sumner's office? Wasn't he the guy in the paper who—"

"Yes. Isn't it awful? I'm packing his personal things for his family."

"Did you know him?"

"Everybody around here knew Matt."

"I'll bet the bank practically had to shut down with everybody going to the funeral?"

"Not as many went as you'd think. The rules for time off are strict. A bunch of managers went, but nobody I know would waste a vacation day for a bastard like him." At my startled reaction, she quickly explained. "I can't believe I said that. I just meant that he could be hard to get along with—a perfectionist who expected daily miracles from his subordinates. But nobody deserves to die like that."

I indicated the photos on the wall. "He must've been devoted to his family."

"Devoted to bailing them out of trouble."

"Oh?"

She didn't elaborate. In the pictures, Sumner's children appeared to range in age from fifteen to thirty. No little tykes.

"Did he have grandchildren?"

"Not that I know of. His oldest son got married this past fall."

Okay. The invitation writer could've been Sumner's girlfriend, with a baby—his baby? If so, someone had to know about them. The question was who? But the woman standing over me wasn't the person to ask.

"Are you feeling better now? I can show you to Ron's office."

"If you wouldn't mind." I rose to my feet.

She closed the door behind us. As she led the way down the corridor, I noticed how nicely her skirt fit. She paused at a door, knocked, then poked her head inside. "Ron? I think I found your errant visitor." She held the door open for me.

"Thanks. For your help." I offered her my hand again. She took it and I held on.

I liked Maggie Brennan.

RICHARD'S BANK ADVISOR WAS more interested in talking about trust funds than his murdered colleague. At my every attempt to change the subject, he'd jump in with some dull fact concerning loopholes and tax benefits Richard could enjoy if he'd entrust all his money to good old Ron. I didn't much care for the man, and I suspected Richard felt the same, although he gave me a few sharp glances when Myers's patience stretched thin. Eventually, I gave up.

From the bank we crossed the street and headed for The Extra Point, a sports bar lavishly decorated with local sports memorabilia—especially the Buffalo Bills. I'd lived away from Buffalo for a long time, and although I still cheered for the team, I'd forgotten what they meant, not only to the city, but to all of western New York. Didn't Richard say he had season tickets?

Seated under one of Jim Kelly's jerseys, we ordered lunch, and my physician watchdog brother actually allowed me to have a non-alcoholic beer. I could only look longingly at his glass of the genuine article.

Over lunch, I filled Richard in on what I'd learned, leaving out my memory of meeting Sumner. He didn't seem impressed.

"Guess you didn't expect all this when you invited me to stay with you."

Richard set down his glass. "No."

"I thought things would be a little less hectic, too."

"Except for this psychic stuff, I expected you to be a lot more belligerent."

"Belligerent? You mean like when I was a kid?"

Richard blinked. "Why would you say that?"

"It seemed to me I was constantly in trouble. How about when I bugged your grandmother?"

He almost smiled. "Maybe. But getting you to talk was as hard then as it is now. In some ways, you haven't changed at all."

I didn't know how to reply to that.

"Belligerent, huh? Like those poor souls in the brain-injury rehab hospitals?"

"Jeff, I don't think you understand how serious your injuries are."

The chip on my shoulder grew bigger and heavier. "I'm not sick."

"Look, don't get angry—"

"I'm not angry. I'm adjusting—slowly—to everything that's happened to me. Let me do it my own way, okay?"

"Okay." He drained his glass. "Where do you want to go next?"

"Public library. I want to check the birth announcements in old copies of the newspaper."

"Has it occurred to you that you're going over the same ground as the police? What do you think you'll find that they won't?"

"I don't think they're looking into the same things I am. Besides, they're not likely to tell me what they know. By the same token, I'm not prepared to tell them what I know. At least not yet. Hell, Rich, I practically witnessed the murder."

He looked around, lowered his voice. "Then go to the police."

"How can I convince them when I can't even convince you? And what am I supposed to tell them? 'Uh, I have a funny feeling about this murder.' They'd send me to a psych ward.

Uh-uh, I can't talk to the cops until I have some kind of hard evidence. Now can we pay the check and get out of here?"

It took longer to find another parking space than to drive the two blocks or so to Buffalo's main library. True to his word, Richard brought his own book along. A heavy medical tome with a long, boring title. He sat and read for two hours while I gave myself one hell of a skull-pounding headache and a good case of vertigo whipping through the microfilmed records.

I ended up checking two months' worth of newspapers for the names of children born the week before and after the January tenth date. I found three possibilities. John Patrick Ryan, Jacqueline Tamara Prystowski, and J. Matthew Walker. I hoped one of them was the Jackie I was looking for. Otherwise, I didn't know what I'd do.

I wrote down the names and addresses. Two of the announcements listed both mother's and father's names. The Walker kid's did not. Not unusual these days.

Closing my notebook, I found my very bored brother, and had him take me home.

Nausea kept me from eating dinner. I took two of the pink tablets and waited for sleep, the only haven of relief from the headache.

The memory of my only meeting with Sumner and the terror and horror I'd felt when touching that invitation kept circling through my aching head. I was onto something. I was going to find Matt Sumner's killer.

EIGHT

I AWOKE LATE THE NEXT morning—perfect timing for calling Sumner's widow. I checked on Richard's availability first. Funny, my brother didn't seem to have a lot to occupy his days.

According to the newspapers, Claudia Sumner had been visiting friends in Florida at the time of the murder. Since she'd found the body, I wanted to talk with her while her memories were still fresh. When we spoke, I'd mentioned my former employer's name, carefully avoiding the fact that I no longer worked for them. Without that ploy, she'd never grant me an interview. Our appointment was set for one. In the meantime I hauled out the phone book. I wasted an hour trying to call the parents of the kids born January tenth. No luck.

Next I called the funeral home. No, they would not discuss the church guest list or any arrangements on the Sumner funeral. Instead, they referred me to their attorney.

Richard and I hit the road about twelve forty, giving us a twenty-minute window to get across town. We hadn't gone far when I pulled down the visor, inspecting my hair in the attached mirror. Maybe I should've asked Brenda to concoct some kind of bandage to cover my unusual haircut. I'd explained to Mrs. Sumner about my…accident…so that when she saw me she wouldn't wonder what kind of nut case had come to visit her.

"What's the matter?" Richard asked, glancing over at me. "Nervous?"

I flipped the visor back into place. "Yes."

"Why? You interviewed six or eight people on Monday."

"Yes, but none of them was the victim's wife, and none of them found the guy hanging in the garage."

"Just what do you hope to learn?"

"I don't know. What I really want to do is get in that garage—"

"To see where it all happened?"

"Not the murder. Just the aftermath."

Richard made no further comment. He still didn't believe me. The logical part of me didn't blame him. The brain-damaged part of me was irritated.

"Look, after we finish here, I'll take you where I go and we'll get you a haircut," he said. "Maybe they can trim it up so that you don't look like a—"

"Psycho?"

Richard smiled. "Nonconformist."

"Thanks," I said, meaning it. The visor came down for another look. Definitely nonconformist.

Sumner's house appeared no different than it had before, except for the uniformed security guard posted at the bottom of the driveway. Mrs. Sumner had found it necessary to hire someone to keep the hounding press at bay.

Richard waited in the car while I checked in with the guard, who waved me through.

I walked past a late-model Lexus. Mrs. Sumner's or a friend's? After climbing the concrete steps, I thumped the door's brass knocker. Seconds later it opened a few inches on a chain, as though she'd been waiting behind it. All I could see were a pair of sharp, gray, schoolteacher eyes.

"Mrs. Sumner, I'm Jeffrey Resnick. I called earlier."

"Can I see some identification?"

"Of course." My old insurance ID worked again.

She scrutinized the card. "I must confess I don't recall Matt having a policy with your company."

Then again, maybe it hadn't.

Just when I thought she'd slam the door in my face, she released the chain.

"May I take your coat?"

I waved off her offer and followed her into the house.

Claudia Sumner was an attractive woman of about fifty. Her short, permed hair was colored an appropriately light shade of brown, and her face was virtually unlined. Either she never had a care in the world, or knew a skilled plastic surgeon. Petite and trim, she wore a beige cashmere sweater, matching slacks, and comfortable-looking leather pumps. I bet she never sat down in front of the TV with a bag of nachos and a pot of salsa.

She seemed to be alone in the house, with no friends or relatives in attendance for emotional support. In fact, her attitude was very businesslike, not at all the bereaved widow I'd expected.

She settled on one end of the overstuffed couch in the living room, motioning me into a chintz-covered wing chair. The furnishings stressed comfort. Antiques and expensive-looking porcelain figurines graced the shelves and tabletops. Several framed photographs were scattered throughout the room, but they seemed to be exclusively of her children. No books or magazines, and no lingering aura of Matt Sumner, either.

"Are you working with the police?"

"I expect to share some information soon," I said, hoping I'd effectively evaded her question. "I'm grateful you agreed to talk with me. It must've been unpleasant to find your husband."

"I really don't care to discuss it."

"Can you give me some background on Mr. Sumner? His interests…?"

"The newspaper was quite thorough. He was active in The United Way. He served as last year's campaign chairman. Matt truly cared about people."

Oh yeah?

"Did he have any enemies?"

She hesitated. "Not that I'm aware of. Matt was…could be," she amended, "very charming."

"Is it possible he might've had financial problems?"

"If you mean blackmail, no."

Her perfectly calm statement took me by surprise, but then she'd probably already been over this with the police. And if she was willing to be blunt, there was no reason for me to dance around certain issues.

"Did he have a girlfriend?"

The widow was not surprised by the question.

"Perhaps. He worked late a lot these past few years. I suspected he might be having an affair…but I guess I didn't want to know for sure. We lived a quiet, comfortable life."

Her cold gaze made me shudder.

"Did he ever mention Jackie?"

She blinked. "I'm sorry?"

"I ran across the name in conversation with someone at the bank."

"I know of no one called Jackie."

I got the feeling she wasn't exactly being candid with me. But then, I hadn't really expected her to.

"When did you last speak with your husband?"

She sighed. "Last Sunday evening. He said he had meetings all day Friday and I should take a cab home from the airport."

"Did you find him immediately?"

"No. I was home for about an hour. I'd unpacked my suitcase and thought I'd go to the grocery store. That's when I found him." She looked away, her eyes filling with tears. I wasn't sure if it was from grief or revulsion. I pretended to jot down a note, giving her a moment to collect herself.

"Who was the last family member to actually see your husband alive?"

She cleared her throat. "Me, I suppose."

"None of the children visited while you were gone?"

"I don't think so. Michael's school is in Erie, Pennsylvania. Diane and Rob haven't lived at home for several years."

Which confirmed what the neighbors had said. "Do they live in the Buffalo area?"

"Yes, Rob does. Diane...." Her gaze narrowed. "Why do you want to know?"

"I'd like to speak with them, too."

She sat straighter in her chair. "I would prefer that you didn't, although I suppose there's no way I can stop you."

I changed my line of questioning. "Did your husband hunt?"

"Never. He could never kill anything."

Maybe not, but as a bank V.P. he'd had the power to ruin someone's financial life with the stroke of a pen.

"Any other hobbies?"

"He golfed. He was quite good at it, too. He was to head a tournament in June. A benefit for one of his causes. At the moment, I can't think which one."

"That's quite understandable. How tall was your husband?"

She looked at me as though the question was ridiculous, but answered it anyway. "Five-eleven."

"And his weight?"

"I don't know. Maybe two hundred and ten pounds."

I jotted it down. "I'm curious; there were no calling hours at the funeral home. Was there a reason?"

She pursed her lips. "You *are* curious."

I was afraid she was going to refuse to answer the question. Then she sighed.

"To be perfectly honest, Mr. Resnick, I want to put this whole unpleasant ordeal behind me. You can understand that, can't you?"

"What about his friends? Wouldn't they—?"

"I telephoned those people I deemed necessary. The church was full of our friends and his colleagues. There was no need to subject my family to a media circus."

A plausible explanation. Yet how could she know of all the

people whose lives her husband had touched? How many would've showed up to pay their respects, people who were genuinely sorry to hear of his passing?

I tried a different tack. "I understand you'll be selling the house."

She called my bluff without blinking. "As a matter of fact, a real estate agent will be here later today."

She really was eager to move on.

And then my mind went completely blank. I couldn't think of a single question that didn't involve finding the body and the entire grotesque situation. She picked up on my hesitation.

"I'm curious about the insurance policy, Mr. Resnick. Can you tell me how much it's worth, and who the beneficiary is?"

Every muscle in my body tensed. "I'm just the investigator, ma'am. I'm not at liberty to discuss such matters."

"But surely you have an idea? Can you give me the policy number, or the date it was issued—anything to help me trace it?"

"I'd be glad to get back to you on that."

Her gaze was steely. "I'd appreciate it."

It was time for me to get to the real reason for my visit. I pretended to consult my notes, posing the question as though it had no real relevance. "May I have a look in the garage?"

Her eyes narrowed in irritation. "I suppose. Although there's really not much to see. I had a cleaning service come through this morning."

I followed her through the house to a utility area. She pointed to the door. "I hope you'll forgive me if I don't follow you."

"I quite understand."

Besides, I didn't need a companion for this phase of my investigation.

The double garage was cold, the only light coming through the frosted glass on the door to the back yard. I flipped the light switch to my left, and a lone bulb illuminated a room I was already familiar with. I'd heard crime scenes, especially where a homicide had been committed, are filled with an aura of anger, desperation, and pain. This place was no different, but Sumner's murder had not been committed here.

With no cars parked inside, the garage seemed cavernous and unnaturally tidy. The police had probably gone over every inch of it in search of evidence. Still, Claudia Sumner had been correct; there was little out of the ordinary to see.

Matching bicycles hung from laminated hooks near built-in storage cupboards. No gardening equipment cluttered walls or shelves, yet I suspected that under the remaining snow the yard was perfectly landscaped and attended to by experts. A garage door opener stood silent vigil over the room. The newspaper stressed there'd been no forced entry. The killer could've used the remote to get in. No mention was made of it being found.

Except for rope marks on the joist where the body had hung, and a brown stain on the concrete, now scrubbed almost clean, there was nothing of interest to see. But the lack of visible evidence didn't mean there was nothing for me to experience.

Closing my eyes, I tried to relax, to open myself to whatever psychic pipeline was feeding me information. In seconds that sick wave of anger and triumph filled me. Fear and a strong sense of revulsion swirled in the mix, but the queasy feelings I received were not from Matt Sumner. From the start, I'd gotten next to nothing from the victim.

Clearing my mind of distracting thoughts, I concentrated, trying to conjure up the image of the deer running across a barren field.

Instead, the vision that appeared before my mind's eye wasn't the tawny buck, but a naked, middle-aged man in bare feet, stumbling across the snow, racing for his life. The pronounced thwack of the arrow leaving the bow jarred me. Sumner's anguished grunt of shock as the arrow connected with its target left my stomach reeling.

The vision winked out. I let go of the breath I hadn't realized I'd been holding. It wasn't so bad now. I was already learning to distance myself from the other's fear—to experience it, but not make it my own.

But maybe that wasn't the way to go. Maybe I needed to delve deeper, immerse myself in that sense of terror to truly understand what the witness had seen, felt. Yet my own sense of fear—survival instinct—kicked in. Someone had literally butchered Sumner, while another terrified someone had watched. I wasn't willing to experience that first-hand.

I remembered that god-awful feeling of despair I'd gotten from the invitation in Sumner's office, muted now that I had no catalyst to reignite it. What was it…?

And then it hit me: Betrayal. Stark, maddening betrayal. Why?

Because the same thing could happen to me.

A thrill of horror washed through me, leaving me clammy with cold sweat.

Needing to do something, I dragged a stepladder across the floor. Once positioned, I climbed. Hauling my left arm and cast onto the joist helped me maintain balance as I reached the top rung. Looking down at the beam, I examined the rope marks. Minute fibers, embedded in the wood, still remained.

I shut my eyes, rubbed the fibers between my thumb and forefinger, making it a Zen experience to become one with the rope. Stupid as it sounds, it worked. The killer's rope was old, had sat coiled in a dark, dank place for a long time before being used—same impression I'd gotten at the hardware store.

Replacing the ladder against the wall, I pulled out my tape measure and checked the height of the joist from the floor. Sumner was five-eleven, so his feet would've hung anywhere from six to ten inches above the ground.

I had no need of the police photographs. With only a little effort I could see a mental picture of every detail. I forced myself to confront the image of Sumner, hanging.

He looked so…dead, his skin tone a flat, bluish white. Yet his opened, unseeing, cloudy eyes seemed to follow me. I looked away.

Heart pounding, I circled the phantom body. Sumner's neck had been broken, probably after death. The rope around his throat had rubbed against his ears and dug a visible groove into his skin. A bruise darkened his left temple, and I found myself absently touching my own, where the baseball bat had collided with bone. We'd both been attacked by a right-handed assailant.

The entrance wound in Sumner's back was puckered and blood-blackened. My gaze traveled the length of his body; his genitals were missing, all right. Had the killer kept them as a souvenir?

Sumner's chest cavity was empty, his sternum gouged and every organ gone. The ribs were totally exposed, reminding me of a rack of barbecue ribs ready for the grill. Bruises marred his shins, and both feet were crisscrossed with cuts, probably received while attempting to escape his murderer across the crusted snow. The bottoms of his heels showed scrape marks, and dust particles clung to his back and buttocks. Had the cops found skin cells on the floor where he'd been dragged across the concrete?

I looked away and the vision was gone. The bloodstained floor drew my attention. The murderer would have to be pretty strong to haul Sumner around, transferring him from the crime scene to his home, hoisting his rigor-stiffened body to hang, and all without leaving a single fingerprint or other clue. There was cruelty in leaving the body for his wife to discover, as though the killer were rubbing her nose in the crime.

The light bulb was missing from the garage door opener. After the murderer strung up the body, he'd probably wanted the garage dark when he opened it to leave. Had the lamppost been on that night? Surely someone had to have seen *something*.

I turned. Claudia Sumner stood behind the storm door.

She'd waited for me—watched me—her arms crossed over her chest in annoyance.

"Thank you for your help, Mrs. Sumner."

She opened the door, reached to touch the garage door control. With a hum and a jerk, the door slowly rose.

"Good day, Mr. Resnick."

As I crossed onto the driveway, the door started its slow, steady descent.

I was glad to reach the car and Richard's friendly face.

NINE

"THE POT'S EMPTY."

Brenda and I looked over our sections of newspaper to stare at Richard.

He turned his coffee cup over to show us it, too, was empty.

"I made supper," Brenda said, her voice flat. "And washed up."

"I can't get the filters out with only one set of fingers," I said, showing him the limited range of motion my cast allowed.

Richard scowled, let out a breath, and got up to make a fresh pot.

Evenings had fallen into a pattern. After dinner, we'd sit around the kitchen table drinking coffee and reading the paper. Later, I'd try to stay out of Richard's and Brenda's way. Things seemed strained between them, and no doubt my presence was a contributing factor. Then, for as long as I could concentrate, I'd reread the newspaper articles on the murder, or maybe glance at the library books, before going to bed. A boring lifestyle, but I wasn't up to much more.

The coffeemaker chugged and Richard took his seat again.

The front doorbell rang.

We glared at one another for long seconds, daring each other to answer it.

It rang again.

Without a word, Richard pushed back his chair and disappeared down the hall.

I turned my attention back to the financial page and felt sorry for old Rich. It seemed like he was doing all the fetching and carrying lately. Did a man as well-educated and professionally situated as my brother feel degraded by such trivial matters?

Brenda got up to pour herself another cup of coffee, as Richard returned with another man.

"Jeff, this is Detective Carl Hayden. He'd like to speak with you." He didn't bother to introduce the plainclothes cop to Brenda.

My stomach knotted. I recognized the name from the newspaper articles. Hayden was the lead investigator on the Sumner murder. He was big—about six-four, two hundred and fifty pounds—and he looked pissed. Crew-cut and heavy-featured, he reminded me of a slow-moving freight train—deadly, not to be underestimated.

"Detective Hayden." I offered my hand, which he ignored.

"Would you like some coffee?" Brenda asked politely, but her body language belied her solicitous words as she eyed the cop with suspicion.

Hayden shook his head, all business, turning his full attention to me. "Sir, Mrs. Claudia Sumner called Orchard Park Police Department this afternoon. Said you'd paid her a visit."

"Yes, sir." I figured I'd better be as polite as he was. After all, I didn't want to be charged with obstructing justice, if that's what he ultimately had in mind.

"You told her you were an insurance investigator. But she doesn't deal with The Travelers."

Neither did I, any more.

"Sir, do you now work for Travelers?"

I carefully considered my answer.

"No."

"Have you ever worked for that company?"

"Yes."

"In Buffalo?"

"No."

I hoped my curt answers wouldn't bug him, but I didn't want to give him any more information than I had to.

"Mr. Resnick, just what is your interest in Mr. Sumner's death?"

"How did you track me down?"

"DMV. Mrs. Sumner's security guard took down the license plate number. Please answer my question."

Polite but firm.

"Like everybody else, I just want to know what happened to him."

"Everybody else doesn't pass themselves off as insurance investigators and visit the bereaved," Hayden said. "Where were you on Thursday evening between four and eight o'clock?"

"You can't suspect Jeff," Brenda cried.

"I was with them." I nodded toward Richard and Brenda. "All day, all evening."

"We can vouch for him," Richard added. "Detective Hayden—" He turned the cop aside and spoke quietly. "My brother recently suffered a rather severe head injury, which can account for—"

"Richard!"

Just what I needed—to be branded a nut.

Listening intently to Richard, Hayden looked at me over his shoulder, his expression grim. He turned back to me with no hint of sympathy.

"Mr. Resnick, I'd appreciate it if you'd refrain from visiting the Sumner family; they've suffered enough. And it would be unfortunate for you if they decided to press harassment charges. Besides, the Orchard Park PD is capable of solving this murder without outside interference."

Defiance flashed through me, but I kept my mouth shut.

Hayden nodded at Richard and Brenda, then headed back the way he'd come, with Richard struggling to keep up.

"Of all the nerve," Brenda said.

"I haven't stepped on anyone's toes," I said, but she wasn't the one I needed to convince. I was out of the hospital on Richard's say-so. As my next of kin, and a physician besides,

Richard held all the power. I wasn't sure of my rights should he decide to have me committed, or—

I forced myself to breathe evenly. No way could I let paranoia get the better of me. It made me react like those brain-injury case studies in the pamphlets.

Footsteps approached. I must've looked panicked, because Brenda moved closer, put a hand on my shoulder. "It's okay, Jeffy. Everything's okay."

Richard's face betrayed no emotion. "We need to talk," he said, voice calm, his attention fixed only on me. He took his seat at the table across from me.

I felt like a kid who'd been caught spying on a skinny dipper. I hadn't done anything wrong. Not really. Certainly nothing too illegal.

He composed himself, and I wondered if he assumed that stance before telling patients they had only weeks to live.

"Something's not right with you, and I don't believe it's physical."

"Why? Because I know about this murder?"

He nodded. "I'm having trouble dealing with this whole situation."

"You're having trouble? What about me? I feel like I'm going crazy. It's like the inside of my brain itches and I can't scratch it. My whole life is fucked, because a couple of street punks needed crack money."

Richard remained controlled, rational. "Just what do you know that you didn't read in the paper?"

My voice rose. "I know that a man was murdered."

"Everybody knows that."

"I know he was killed in a field. I know that a little kid witnessed it."

"What little kid?" Brenda asked.

"Jackie."

"The kid on the invitation you saw in Sumner's office?" Richard asked.

"Yes."

"And how did she witness it?"

"I don't know—*he* just did."

They were both staring at me; Brenda aghast, Richard incredulous. But the impact of my words had only just hit me. Until that moment, I hadn't known Jackie was a boy or what he'd seen, but I was as sure of it as I was about my own name.

"If you don't want to talk to me or Brenda, I think you should talk to someone else," Richard said, his voice deadly calm. "You need professional help to get over the trauma of your...accident."

"It wasn't an accident—it was an unprovoked attack. A robbery. And they got a whole lot more than just my money. They took my life!"

"Which proves my point. You need to work through this anger. Until you do, your subconscious is going to keep harping on it, which is why you're obsessing on this murder."

"No." Our gazes locked. "I know what I know. I had those dreams in the hospital before Sumner was murdered."

"Do you actually believe you have psychic power?"

"Whatever's happening to me is real. It's not a psychotic reaction, or a delusion, or something I'm making up to get attention."

"You must admit your behavior has been a little strange."

"How so?"

"The fact that you can't go upstairs, for one."

Just thinking about it filled me with dread. "It's because of your grandmother."

"Oh, so now you think the house is haunted?"

"Richard!" Brenda chided.

He whirled on her, eyes blazing. "Stay out of this."

"Just who do you think you're talking to?"

"Him!" He turned back to me. "Well?"

"I don't believe in ghosts—but there's something of her up there. It's leftover anger—rage. I don't understand it, but it's there and it hurts like hell."

I changed the subject. "What happened to the sympathetic doctor I spoke to the other day, the one who wanted to help me? Now, because the police got wind of my investigation, you want to shut me down, hide me in a closet, and pass me off as some kind of brain-damaged fool!"

I bolted from my chair. I didn't have the stamina for an extended battle with Richard.

"Where're you going?" Richard demanded, following me through the house.

"Out." I grabbed my coat from the hall closet, struggled to get it over my cast, and opened the front door.

"Jeff."

"Let him go," Brenda said, as I stormed out into the cold.

"Jeff, come back!" Richard called after me again.

I stalked off toward Main Street, my breath coming out in foggy wisps. The cold air felt good, cleansing. With every step I felt empowered, even though I hadn't won the argument.

The Snyder business district was to the right. I headed for it.

Biting my lip in frustration, I faced the reality of my situation: Richard had lost all patience with me. That meant no more lifts around town. No more getting me in places like the bank. The strings were now firmly attached, and I would either have to play the game his way…or get back on my feet. To do that, I needed a job.

The answer seemed simple, but was I physically ready to work? The headaches weren't as bad, but they still came daily and probably would for some time. I couldn't even remember how much longer I needed the cast on my arm. I had no money and nowhere else to go. I'd paid taxes—I might be eligible for Social Security. But how long would it take to get it, and what was I supposed to do in the meantime?

I paused, looking around. Where the hell was I going, anyway? In the back of my mind I remembered a cozy little bar up ahead, next to the fire station.

The penetrating wind made me huddle deeper into my

unzipped jacket. What was the name of that tavern? Oh, yeah, McMann's. Richard had taken a few hours off from the hospital to take me there on my eighteenth birthday. My first legal drink. We'd stood at the bar, sipping our beers, surrounded by a bunch of old geezers, and shared a fleeting moment of camaraderie. Afterwards we'd returned home to find Richard's grandmother waiting for us. Her shrill voice cut my soul as she ranted about our alcoholic mother.

I'd been a forgotten bystander as Richard argued that as my guardian he could take me where he wanted, do exactly as he saw fit. It hadn't occurred to him that on that date I could legally make my own decisions. That same night I decided I'd enlist in the Army at the end of the school year.

Richard tried to talk me out of it—he wanted me to go to college. But I wouldn't listen and traded one four-year sentence for another. I wanted to get away from that old woman the way I now wanted to get away from him.

The wind whipped around me and I stopped dead. Déjà vu dragged me back to the night of the attack. The circumstances were the same: a lonely street, a bitter cold night. Panicked, I looked ahead and behind me, expecting two shadowy figures.

No one.

Slower, my feet crunched the crusted snow once more.

Time to play devil's advocate. What if Richard was right? Could some injured, twisted part of me be fooling me into thinking I knew things I couldn't possibly know?

No.

I'd seen Sumner's face in my mind before Brenda showed me his picture in the newspaper. I don't know why I was blessed—cursed?—with this knowledge, but I trusted it. If I didn't believe there was a reason for this happening to me, it would drive me crazy.

A look around helped me get my bearings. Up ahead, the lights of my alma mater, Amherst Central High School, illuminated an entire city block. On really bad days, Curtis the chauffeur would drive me…unless Mrs. Alpert rose early. Then she insisted he be at her beck and call. She always picked the stormiest days.

I hated that old woman with a passion I've never felt since, and I wanted to get out of that house so badly….

Why did it always come back to her?

Forcing my thoughts back to the present, I continued walking.

A bakery sat at the crossroads. What had been there years ago? I'd already walked past the Snyder fire station before realizing something was wrong. Hadn't McMann's been right there? The fire station looked big and new and had obviously been expanded to sit where that quaint little tavern had been.

Confused, I glanced around me. The cold seeped through my thin-soled shoes. I was too far from home to start back without first stopping to warm up. All the little stores were dark and the night seemed to be closing in.

An elderly woman peered through the bakery's plate glass window. She'd rubbed a hole in the condensation and motioned to me. I looked around. No one nearby. She *was* beckoning me.

I waited for a car to pass before crossing the street, not knowing why I felt drawn. She met me at the door.

"Come in—come in. It's too cold to be out on a night like this."

The dead bolt snapped behind me, sending a shiver up my back. She led me to the rear of the shop, the aroma of fresh-baked bread and cakes still heavy in the warm, moist air.

A storeroom acted as a buffer between the storefront and the actual bakery; a bare bones affair, not much more than stacked crates and boxes, a card table, and a couple of chairs. On a shelf over a sink sat an ancient hot plate—a dangerous arrangement, but the old woman seemed unconcerned. She filled a saucepan with water and turned the burner on high. Taking two cups from the shelf, she carefully measured cocoa from a canister.

"All I have is instant. Not very good, but it warms me."

"Look, I don't want to put you to any trouble—"

"It's no trouble."

In her late seventies and heavyset, she moved stiffly, as though with arthritis. Her accent was Polish, her wrinkled face careworn, but her eyes were bright and loving—an odd assessment coming from me. I don't take to people right off. Yet her whole demeanor encouraged trust, like you could tell her all your troubles.

Why had she invited me here? I was a stranger—a man. She should be afraid of me—instead, I was leery of her.

I shoved my good hand into my jacket pocket, feeling self-conscious. "What am I doing here?"

"You look like you need to talk. I need to listen. Sit," she said and ushered me to a folding metal chair, taking one on the opposite side of the wobbly table.

"You here all alone?"

"Yes."

Why didn't that question frighten her? I could be an ax murderer, for all she knew.

"My son—he's a big shot with his own business downtown," she said. "He wants me to move to Cheektowaga to live in one of those old folks' homes. But I like living over the shop."

"I lived over a bakery when I was a kid."

"The bread smells so good in the mornings, yes?"

"That was the only good part about living there."

"That's not true. I'll bet there were many good things. You just don't want to remember."

"Why do you say that?"

She shrugged theatrically, her smile enigmatic. "I've been waiting for you."

"For me?"

"For a week. Maybe two."

"But I've only been back in Buffalo a week."

"But it's good now that you're here, eh?"

I shook my head. "I should've stayed in New York."

"There's nothing for you there. Here you have a girlfriend, your family."

"I don't have a girlfriend. My brother is my only family."

"See," she said, the creases around her eyes doubling, her smile warm.

I leaned back in my chair. This was too creepy.

"You need to talk," she repeated. "I'm here to listen."

"Why would I tell a stranger about myself?"

"Maybe I understand—tell you something about yourself you don't know. Maybe I'll tell you something about yourself you already know."

The hair on the back of my neck bristled. "Like what?"

"Give me your hand."

Her creased hands caressed mine; her clear brown eyes looked into my soul. She shook her head, released it. "First I'll tell you about me; then you can decide if you want to tell me about you. My name is Sophie Levin. Look." She pulled back her sweater sleeve to reveal a tattoo—numbers.

"Buchenwald?"

"See, you know."

"A good guess."

She shook her head. "No, this you know. Like lots of other things you know, eh?"

I wasn't sure how to answer.

The water began to boil. She got up, poured it into the cups, and stirred. Then she disappeared into the shop and came back with a *placek*. I hadn't tasted one of those sweet crumb loaves in years. She cut thick slices and put them on napkins from the shelf, set one in front of me.

"Now, I'll tell you how I survived the camp. I would volunteer for the work groups. I did anything they said. Dig holes, bake bread—anything. And I knew when to be away from the barracks. To stay was to die."

"How'd you know?"

She tapped her temple. "I knew. Like you know. For me there are colors. Everyone has colors that surround them. I would watch certain guards and when their color was black, it meant death. I knew to stay away. Right now you are red. Very angry. Your brother—don't be hard on him. He loves you, you know."

"How do you see these colors?"

"Not with my eyes, with my mind. It's not wrong, it's not bad. Just different. You see things a different way, too. But then you always have."

"No."

She shook her head, dismissing my protest. "Of course you did. I can tell you many times—but it's better you remember yourself. Little things. Finding lost things. Waiting for a letter—a phone call."

I hesitated, afraid to ask my next question.

"Are you…psychic?"

She shrugged. "I just see colors…and then I know. You feel things, deeply. Before this happened…" She reached across the table, traced a finger down my shorn temple "…you never let yourself. Now you have to. The plug is pulled—the feelings leak out—other people's feelings find you. It's very hard for you, but good things will come of it. They will," she insisted. "But sometimes things will seem worse because you can't understand them. Sometimes it's hard to understand."

I wanted to believe her. Hadn't I just been telling myself the very same things? Yet suddenly I was as skeptical as Richard.

"I don't know what you're talking about."

She thought for a moment. "You like to take photographs, eh?"

I nodded uncertainly. How could she know these things?

"You take a picture—it's there, in your camera. Even when it's not developed—it's still there."

"A latent image?"

"Yes. These things you know, it's a latent talent. You

always had it, but it wasn't developed. Now you can develop the pictures in your head. You can see them when others can't. You can know things when others don't."

"My brother wants me to have tests—"

"How will knowing the science of it help you? If they can even tell you."

That was pretty much how I felt about it, too.

"Still, you must be careful. Believe what you know, and be watchful. Even innocent situations can hide great danger."

She held out her hand. "Now, tell me about me."

I felt her pulse thrumming rhythmically in her fingers, her smile encouraging.

"Well?"

"You're a nice lady. You want to help people." I didn't know what else to say.

She took back her hand, frowned. "You'll get better at it." She picked up her cup, took a sip. "Not bad for instant, but better with marshmallows. That's what my granddaughter says."

She launched into a monologue about her grandchildren, giving me a chance to digest what she'd said. I think she knew I wasn't listening, but she seemed to like the sound of her own voice.

She was right. I'd always been good at finding lost objects. I assumed it was a matter of remembering where you'd last seen the missing item. That and begging help from St. Anthony. Were emotions the psychic key for me? I remembered returning home from school and knowing, before I opened the apartment door, when my mother would be passed out drunk in front of the TV. And I'd learned early to keep the hurt, anger, and humiliation inside.

Most of what I knew about Sumner's murder hinged on emotions. Those of the killer—and a witness. Anger and triumph and terror, all mixed up.

I looked down at my empty cup.

"Time for you to go," Sophie said, rising. "My son would

be upset if he knew I entertained a gentleman here." She patted my shoulder. "It's a long walk home. I'd let you call your brother to come get you, but my phone hasn't worked all day. The bar down the street has a pay phone. You call from there."

I followed her back into the shop. Snow fluttered and settled on the empty parking spaces outside.

"That's okay. I think I'll just head on home."

"Oh no—it's too far to walk in the snow. You're not as strong as you think. You must promise me you'll go to the bar." Something about her tone made it seem like an imperative.

"Okay, I promise."

"Good."

She clasped my hand and I nearly staggered at the burst of unconditional love that suddenly enveloped me. I looked into her smiling, wrinkled face, and didn't want to leave.

"Can I come back and visit you again?"

She shrugged. "Sometimes I'm here. Sometimes I'm not. Best you come at night. Alone."

"Why?"

"It's just best." She winked at me. "Good-bye, Jeffrey."

She locked the door behind me, and waved. As I headed down the sidewalk, I realized I'd never introduced myself. I looked back. The shop was dark, but a light blazed in the apartment overhead.

My anger toward Richard had waned, but the sour feelings it evoked lingered, depression settling in.

I had other things to think about. Like what inspired Sophie to direct me down the road instead of going home.

Curiosity got the better of me.

I headed for the bar.

TEN

THE GLOW OF A NEON BEER sign drew me half a block to a working-class sports bar called The Whole Nine Yards. Its dry warmth enveloped me as I pushed open the heavy glass door. A scattering of patrons watched a basketball game blaring on the tube. Football jerseys, hockey sticks, pennants, and signed photographs dotted the walls, but the budget for decor was a lot less than at The Extra Point downtown. It had the feel of a business on a downslide.

I avoided the pay phone. I had no intention of calling Richard.

The bartender interrupted his conversation with an older man at the other end of the bar when I took a seat. Weariness clung to him. I guessed him to be the owner, who looked like he'd been on his feet all day. "What can I get you?" he asked.

I considered my nearly empty wallet and my belly full of cocoa. "Club soda."

His expression said "no tip," but he poured me a glass from the well soda trigger. "That's a buck."

I put a five-dollar bill on the bar. He grabbed it, rang up the sale on the old cash register, gave me my change, and went back to kibitzing.

Four bucks—my total net worth. I'd have to nurse my drink for a while, but that was okay. I was willing to park here for a couple of hours.

I'd tended bar for a while after my stint in the Army; I could do it again. Sure, a part-time job at a place like this, maybe within walking distance. But who'd hire a broken-armed jerk who couldn't lift a case of beer or hold a lime to cut garnishes?

My mind wandered back to the ugly scene back home. Richard's house was not my home. It was a place to stay until I got back on my feet; at least that's what he'd said at the hospital.

The memory of that conversation came back to me.

HE'D BEEN GONE ALL DAY, leaving me alone in that cell of a room. We hadn't had many meaningful discussions since I'd awakened from the coma two days before. Still, I'd gotten used to him being in the background.

"So, where've you been all day?" I'd asked, when he finally showed up that evening.

Richard settled his coat over the back of the room's only chair. "I had things to do."

"Business? Sightseeing?"

He straightened, as though tensing for battle. "Getting estimates from movers to take your stuff to Buffalo."

"Look, I never said—!"

"I know what you said. I was only getting estimates, okay?" A pause, then, "I spoke with your apartment manager."

My insides squirmed.

"Your back rent's taken care of."

"But I owed—"

"I said it's taken care of."

I was about to spew like Vesuvius when he interrupted me again.

"The last few times I've seen you, you've been distant and pissy. Have I done something to offend you?"

"The cultured, refined Doctor Alpert never offends anyone."

"Then stop acting like you've got a stick up your ass and tell me what's eating you."

"All right, you want an answer—the problem's you. You being so goddamned rich makes me feel like I'm shit. You're always shoving it down my throat and I'm sick of it!"

That wasn't even remotely true, but it sounded good and fit my mental state at the time.

He stiffened. "I'm sorry my financial status offends you, but I'm still your brother. I care about what happens to you, you dumb shit. Why else would I be here?"

He'd never spoken to me in anger. I'd never known him to swear.

"Guilt," I shot back. Richard blinked, taken aback. "Yeah, guilt—for the way your family treated our mother. Maybe you're only here for me because you weren't there for her!"

Richard looked away. My words had hit a nerve, all right, though I knew indifference hadn't kept him from knowing my mother and me. The legal maneuvers his grandparents used to keep my mother from him had cut him off from us, too. Yet I couldn't admit that to him in the heat of anger.

"Neither of us can change the past. But, in case you hadn't noticed, we're all the family we've got. When will it penetrate your thick skull that you're important to me?" He paused. "You never told me about Shelley until it was all over. Christ, your landlord told me you'd lost your job. Why didn't you call—why didn't you come to me?"

"Rich, you can't take care of me the rest of my life."

He spoke slowly, holding back his own anger. "I'm offering to help you 'til you get back on your feet. No strings attached. If you're too damned proud—" Richard broke off, struggling to regain his composure.

"I don't want to fight about this. That's the last thing you need right now. All I ask is that you seriously consider coming back to Buffalo with me—at least until you recover. After that, you can do as you please."

I'd exhaled raggedly, defeat seeping into me. Sick, hurting, and broke, I had nowhere else to go.

"Okay. I'll consider it."

Neither of us spoke for long minutes, then Richard grabbed his coat.

"I'm going to find something to eat. Want me to bring you a sandwich?" I shook my head. "Okay. See you later, right?"

"Yeah, right."

Richard shuffled toward the door, paused. "I'm sorry, Jeff. I hoped things could be different." Genuine regret colored his voice. I felt like a heel. Then he was gone.

I sank back in the bed. Dr. Klehr said a head injury like mine can lower all defenses. He'd been right. For the first time since my wife's death, I buried my face in the pillow and let the tears flow—like I had all those years ago when my mother died, when I first found myself totally on my own.

It took a while before I could think rationally. So, I'd finally told Richard off. Instead of feeling better, shame burned within me.

I hauled myself out of the bed, my arm aching. Leaning against the window sill three floors above the street, I stared at the bleak winter sky. The shit was just piling higher and higher.

Richard was right. What kept me in Manhattan, anyway? No job, no significant other, no close friends. The city held nothing but bitter memories. Richard was the only family I had. He was all I had on my side—if I hadn't just blown that, too.

A noise at the doorway interrupted my thoughts. I turned to see Richard, hands thrust into his coat pockets.

"I—I came back to apologize."

"What for?"

He inched closer. "Because maybe part of me thought I could come down here and play savior for you. It was arrogant of me. I'm sorry." Eyes downcast, he stared at his polished shoes. "I guess I still think of you as that skinny fourteen-year-old kid who desperately needed a home."

This was a Richard I'd never known—had never bothered to get to know.

He met my gaze and continued. "I came here because I'm sincerely worried about you and thought I could help. I hoped that after all these years maybe we could be friends. I don't know about you, but I can always use another friend."

My throat tightened until I thought I might choke. "That's funny. I was just thinking the same thing."

Richard moved forward, his arms open to capture me in a hesitant, gentle hug. And for the first time in my life, I hugged him back. Then suddenly we were standing face-to-face, embarrassed and uncomfortable.

"Please come to Buffalo. There's nothing for you here. Besides, I've got Bills season tickets, and Brenda hates football."

"Okay, but I've got to have my own space. And when it's time to leave, I don't want an argument."

Richard raised a hand. "Fine."

A CHEER BROKE THE QUIET—and the buzzer signaled the end of the first period on the bar's TV.

I took a sip of my club soda. I owed Richard a lot, yet bitterness gnawed at me because the tentative trust I'd put in him—and he'd shown in me—had been so easily erased.

I couldn't let Richard browbeat me. If I didn't pursue my own investigation, Sumner's murderer might go free. And then there was the small boy who'd witnessed that terrible crime. It was his mental SOS, his fear, I'd experienced—not Sumner's. I'd never gotten anything from the victim—as though he had expected to die....

The door opened and closed, and the light tap of footsteps interrupted my reverie. "Do you have a phone?" a woman asked.

The bartender pointed. "Over there."

I looked over my shoulder, surprised to see the woman from the bank. She dropped a quarter in the slot and dialed a number off a card in her hand. She caught my eye and I looked away.

I gazed into my drink. My arm itched. I wished I'd brought the chopstick.

A minute or two later, she joined me at the bar. "Hi, remember me?"

"Maggie Brennan."

She nodded and sat down on the stool beside me. "And you're Jeff."

She remembered.

"Car trouble?" I guessed.

"I hit a pothole. My right front tire blew."

I proffered my broken arm. "I'd like to give you a hand, but—"

"That's okay. Triple A will be here in a while."

"Can I buy you a drink instead?"

She eyed my glass. "I'll have what you're having."

I caught the bartender's attention. "A club soda—with a twist—for the lady." Somehow, she didn't seem surprised by my order. Moments later, the bartender put a fresh napkin on the bar and set down the glass. I left another dollar for him and indicated a table in the back, away from the noisy TV.

Maggie draped her coat over the back of the chair that I'd pulled out for her, then sat down. "Thanks. I'm taking a writing class at Daemen College. I was on my way home when I hit that damn pothole. I've never even been in this place before. I'm glad you were here."

"But you don't even know me."

She shrugged. "At least you're a familiar face. Hey, you got your hair cut. It looks good."

I raked a hand over my head. "Thanks. I'll feel better once it all grows in. In the meantime, I don't feel so much like a freak."

She gave me the once-over. "You don't look like a freak."

"But what if you'd walked in here and hadn't known me, and I'd tried to hit on you?"

"Would you?"

I felt a smile tug at my lips. "Maybe."

She took a sip of her drink. "You told me a fib the other day."

"Me?"

"You acted like you were sick."

"It wasn't much of an act. If you hadn't caught me, I really would've keeled over." I gazed into her pretty blue eyes. Something about them inspired tranquility.

"What were you really doing at the bank?"

I stared into my glass. The bubbles on the side had just about dissipated. "Hanging out with my brother."

"Doctor Alpert? But your name's—"

"Resnick," I supplied, and she nodded. "We're half-brothers. Bet you wouldn't know that by looking at us." She frowned, and I regretted the smart remark. I looked back down at my glass and sobered. "Okay, I'm looking into Matt Sumner's death."

"Are you a cop?"

"It's a personal matter. Can you tell me more about him? Who his friends were? How he spent his time away from work?"

She leaned back, her face growing cold. "I didn't know him well, and I didn't want to know him any better."

Great. My only remaining source on the man had just dried up.

Her expression softened. "But, maybe I'd like to get to know you a little better."

I gave her what I hoped was a reassuring smile. "That would be nice."

The corners of her mouth rose—a really nice smile.

"So, tell me about yourself," I said.

"I'm thirty-nine and not ashamed of it. Depressed some days, but not ashamed. Like everyone else these days, I'm overworked and stressed-out. I'm also divorced and childless. How about you?"

"I'm an unemployed insurance investigator, a widower, and currently sponging off my wealthy older brother."

"Widower?" she asked, as though not hearing the rest. "I'm so sorry. How long ago?"

"Two years."

She hesitated, curiosity getting the better of her. "H...how—?"

"Cocaine. At first she'd have a hit or two on weekends. Then it was a couple of times a week. I worked late—trying to keep my job while downsizing went on all around me. She got fired as a travel agent when she was arrested for selling coke to an undercover cop. After that, she promised me she'd stay clean, but she was already too far gone. Six months after she left me, the cops found her dead in a bathroom at Grand Central Station. Shot execution-style. They figured she tried to rip off her supplier."

Hey, I'd told the entire tale—albeit much abbreviated—and hadn't gotten angry. Real progress.

"How awful for you." She tapped the cast on my arm. "You said you were mugged?"

"All I remember is that baseball bat coming at me. They took my wallet, my keys, ransacked my apartment, took everything I had that was worth anything, and ruined just about everything else."

"Oh, Jeff!"

Again, the compassion in her eyes captivated me.

"Anyway, my brother rescued me and here I am." My God—I was spilling my guts to a virtual stranger—but she was so easy to talk to. I leaned back in my chair. "Sorry. Didn't mean to dump all this on you."

She took a sip of her drink. "My husband was gay. Only he didn't tell me that until we'd been married eight years. After he left, I'd get myself tested for AIDS every six months. I didn't know anything about his secret life, or how many men he'd been with."

I nodded. "Came the end, Shelley would sleep with anyone for cocaine. Scared the hell out of me. For a while, celibacy was my way of life."

She reached across the table to shake my hand. "Amen."

Her fingers were warm. I held on longer than was absolutely necessary. Our eyes met and an odd sensation passed through me, an unexpected sense of well-being, yet my heart pounded.

"Um…my hand." She smiled. "Didn't we just go through this at the bank?"

Embarrassed, I relinquished my hold and felt a tug inside me. She hadn't told me everything. But then why should she?

"You live around here?" she asked.

"Down on LeBrun. I'm just staying with Rich until I get back on my feet."

"Doctor Alpert's older than you, isn't he?"

I nodded, draining my glass. "Twelve years. My mother was a staunch Catholic. She married well the first time. Richard's father was handsome and an heir to millions. He didn't expect to die young and leave his wife penniless. Mom had a nervous breakdown and ended up in the State hospital. They didn't even have the decency to put her in a private hospital."

"Who?"

"Richard's paternal grandparents." I shook my head. "While Mom was in the hospital, they got legal custody of Rich, saying she was unfit."

"Where do you fit in?"

"Years later, Mom married Chet Resnick, a Jewish dry cleaner. He left us when I was four. My mother wouldn't talk about him—except to say he gambled and drank. I heard he was dead."

"So, how did you and your brother ever get together?"

"He found out Mom had cancer and came by the apartment the Christmas before she died. He was in his first year of residency at the time." A lifetime ago. "She was really proud of him. He was curious about us, said he'd like to get to know us. But two months later, Mom was dead. He took me in."

"How long did you stay?"

"Four long years." I paused. "Can't we talk about something else?"

She nodded and took another sip of her drink. "You said you were looking into Matt's death. What does that mean?"

"Right now, nothing. Claudia Sumner sicced the cops on me. Now I won't be able to talk to their kids."

She studied my eyes. "This is really important to you, isn't it?"

"Yeah. It is."

"Why?"

Because I got whacked on the head and now I know things I'm not supposed to know, and I've seen things I wasn't supposed to see. And I'm probably crazy or stupid—or both— and I have a ridiculous debt to repay to Matt Sumner, but I have to find out the truth for myself.

"It just is."

Guilt darkened her eyes. "I didn't tell you everything I know about Matt. I mean, I don't know what might be of use to you. But I like you. You seem…trustworthy."

"And I'm not even wearing my sincere suit."

Her smile disappeared. "This may not be important, but Matt recently fired one of the loan managers. The police have been digging around and it came up. To tell you the truth, I'd almost forgotten about it."

"What happened?"

"They said Don Feddar was approving loans without the proper documentation. There was a big blow-up and Matt fired him."

"How long ago was this?"

"Just before Christmas."

"That's a possible motive for murder."

"But Don's a sweetheart. He's not capable of doing what was done to Matt."

"That's probably what people thought about Jack the Ripper before his first crime." She conceded the point. "Does this guy have kids? A little boy named Jackie?"

"I think he has three daughters." She looked up, her attention caught by flashing yellow lights in the parking lot. "Hang on. The tow truck's here." She snagged her coat and went out to talk to the driver.

I watched while the guy changed her tire. It wasn't until he finally climbed into the cab to leave that she came back into the bar. Her cheeks were pink and her hair was wind-blown. She looked terrific.

"Well, I guess I should get going. You need a lift?"

I didn't want to go home. I didn't want her to go, either. "Sure."

I took our empty glasses over to the bar, left a dollar tip for the bartender, then shrugged back into my jacket. Outside it must've been twenty degrees, as a light snow still fell. Maggie unlocked the passenger side door of her Hyundai and I got in.

The drive to LeBrun was awkward. I'd felt so at ease with her in the bar, yet now I was tongue-tied. I studied her features in the strobing lamplight as she navigated through the slick streets. Why couldn't I think of something—anything—to say?

She turned onto my street, slowing. "It's halfway down," I told her. "There."

She pulled into the driveway, then turned to me. It seemed like she wanted to say something, but she didn't speak. So I did.

"Can I call you?"

She reached for her purse, her smile radiant. Tearing a sheet from a notebook, she jotted down her number. It took all my willpower not to kiss her right then. I took the paper from her. "I'll call."

Then I was out of the car, standing in the silent, falling snow, watching her little blue car pull out of the driveway. She waved before she started off toward Main Street.

Hot damn, I liked Maggie Brennan.

ELEVEN

I KNEW WHEN I SHOWED up for breakfast the next morning that it wasn't the time to announce I'd made a couple of new friends. Brenda and Richard weren't speaking, and I more than half suspected I was the cause.

Richard announced he'd made an appointment for me at UB Medical Center with an orthopedic specialist for that afternoon. I didn't argue.

Plaster is old-fashioned. My new physician gave me the option of a fiberglass cast—in designer colors, no less—or a removable plastic-and-Velcro brace. I chose the latter, glad to be rid of the anchor-weight cast. An x-ray showed my ulna to be healing nicely.

No one mentioned sending me to a shrink.

Even so, I wasn't feeling cocky as I left the doctor's office. Something was definitely up with Richard.

We walked in silence back to the car. Richard had accompanied me to the clinic, and sat in the waiting room until I'd finished. He didn't ask how things had gone.

He unlocked the car door for me, walked around to the driver's side, and climbed in. He turned the key in the ignition and cleared his throat.

"Anywhere you want to go?"

I shook my head. "Let's just go home."

Snowflakes began to fall, dancing on the windshield before being blown away, replaced by new ones. I gazed at the traffic whizzing by and remembered what Richard told Brenda days before: "He's different."

He was right, I was different. And I looked at everything in a new, harsher light—especially myself.

I didn't like what I saw.

Minutes later we were home. Richard stopped the car in the driveway, letting me out before he parked the Lincoln in the garage. I started for the house, but paused. I couldn't let this go on. Pulling up my collar, I waited for him. Although it was only three o'clock, the sky had darkened to the west—a storm was brewing.

The garage door closed and Richard came out the side door, shoulders slumped, head down. He looked as bad as I felt. He glanced up, surprised to see me.

"Wanna take a walk?"

He took in the sky. "In the snow?"

"Why not? Besides, I want to talk."

He blinked at me. "You never want to talk."

"I never had a crack in my skull before, either."

"You think that makes a difference?"

"Yeah, I do."

Richard sighed. "What's the point?"

The defeat in his voice scared me. "You giving up on me already?"

"No. It's just—I don't like things being so awkward."

"That's kind of what I wanted to talk about."

We started down the driveway at a snail's pace. Awkward was a good description for how I felt. And he was right. Expressing myself was something I'd never been good at.

I took a breath for courage.

"Back in New York I said something I'm not proud of. That you're always rubbing my nose in the fact that you have a lot of money. It isn't true. You've never treated me with anything other than kindness. In return—"

"Jeff, don't—"

"Let me finish. In return, I've been an ungrateful son of a bitch, too proud to accept your generosity gracefully. I'm sorry."

"You're my brother. You've been through hell."

"Well, I just wanted to say thanks. I've asked a lot of you and…I have a feeling I'll be asking more before this is over."

"You mean this stuff with the murder?"

I nodded.

He forced a smile, but his eyes were still troubled.

For all I seemed to know about Sumner's death, I was unable to read anything on my own brother. Time to risk it all. "What's going on with you and Brenda?"

Richard's gaze remained fixed on the sidewalk ahead. A muscle twitched in his jaw. "I wish I knew."

How arrogant of me to think he'd be preoccupied by only me and my problems.

"Once my arm heals, I could be out of your hair in a month or so."

He looked at me, his eyes pained. "You going to abandon me, too?"

"What do you mean?"

He looked away. "Brenda's thinking of going back to L.A. Something about the climate here not agreeing with her." His voice sounded shaky.

Major guilt trip. "Oh, man, Rich."

"It's not your fault. This has been brewing for a while— ever since we came here."

"I don't understand. When we got off the plane, she seemed so glad to see you. I could feel she really loves you."

"We've been together a long time," he admitted. "She knows I love her. I know she loves me. But she says we don't have a life here—that I'm ashamed of her. That's bullshit."

"Is it a race thing?"

"I don't know. Maybe."

"Well, you ever take her out?"

"Where? This is Buffalo, for chrissakes."

"There have to be some nice restaurants. Toronto's only

ninety minutes away. Go to a movie, join a country club, I don't know."

"It goes deeper than that. A lot deeper."

"How?"

"She says I don't trust her any more. That I used to ask for her opinions—trusted her judgment. She says I don't any more."

"Why?"

"Mainly because I haven't been supportive of you and this psychic crap. She fell for it hook, line, and sinker."

"These things are really happening to me."

His voice was gentle. "I know you believe that. But things are different here. Buffalo's a working class town. I've heard it called a city of no illusions." He paused. "Maybe she's right. I was open to more possibilities back in L.A. We dabbled in so many things at the Foundation. Our team collaborated with Stanford on experiments with extrasensory perception. We studied a psychic with frightening psychokinetic powers. Things like that don't exist in Buffalo—certainly not with my own brother."

I wasn't comfortable talking about that. "Maybe you're going through a mid-life crisis. You could sell the house, go back to L.A."

"No, I belong here. I can't explain why, but I can't leave again. And because of that, I'm going to lose Brenda."

"I think you need a job—both of you."

"It's not that simple."

"Isn't it? Here I am, wondering if I'll ever work again. I'm thinking maybe I could tend bar—something part-time. Something where I won't fail. Damn it, Richard, you're a doctor. And you're good."

He shrugged. "I used to be. But I don't want to start a practice at this stage of the game."

"How about volunteering somewhere? There's gotta be clinics just crying for someone with your talent to work gratis. You could probably name your hours, do as much or as little as you please. But you've got to do something. You've worked too hard to just let your skills—and Brenda—slip away."

He nodded, but I could see he wasn't convinced. We walked half a block in silence.

"Thanks," Richard said finally.

"For what?"

"A different perspective. Maybe I do need to get back to work. And maybe I have been ignoring Brenda. Maybe if we did something together...." His words trailed off, but he seemed to warm to the idea.

An inch or more of snow had fallen in the short time we'd walked, covering the sidewalks, the wind whipping it into peaks. Fooled by the premature darkening of the sky, a few of the street lamps flickered to life. Lights were blazing in the house as we approached, welcoming us.

Once inside, Richard clapped me on the back before disappearing into his study.

After I showed Brenda the brace, I grabbed a cup of coffee and parked myself by the phone. Thanks to a helpful library aid and the city directory, I tracked down the employers of several of the three little Jackies' parents and talked to the two fathers. Neither admitted knowing Matt Sumner, but then why would they? One hung up on me. I needed to talk to Maggie. Maybe she could check to see if any of the parents had accounts with Bison Bank. And it would give me an excuse to call her.

Donning a sweatshirt, I wandered out to the sun room—a misnomer on that chilly, dark day, but a great place to think. I borrowed Brenda's portable radio, listening to mellow jazz while I froze my butt off watching the wind make snow sculptures. The winter storm watch had turned into a full-blown blizzard, and the snow began to drift out on the driveway. I was glad I didn't have to drive in this weather, although I'd have to get the hang of it if I decided to stay in Buffalo.

The thought didn't seem as appalling as it had just a week ago.

In addition to the weather, the hourly newscast reported that the police had found Sumner's car in a mall parking lot in Erie, Pennsylvania—the same city where his youngest son went to school. Interesting. Seeing the car was a pipe dream. The cops would impound it, though they wouldn't find much to further their investigation. It's harder to get a decent fingerprint than most people think, and I suspected the murderer hadn't been stupid enough to leave them.

Eventually Richard came out and hauled me in for dinner. He and Brenda were back on speaking terms, albeit extremely polite.

Afterwards, I volunteered to clean up the kitchen. Being one-armed, the job took longer than I thought. By the time I finished, every pan was clean, the table wiped, and the floor had been swept. Maybe I could find employment as a domestic. Meanwhile, I must've glanced at the phone a hundred times, trying to work up the courage to call Maggie.

Finally, I punched in the seven-digit number I'd memorized the night before. It rang once. Twice. Three times. I was sure an answering machine would kick in when a breathless voice answered, "Hello?"

"Maggie? It's Jeff Resnick. Is this a bad time?"

"No. I just came in from walking the dog." She sounded pleased. She might not be after I begged my favor. "How are you? How's your arm?"

"Better. Some snow, huh?" I wasn't showing her my most articulate side.

"Yeah. But, it's late in the season. It'll probably melt in a day or two."

"Yeah." A lengthy silence. "Uh, I'm a little out of practice. You know, with this dating stuff."

"Yeah?"

"So, you want to go out?"

"What did you have in mind?"

"Well, that's kind of a problem. See, I'm not working, and I might not be for a while. I don't have a car, either."

"Oh."

"Did I just blow my chances?"

I envisioned her smiling. "Well, my mother wouldn't say you were a hot prospect, but I've always rooted for the underdog, so you haven't blown it. Yet."

I might now. "Could you check on something for me at the bank?"

She hesitated. "Does this have anything to do with Matt Sumner's death?"

"Yeah."

"Are you using me? I mean, I could still do whatever it is you want, but do you really want to get to know me better, or are you just feeding me a line?"

"No. I think you're nice. I'd like to get to know you better. I don't have any friends in town." My foot was jammed so far into my mouth, it would take major surgery to remove it.

Silence, then she laughed. "Okay, what do you want?"

She listened patiently while I explained the situation.

"Because of privacy laws, I can't give you specifics. I can let you know if they've got accounts or loans with us, but that's it."

"That's all I need. Thanks."

"Okay. What about going out? Can you swing lunch? Dutch treat?"

"Yeah. Where?"

She gave me the address of a place close to the bank and we agreed to meet the next day.

I found Richard and Brenda in the study. As usual, Richard sat behind his desk, his nose buried in a book. Brenda had parked on the leather couch by a lamp, doing some kind of needlework. They both looked up as I knocked on the door jamb.

"I need a favor tomorrow. A ride. I sort of have a date."

Brenda's eyebrows rose. "A date?"

"I met this lady at the bank the other day. We're going to lunch tomorrow. I thought maybe you two could go out, drop me off, then pick me up later."

"You mean you don't want us to join you?" Richard asked. There was a lightness in his tone that had been absent for days.

"No!" This wasn't my night for conversation. "I mean, sure, if you want. But—"

"No one's taken me to lunch in ages. Richard?"

He smiled at her. "Sure."

I figured I'd better make a fast escape before my foot became permanently lodged in my mouth. "Thanks."

RICHARD DROPPED ME AT Ted's Place, a little diner across the street from the main branch of Bison Bank in downtown Buffalo. He and Brenda were headed to a much more upscale restaurant down the street, where linen napkins and salad forks were standard at every place setting.

I stood in the café's crowded entryway, waiting for a table to open. The place smelled of bacon, coffee, and greasy fries, and was an obvious favorite with downtown office workers who'd donned heavy coats and boots to trudge past thigh-high snowbanks to get there.

A waitress seated me in the last booth. As I perused the menu, Maggie flopped down across from me.

"Hi! Sorry I'm late. You order yet?"

I shook my head. "Good to see you."

She struggled out of her bulky down coat and set it beside her on the bench seat. She wore a navy knit sweater over a dark wool skirt. The thin gold chain around her neck made her look dressy yet casual.

She glanced over the menu. "I'm starved. I had to shovel the driveway, so I didn't have time for breakfast, and nobody brought in doughnuts. God, I hate winter."

"I guess I shouldn't mention that some guy in a pickup with a plow did our drive about six this morning."

She stuck out her tongue at me, then went back to the menu. The waitress showed up with steaming coffee pots— regular and decaf—in each hand. We ordered, Maggie settling for chicken salad, and I asked for beef on weck—rare roast beef, piled high on a salty, caraway seeded kimmelweck roll, served with a Kosher dill, sinus-clearing horseradish, and au jus. For me a New Orleans po boy or a Philly cheese steak sandwich would never beat Buffalo's beef on weck.

After the waitress had gone, Maggie opened her purse and took out a sheaf of folded papers. She looked around, decided it was safe to speak, and motioned me closer. "I could get fired if anyone found out about this." She handed me the pages.

"I won't say a word."

The first was a typed list of the three names I'd given her. The Ryans had a VISA account with the bank, the Prystow-skis had none. Under the third name was a lengthy paragraph, which I skimmed.

Sharon Walker had no current accounts with the bank, but her father's construction business had many loans with Bison Bank over the previous two decades. The text concluded with a terse statement: Walker Construction had gone bankrupt three years before. At that time, Sharon Walker headed the company. Matt Sumner was the executive in charge of those loans. I wondered if that alone could get Maggie fired, and swallowed a pang of guilt. As I stared at the Walker woman's name, something in my gut twisted.

I shuffled through the next several sheets, photocopies of Sumner's appointment calendar the week of his death. Interesting.

"I had to do some digging on that third name. I threw in the calendar as a bonus. Hope it helps."

I folded the papers and put them into my coat pocket. "Thanks. I really appreciate it."

"No problem," she said, but sounded nervous and quickly changed the subject. "Hey, your cast is gone."

"The brace is better. And I only have to wear it another twenty-seven days." I took a sip of my coffee. "You never told me exactly what you do at the bank."

"I'm an administrative assistant—a glorified title for secretary, except that I have a secretary. She does all the piddly work, I deal with the directors and handle the more complicated assignments—like coordinating this conference, which is driving me nuts." She paused to sip her decaf coffee. "I've been there fourteen years. The way things are going, with so many banks consolidating, you never know how long you'll last."

"A familiar story. I worked my way up to supervisor, only to be busted back to field investigator, then out the door, after a major re-engineering at Travelers. Thinking about it depresses the hell out of me."

The sandwiches came, but I was more interested in listening to Maggie than eating. She seemed nervous and began to chatter.

"If you need a dentist, my brother-in-law has a practice in Tonawanda. He's wonderful. Totally painless."

"Totally?"

"Well, it depends on how well you take care of your teeth."

"You live in Tonawanda?"

"Out in Clarence. Me and my dog, Holly, a golden retriever. I got her for Christmas a couple of years ago. She's a big dog and needs to be walked at least once a day. Then there's the yard work." She rolled her eyes, making me laugh.

We talked while we ate: the Buffalo Bills, the weather, how she dabbled in interior decoration as a hobby. Occasionally she'd look down at her plate, bite her lip like something bothered her. Then she'd find another safe topic and start again.

The check arrived and I grabbed it. Brenda, bless her heart, had slipped me a twenty.

Maggie donned her jacket and pulled a white knit beret over her hair. I stood to follow her and pay the check at the register.

"Bye. Thanks for lunch," she said, took a few steps, and turned back. She gave me a quick hug before hurrying out the door.

People crowded past me on their way in or out, but I hardly noticed. I just stood there and smiled.

I WASTED THE REST OF THE day with mundane tasks—namely laundry. After dinner, I returned to my cramped room. I needed a desk. I needed more space. I needed my *own* space.

I studied the copy of Sumner's calendar Maggie had given me. The daily register was broken down into half-hour increments. Most of the entries were downright cryptic. Maggie had included a Rosetta-stone-like key for me. Merrill, R1010C translated as a meeting with Bob Merrill in Conference Room 1010. Most of Sumner's appointments had been right at the bank, the entries made in neat, fat, girlish script—the secretary's, no doubt. The last entry for Thursday, four-thirty, was made in a messy scrawl, which I assumed to be Sumner's own hand. According to the newspaper, he left the bank about four o'clock and was never seen again.

I stared at the entry: Ron. Ron Myers? He was a colleague on the same floor. Surely the cops had talked to him—and every other Ron in the building. I'd have to ask Maggie.

My mind wandered to thoughts of Sumner's remains…or lack thereof. According to the deer hunting book, the internal organs were usually left in the field. Hunting season in western New York State occurs in the fall, when only a deep frost is expected. It had snowed less than an inch in Amherst the night of the murder; it may have snowed more than that on the outskirts of town, and since then we'd had a major snowstorm. I couldn't remember the weather patterns in and around Lake Erie to know just where the snow belt lay. Instead, I thought about the steaming pile of organs left in the cold night air. What if the raccoons hadn't gotten them? What if…?

Richard didn't have a map of western New York, but he said Brenda had one on the back seat of her car—a Buffalo atlas, which included all of Erie county. My shoes were snow-caked from trudging through the ever-forming drifts to retrieve it. I sat at the kitchen table and flipped through the atlas pages, with no idea where to start looking.

Brenda shuffled into the kitchen on slippered feet. Although it wasn't late, she was dressed in a blue quilted bathrobe. "Is that from my car?"

"Yeah. Rich said I could—"

"Okay, but I want it put back where it belongs. You want some hot chocolate?"

"Sure."

She got the milk out of the refrigerator and heated it in a saucepan on the stove. No instant stuff for Brenda. She had a cylinder of Ghirardelli sweet ground chocolate and cocoa, and scooped teaspoons of the stuff into large mugs.

I turned my attention back to the atlas, still with no clear idea of what to look for. The pages flipped past. Whole sections of the book were devoted to the outskirts of Buffalo. I ran my hands over the paper, hoping for some kind of impression.

Brenda plunked a steaming mug, heaped with fluffy clouds of Reddi-Wip, in front of me, taking the adjacent seat. I took a sip. Better than the cheap stuff, for sure.

"What're you doing?" she asked, took a sip, and ended up with a whipped cream mustache.

I kept fanning through pages, running my hand over the type—waiting for…something. "I'm looking for Sumner's guts."

"Are you kidding?"

"No, I'm not."

She wiped her lip with a paper napkin. "What'll you do if you find them?"

"I have no idea."

She took another sip, watching me as I continued to run my hands over the pages. "What're you hoping to come up with?"

"I'm not sure. But as far as I know, the cops haven't found his insides. What do you know about DNA testing?"

She looked thoughtful. "I'm sure they took tissue samples

during the autopsy. It would be easy to match them." She glanced down at the page in front of me. "If you find them."

My index finger rested on the town of Holland. "I think I already have."

TWELVE

"YOU WANT TO WHAT?"

To say that Richard wasn't enthusiastic about my plan was definitely an understatement.

"I'm pretty sure I know where to find the rest of Sumner's remains, but I need your help."

His eyebrows drew close in consternation.

"Think of it as archeology, Rich."

"Do you realize how much it's snowed in the past week?"

"It's in the country. Snow blows away in an open field. I'll bet we can find it easy."

Skeptical doesn't begin to describe the expression plastered across his features.

I awoke early the next morning. Too psyched to eat breakfast, I wandered around the house, waiting for Richard and Brenda to get up. I dressed in my oldest jeans and sneakers. The only pair of boots I owned were more suited for line dancing than foraging through deep snow. With no heavy jacket, I dressed in layers—cotton, flannel, and wool—and hoped I wouldn't freeze to death. That was unacceptable to Richard, who, when he finally got up, loaned me one of his jackets—easily two sizes too big. I talked him out of cashmere and into flannel, but when he reappeared in his grungies, he still looked like a walking advertisement for Neiman Marcus.

By raiding Richard's bar and the broom closet, I'd collected a plastic grocery bag filled with tools that might come in useful, and plunked them in the back of Brenda's Ford Taurus. I figured Richard wouldn't want the back seat of his beautiful Lincoln cluttered with broom, shovel, and the like, and Brenda was accommodating, as usual. She informed us she intended to read up on frostbite remedies while we were gone. She had no desire to spend the better part of the day in sub-freezing temperatures.

It was after eleven when we finally started out. The day was bright and sunny. As Maggie predicted, the snow was melting and the roads were clear and dry as we headed south. For the first time in what seemed like ages, I felt good. Useful. Richard drove the twenty-some miles in silence, making me glad to have the radio for company.

We passed naked trees, closed ice-cream stands, and mile after mile of snow-covered fields. One thing was apparent: the road was not well-traveled.

The perfect place for murder.

The Holland town line sped past. "Slow down, will you? I'm not exactly sure where we're going."

"Anything look familiar?" Richard asked.

I shook my head. "I've got no mental picture of our destination, just a funny feeling in my gut, which, I'll admit seems pretty insubstantial."

Richard slowed the car. Instead of looking at the countryside, I concentrated on the thrumming inside me.

"Stop!"

"Here? It's the middle of nowhere."

"We're getting close."

Plow-piled mounds of dirty snow flanked the road. The shoulder was virtually nonexistent. Richard parked as close to the snow as possible before activating the hazard flashers.

"If this car gets hit, you're going to explain it to Brenda. Not me."

I closed my eyes and concentrated. That shaky feeling inside grew more pronounced.

"What is it you feel, anyway?"

"I don't know how to describe it." I frowned, thought about

it for a moment. "It's like being a Geiger counter. But instead of a noise, I have this tense feeling inside me. Like a guitar string tightened too much." That didn't come out exactly right, but he seemed to accept the explanation.

I got out of the Taurus, opened the rear door, and took out the grocery bag, shovel, and broom.

Richard surveyed the waist-high snow. "This isn't going to work."

"Of course it will. Beyond the road, the snow can only be a foot or so deep." I knew I was being optimistic, but I didn't want him to crap out on me before we even got started.

We struggled over the snowbank, and I took the lead. The shoulder sloped into a gully and, because of the drifted snow, it was hard to tell where the terrain became level again. After only a couple of feet, I realized that thanks to my bum arm, my center of gravity was off. My foot caught in the crusty snow and I went down. I rolled onto my right side, protecting my already-broken left arm. The air turned blue and I'm sure Richard learned a few new curses to add to his growing repertoire.

He crouched beside me. "You okay?"

I glared at him. "Great bedside manner."

He frowned, helped me to my feet, then thrust the broom at me. "Here, use this as a walking stick."

I jabbed the pole into the snow, taking a tentative step forward. I wished I'd thought to bring sunglasses; the glare was unrelenting. Shading my eyes, I looked around to get my bearings. "This way."

We started off to the southwest, and it was anything but easy going. Traffic passed behind us on the road, but the winter landscape before us was absolutely desolate. It took almost ten minutes to walk some twenty yards; my feet were wet in less time than that. The ice-crusted snow broke around my toes in jagged hunks. I looked back and saw that, instead of a straight line, we'd made an uneven path. No wonder people get lost in the desert.

"Why I ever agreed to come along…" Richard muttered behind me.

"You won't let me drive, remember."

"I could've stayed in my nice, warm house. But, no—I'm trudging through snow—"

I listened to him gripe for the next five minutes. It took all my self-control not to turn around and clock him. As it was, if we found nothing, I was sure he'd start filling out the commitment papers for me when we returned home.

That funny feeling vibrated right through me. I stopped, gazed around us at the crystalline snow. "This is a good place to start digging." I nodded toward the shovel.

"You want me to dig?"

I rubbed my broken arm. "Well, I can hardly do it."

If looks could kill, I'd have been as dead as the object of our search. Grumbling, Richard thrust the shovel into the snow. I watched as he cleared a one-foot square patch. Nothing. He started shoveling around that small area, pushing aside the snow until there was only flattened grass underfoot. Nothing.

Minutes later, he'd cleared an area about the size of a back yard pool.

"Take a rest," I said, and he gratefully leaned on the shovel. Although in good shape for his age, Richard was not used to physical labor. His flushed cheeks and labored breathing were accompanied by a thin film of sweat across his forehead.

"This is useless," he puffed. "Like looking for a needle in a haystack. A wild goose chase. A complete and utter waste of time."

"Can you come up with any other clichés?"

I took the shovel from him. We were close to finding it— very close. Awkwardly, I tried to scoop away the snow, but it was just too heavy.

"Don't," he told me, grabbing for the handle, which I held onto. "How're your feet?"

"They're okay."

"They're wet. It's below freezing. You'll get frostbite. Let's call it quits."

"No." Stubborn, I tried again. This time I managed to move some snow, but not enough to make a difference.

"Stop." He took the shovel from me. "I'll give you five more minutes, then we're heading back to the car." He meant it. But I didn't have to wait five minutes.

Richard jabbed the snow and hit something solid. "What the hell?"

"That's it!" I fell to my knees, scooping away snow with my good hand. Fumbling with the grocery bag, I brought out the hand brush and removed the last of the snow from the dark, icy mass. Richard paled as I handed him an ice pick. "You can have the honors."

Richard knelt beside me in the snow, then carefully chipped away at the mound. He stopped after about a minute, studying it.

"Well?"

He pointed to an ice-encrusted protrusion. "See this, it's a pancreas."

"Human?"

"It sure looks like it to me." He straightened, looking at me expectantly.

"I think I'm ready to warm up my feet now."

We gathered our things, all but the shovel. I rubbed it down with my snowy glove to remove any stray fingerprints. We left it standing in the snow to mark the spot, and trudged back to the car.

I noted the odometer reading while Richard made a U-turn, then we headed back toward Holland. "Now what?" he asked.

"I guess we report it."

"How do you report something like this?"

I hadn't thought of that. "You have a lawyer in Buffalo?"

"Yes."

"Before we do anything, maybe you should call him. I don't want to be interrogated by the cops without one. Hayden already warned me off. When he finds out what we've found—"

"We?" Richard echoed.

"You were there, too."

His expression was grim. "What if we reported this anonymously?"

"Smart move. Otherwise how are we going to explain this? 'Uh, hi, I'm a nut-case fresh from the Big Apple. I found these guts on the side of the road.'"

He was not amused.

"And I'll tell you something else. Who do you think will be the prime suspect?"

Richard stared at me. "You, of course."

I shook my head. "I'm not the expert on anatomy."

It took a moment for that statement to sink in. He blanched. "Jesus."

I consulted the atlas. "Take the next cutoff. We have to get out of the area fast. Someone might remember the car. 'Course the California plates will confuse the cops for a while," I said, thinking aloud.

"We are going to report it, aren't we?"

"Sure, but I'd rather wait until we get back to Buffalo. From a pay phone. Then we'll hide Brenda's car in the garage." I stopped myself. "Do I sound paranoid?"

"Just a little," he said, and smiled. He was quiet for a while. "I owe you an apology."

"What for?"

"You knew where to find…." His words trailed off. "I didn't want to believe you."

"Yeah, but you humored me."

"I was determined to prove you wrong once and for all. But this—this is creepy."

"Tell me about it. You're not the one it's happening to. But if you want the truth, I didn't know if we'd find them. On a gut level, I trust these feelings, yet I'm afraid to. I'm afraid to look like a fool. I keep hoping this blasted insight will just go away."

It was after two when we returned to Amherst. I dialed 911 from a pay phone in the parking lot of a Jubilee grocery store. Disguising my voice with a lousy Texas accent, I told them where to look, and hoped like hell they'd take me seriously. If not…I suppose it wouldn't matter; finding frozen viscera wasn't going to solve the case. But it was a stepping stone for me. Time to start adding things together.

I FOUND RICHARD STARING out his study window, sipping a dark Manhattan. Under my arm was the dog-eared manila envelope.

"Is the sun over the yardarm?" I asked.

"It is for me. It's not every day I find that kind of buried treasure."

"I can't wait to see the six o'clock news." I sat down behind his desk, moving his papers, books, and mementos aside. He watched as I spread out the newspaper clippings, my notes, and everything else I'd collected on the Sumner murder.

"I've got some ideas on who the killer is, but I want to bounce them off a neutral party."

"I don't know how neutral I can be, after this morning."

"Well, I figure we're in this together now, right?" He didn't say no, so I took that as assent. "You read the newspaper profile of the killer?"

"Yes."

"What do you think?"

"I don't have an opinion."

I handed him the clipping and he read parts of it aloud. "The assailant is probably between the ages of thirty-five to sixty, strong, an active outdoorsman or hunter. No known motive."

"I think they're wrong. I think the killer is little Jackie's mother."

"Which little Jackie? Which mother?"

"Sharon Walker. I have this funny feeling…and lately my funny feelings have been correct."

"What do you know about this woman?"

"Virtually nothing. She had a child on January tenth four years ago. I know her father had business dealings with Sumner. I know her father's company went bankrupt. That's it."

"That's what your friend, Maggie, told you, right?"

I nodded.

"How can you conclude she murdered him with just that?"

"I can't. That's why I have to find a way to prove it." I sat back in his chair. "Obviously there's no paper trail to lead the police to her."

"You mean checks, love letters—that kind of thing?"

I nodded. "That invitation I found in Sumner's office may be the only thing he kept."

"Are you sure it came from her?"

"Am I positive?" I thought about it for a moment. "No. But it seems likely."

"So what's her motive for murder?"

"I have no idea. But I'll find out."

Richard took a deep swallow of his drink and pulled up a chair beside me. "Okay. What've you got in mind?"

I savored the moment; he was hooked.

"First of all, a trip to the library downtown. They should have all the newspapers on microfilm or CD-ROM for the time when Walker Construction went under. I can lift names and interview the former executives or employees. If I can get a fix on this woman without tipping my hand—"

"But aren't her former co-workers likely to go straight to her and warn her about you?"

"Not if I can find a disgruntled employee or two. Someone with an ax to grind is likely to tell me the dirt that went on before the company collapsed."

Richard took another long pull on his drink. "This really is a nasty business you're in."

"Murder is a nasty business, and I think Sharon Walker killed Matt Sumner. And she did it in front of her son."

"You said that before. How do you know?"

"I kept getting all these feelings: fear, triumph, horror. It took me a week to sort it all out. The emotions came from all of them at the time of the murder. Somehow I got caught up in it. What's weird is I started feeling all this before Sumner was murdered. And, let me tell you, it's bad enough to have your own fears without experiencing somebody else's."

Richard studied me. "I still think this would make a fascinating study. You really should let UB's Psych Department—"

"No way! I'm not going to be anyone's guinea pig."

"Oh." He sounded disappointed.

"What do you have in mind?"

"I keep thinking about my grandmother. What is it you sense upstairs? What is it of her that's left up there? And why is it in my grandfather's room?"

"I've been wondering about that myself—trying to work up the courage to face it."

He downed the rest of his drink in one gulp. "Well, I'm fortified. Let's go."

This wasn't how I'd planned to spend the rest of the afternoon. But I found myself following in his wake, glad it was still daylight. I didn't think I could face the old lady in the dark of night.

I started up the stairs, dread closing around my chest. Richard paused at the landing. As I topped the last step, he reached for my elbow to steady me. "Maybe this wasn't such a good idea," he said.

Panic churned through me. I was tempted, really tempted, to run back down the stairs. But—

"If not now, it'll still be waiting for me tomorrow or next week."

My words sounded a whole lot braver than I felt.

Richard opened the bedroom door. The sun had disappeared behind the trees, leaving the room gloomy with shadows. Because I was prepared, whatever loomed inside did not reach out for me. I took a steadying breath and entered. The furniture was mahogany, just as I remembered it from glimpses years before. A faint odor of fresh paint still clung to the off-white walls. The new carpet was beige wall-to-wall. The room was pleasant, neutral, with absolutely no soul of its own. I stood in the center and concentrated. Murmuring voices echoed. Something that wasn't from the here and now?

"Well?" Richard asked.

I cocked my head, listening. "I hear something. Like voices behind a wall." I walked around the room and paused at a highboy, ran my hand across the top. The dread grew stronger, threatening to choke me.

Bright light flared behind me.

I whirled to find the shadows replaced by morning sunlight flooding through the windows. The rose-colored cabbage-flowered wallpaper was back. Mrs. Alpert stood in the doorway where Richard had been only moments before. Dressed in a drab wool skirt, with a crisp white blouse under a navy sweater, she looked like an ancient, stern librarian. She leaned on the cane in her right hand; in her left she clutched a piece of paper. Her bloodshot eyes bulged in anger; her paper-white skin was wrinkled ten years beyond what I'd ever seen.

"What is this?" she nearly screamed, her thin voice shrill in the virtual silence.

I turned to see what she was looking at. Old Mr. Alpert stood in front of his closet, fastening a cardigan, his skeletal, heavily veined hands fumbling with the buttons.

"None of your business," he said, and closed the door.

"You bought her flowers, didn't you?"

"Yes, I did. It's the least I can do for her now. Goodness knows I should've done more for her in life."

"How dare you say that to me? She took my boy. She stole him!"

"And you stole her child."

Dizziness rolled over me as I realized who and what they were arguing about.

The scene wavered, images colliding like a double-exposure. I could just make out Richard standing where I'd left him in the open doorway. His mouth moved, but I couldn't hear what he was saying.

As Mrs. Alpert stepped between us, the past obliterated him.

She leaned heavily on her cane, spittle flying as she spoke. "I took what was mine. Flesh of my flesh."

"You destroyed her—drove her insane."

Furious, she came at him, smacked him on the arm with her cane. "How dare you talk to me like that!"

Old Mr. Alpert glowered at her for a long moment, then without a word turned for the closet. He took out a suitcase, set it on the bed, and opened it. He crossed to the dresser.

"What are you doing?"

"Packing." He took out shirts, set them in the suitcase, then turned to another drawer, taking out underwear and socks.

"Where do you think you're going?"

"California. To visit Richard."

Torrents of her anger drilled through me, made my head pound, my pulse race. All these years later, that old, fragile-looking woman still scared the shit out of me.

"Why?" she demanded.

Mr. Alpert turned toward his bathroom. "Because I can't take being with you any more. I don't want to be with you any longer."

Her hand crumpled the paper; then she dropped it onto the floor.

He crossed the marble threshold between the carpeted bedroom and the ceramic tiled bathroom.

She followed.

I did, too.

Oblivious to her, Mr. Alpert reached into the bathroom cabinet for his shaving gear. Her face twisted as she hauled back and slammed the cane against his skull. He went down as though pole-axed.

I jumped forward to stop his fall, but he passed through my hands. His temple smacked the side of the claw-footed tub and he crumpled on the floor.

Mrs. Alpert glared down at him, watching his scarlet blood pool on the cool white tile. Her smile was thin-lipped, triumphant.

She turned for the bed.

I followed, watched as she returned the old man's clothes to the highboy, then placed the suitcase back in the closet. Without a backward glance, she headed for the hallway and closed the bedroom door behind her.

Seconds ticked by.

Mr. Alpert lay unmoving in the bathroom.

The emotions tied to that incident still clung to these rooms: the old man's despair at betraying my mother, his wife's fury at my mother for stealing the affection of Richard's father—her only child.

The crumpled paper the old woman had discarded lay at my feet. I bent down, picked it up. Smoothing it out on my knee, I read the typed script, an invoice from Mankowski's Florist Shop: $35 for flowers, placed on Plot 58975, Elizabeth O. A. Resnick.

The room shimmered back into the present.

I stood upright again—back where I started. The overhead light blazed. Richard gripped my shoulders, gently shaking me. I took in a sharp breath, staring into his worried blue eyes.

"Jeff? Jeff, snap out of it!"

Brenda appeared in the doorway. "Richard Alpert, what

have you done?" Then she was between us, her arms wrapped around me. I let her steady me. "It's okay now," she soothed. "It's over now."

I took a ragged breath and suddenly realized I was okay. No residual anger, fear, or hatred remained. The room was just like any other in the house. I wiped at my eyes and coughed.

"Are you all right?" Richard asked. "Christ, Jeff, what the hell happened? You were practically catatonic."

I cleared my throat, pulling away from Brenda. "Got any Irish whiskey?"

Ashen-faced, Richard nodded, then disappeared.

I collapsed onto the edge of the bed.

Brenda joined me. "You okay?"

"Yeah." I ran a hand through my sweat-dampened hair. "She killed him, Brenda. Old lady Alpert whacked the old man over the head—killed him right in the bathroom."

She rubbed my back like a mother comforting a child. "I knew something bad happened here."

I looked at her, confused.

"I always got bad vibes in this room," she explained. "But not like you. My grandma would've said you've got the second sight."

"You, too?"

She shook her head. "Not like you." She rose from the bed and opened a drawer in the dresser, took out a yellowed piece of paper. "I found this while we were redecorating. I don't know why, but I never showed it to Richard."

A cold shadow darkened my soul. The same florist bill I'd seen only minutes before.

"I can't tell Richard. He loved the old hag."

"Then don't."

"He's already asking—"

"He doesn't have to know everything."

She was right.

Richard arrived with a highball glass filled to the brim with ice and good sipping whiskey. I wondered how he'd managed to get all the way upstairs without losing half the glass's contents.

I tasted it and coughed. "Damn fine."

"What the hell did you see?" he demanded.

I glanced at Brenda. Her nod encouraged me to explain.

"The day your grandfather died, he had an argument with your grandmother. About this." I handed him the aged invoice.

He studied it. "She found out."

"Found out what?" Brenda asked.

"Grandfather always bought Betty flowers on the anniversary of her death. Before his arthritis got too bad, he used to go to the cemetery. I drove him a couple of times." He looked wistful. "He was a good man, Jeff. The only father I ever knew."

"At least you *had* a father figure." That came out sounding a lot worse than I'd meant, but Richard had the grace to ignore it. As a kid, I'd had none of the privileges Richard had. But for all the advantages of wealth, I bet he was nearly as miserable as me. We had more in common than I thought.

The light outside continued to fade, the shadows growing more dense.

"Anyway," I continued, "they argued and she…she went off in a huff. He…uh…slipped in the bathroom."

Brenda gave me a comforting smile, but Richard was looking at me, not her, and didn't see.

"You going to be all right?" he asked.

I took another sip of that damn fine whiskey. "Sure."

"Then let's get out of here," Brenda said. "It's close to dinner time and I can use some help in the kitchen." She rose from the bed and left us. I heard her soft footfalls on the stairs.

Richard looked around the room, apparently caught up in his memories. He seemed content with the shorthand account I'd given, which satisfied me. I had no desire to destroy whatever illusions he had of his little old grandmother.

I took another sip of my drink.

"Aren't you still on medication? You're not supposed to be drinking," Richard admonished.

"You going to report me to my doctor?" I stood. "Come on. Brenda wants help in the kitchen. Think we got any cheese and crackers?"

"I expect so." Richard led the way.

I took one last look around the room. I'd faced and conquered my fear. I felt like Neil Armstrong on the moon: one small step—and one giant leap toward getting my life back.

THIRTEEN

WE SAT DOWN TO EAT dinner watching the kitchen TV. The top story on the six o'clock news was indeed the anonymous tip the cops had received on where to find the last of Sumner's remains. The reports sounded so sanitized. The man was viciously killed, gutted like a deer, and the news media tiptoed around the truth. I suppose they were looking out for the tender sensibilities of children in the audience, but was the reality of Sumner's murder that much worse than the violent fantasy of network dramas?

A brown-eyed blonde reporter with big hair from Channel 7 stood by the roadside with a live report. We even saw our shovel. I was surprised she didn't try to interview it. She hinted it was the murderer who'd tipped the cops.

Yeah, right.

After dinner, I went back to my room to draw up a research list for the library, but found I couldn't concentrate. I tried going over the news clippings, with the same results, and instead toyed with the idea of calling Maggie. I thought about her a lot lately. I wondered what her apartment looked like, where she shopped for groceries, what she liked to do on cold winter evenings, if she slept in flannel or nothing at all…. And I wondered if it was too soon to call her again.

I had to force myself to think of other things. Something bothered me about my first visit to Sumner's neighborhood—nobody seemed to have seen anything the night the body was dumped. People usually want to be helpful, especially in a murder investigation. Of course, I hadn't spoken with all the neighbors. If I had my own car, I might've spent a day tracking down everyone.

Someone had to have seen something the night of the murder.

Stretching out on my bed, I realized that so far I'd been pretty timid in pushing this investigation. Not my usual style. But I'd been busted down to field investigator, and then unemployed for so long. And that stupid mugging…. Richard's reluctance to believe in me hadn't helped, either. But ultimately, the problem was mine. So what was I going to do about it?

I'd been a damned good investigator, so why was I holding back? Despite my success earlier in the day, I knew I couldn't depend on my funny feelings to solve the case. I had to do some real, hard-nosed digging. I wanted to talk with Sam Nielsen, the reporter from *The Buffalo News,* and I needed to make my peace, or at least attempt it, with Detective Hayden.

I hauled myself up and headed for the kitchen. Searching the cabinets, I found an unopened package of rainbow chip cookies. I stared at the drawing of the little hollow tree. My mother had drilled into me that you should never, ever take cookies from an unopened package when you hadn't paid for them yourself. Despite the fact that Richard's millions could buy a lot more cookies, the rule still applied.

I closed the cupboard door and again longed for my own car, so that I could go buy my own cookies or nachos or beer. Having no money put a definite crimp in that scenario. I hadn't owned a car in years, although I'd always kept my license current. In Manhattan, a car was pointless; murders occurred to protect parking spaces. But occasionally Shelley and I would rent a car and spend summer weekends at quaint little bed-and-breakfast inns in Cape May or head for the Green Mountains of Vermont.

I shook my head clear of the memories, then realized I'd remembered something good about my time with Shelley. Two years after her death, it still hurt to think about her.

Standing in the middle of the kitchen, I realized that for the first time since the mugging I felt downright bored. I truly was on the mend. I looked around and caught sight of the phone book on the counter. What I really wanted was to call Maggie.

And say what?

Instead, I found myself flipping through the white pages, searching the columns of six-point type. I already knew Sharon Walker's name wasn't there, but there was a James M. Walker listed at an East Aurora address.

My finger traced back and forth under the name. All I had to do was pick up the phone, call old Sharon, and maybe we'd have ourselves a real nice conversation. Excuse me, ma'am, did you kill Matt Sumner?

A glance at the wall clock reminded me it was getting late to pull that kind of a stunt. The worst that could happen was she'd hang up.

Grabbing the phone, I punched in the number. What the hell.

One ring.

Suddenly nervous, I wished I'd taken time to write a script. Hello, Ms. Walker, I'm taking a survey.

No.

Two rings.

Maybe she wasn't home.

Three rings.

I hoped to God she wouldn't use the phone's call-back feature—or have caller ID.

"Hello?" A woman's voice.

Ready or not.

"Hi, this is Ken with Niagara Associates. I'd like to ask you a few questions about the Buffalo media."

For a moment she said nothing. I heard a TV in the background. "A survey?"

So far so good.

"Do you regularly read *The Buffalo News?*"

"On Sunday. I get it for the coupons."

Had I expected a quaver in her voice? Maybe some kind of intuitive message that screamed she was Sumner's murderer? Instead, she sounded like any ordinary person answering an annoying phone call.

"May I ask your favorite local television and radio stations?"

"Well, I watch Channel 7 news at six o'clock most nights. And I listen to WMJX in the mornings."

Time to risk it all. "How do you feel the local media has covered the Matt Sumner murder?"

A long silence, followed by a click.

I replaced the phone on the hook, knowing I'd pushed her too quickly. I'd gotten no insight and didn't know anything I hadn't known before.

Stupid. Definitely a tactical error. After all, the news had been filled with our little treasure hunt. Had I inadvertently tipped her off that she had not gotten away with murder, and that someone was now hunting the hunter?

What if I spooked her into leaving the area? Or worse, what if my call pushed her into doing something potentially lethal to someone else?

Suddenly, taking the timid approach to my investigation seemed a lot smarter than pushing things—or potentially dangerous people. And yet, I never asked the woman's name. What if the telephone number had been reassigned? Maybe I'd never even spoken to Sharon Walker.

Antsy, I wandered over to the refrigerator and looked in. The six-pack of Canadian ice beer looked inviting, but I wasn't supposed to drink while on medication. I'd already pushed my luck with the whiskey earlier. I needed to get some non-alcoholic beer to tide me over. Such thoughts reminded me once again of my transportation—and monetary—deficit.

Brenda's key ring hung on a decorative brass rack near the door. Their bedroom and Richard's study were in the back of the house, away from the garage. I could sneak Richard's car out. They'd never hear a thing.

Instead, I headed for the study. Richard was still up, reading from some leather-bound medical tome.

"Don't you ever sleep?"

He glanced at the grandfather clock across the way. "It's not even ten o'clock."

"I know, but if you were asleep I could steal your car and joyride around town."

He looked at me with suspicion. "Where do you want to go?"

I shrugged. "Somewhere for junk food. Hang out."

"Hang out where?"

"Maybe Orchard Park."

He sighed, letting the book slam shut. "Why?"

"I want to see Sumner's neighborhood at night. See whose lights are on. Nothing special."

He looked...resigned? Maybe he still felt guilty for goading me into confronting my fears upstairs. He shoved the book aside, stood, then neatly pushed in the chair. "Okay. Let me tell Brenda."

"Ask if she wants to come."

That cheered him. "Okay."

I went back to my room, changed into some shoes. By the time I found my jacket, Richard was waiting for me in the kitchen.

"Brenda said she isn't into male bonding. But if we get wings, to bring some home for her."

We trudged out to the garage, stamped the snow from our shoes before getting into the Lincoln. In a minute or so the big car's heater kicked in and we'd reached Main Street. Richard turned right, heading for the Thruway.

I watched the streets flash past. Traffic was light. We'd make it across town in no time, which was good, because through the power of suggestion, the thought of spicy Buffalo wings began to get to me.

Richard pulled into the turn lane. "Why do you really want to go to Sumner's neighborhood?"

"I don't know. I keep thinking about it. I feel like I need to be there. Tonight."

"You're not expecting the murderer to return to the scene of the crime, are you?"

"It's not the scene of the crime. And no, I don't know what to expect. I just expect…." Anticipation gripped me. "Something."

He turned onto the entrance ramp. "You want to get something to eat first?"

"What did you have in mind?"

"I didn't want anything until Brenda mentioned wings. Now that's all I can think of."

I laughed. "How about on the way back?"

He nodded, his gaze still fixed on the road.

"Things seemed to have thawed between you and Brenda. Everything okay?"

"We're negotiating."

"What does that mean?"

"We're going to look for ways to expand our horizons."

"You don't sound thrilled."

"Right now I'm willing to try anything to please her. Besides, like you, she thinks I need a job. She's been calling clinics and gathering information. She's got it in her head we're going to volunteer as a team."

"What do you think about that?"

"The idea's still too new. I haven't had a lot of hands-on experience in a long time."

"Is that why you've been burying your nose in books?"

He laughed. "It can't hurt to brush up."

The conversation petered out. I considered telling him about my call to Sharon, but what good would it do? I could berate myself without his input.

Richard took the Orchard Park exit. We drove in silence to Sumner's quiet neighborhood. The roads were empty on this snowy March night.

Still as death.

At ten-fifteen we rolled slowly past the Sumner place.

Lights blazed in the living room and other parts of the house. Was Claudia home alone, or had she gone out, leaving the lights on a timer to fool burglars?

We went to the end of the street. Richard pulled into a driveway to turn around. "Now where?"

"Can we stay a few minutes? I feel like I have to wait for something."

"Another psychic message?"

"I don't know."

He looked jittery. "We can't just park. Someone's bound to call the police. I mean, the neighbors have to be nervous after what's happened."

He had a point.

"I'm probably making more out of it than I should. I just felt like I should be here tonight."

He nodded and started down the street, putting on his left turn signal, even though there was no one behind us. I too looked both ways for oncoming traffic and saw a man and his dog jogging farther down on Freeman Road.

"Turn right, will you? I want to catch up with that jogger."

In seconds we were moving parallel to a guy who looked to be in his mid-thirties. I hit the power window control. It slid down with an electronic hum, the cold air blasting in.

"Sir? Sir?"

The man looked straight ahead, picked up his speed. The dog barked, but he yanked it along with him.

"Sir?"

He glanced over to me. "I don't want any trouble."

His words startled me. Hadn't I said the same thing to the muggers just weeks before?

"I'm investigating Matthew Sumner's death. You jog this neighborhood on a regular basis? Maybe you saw something."

He slowed, and Richard braked along with him. He stopped beneath a street lamp, giving us the once-over.

"What do you want?"

I got out of the car, handing him my business card. "I'm investigating Matt Sumner's death," I repeated.

He examined the card, gave me another quick once-over.

"Did you jog around this neighborhood a week ago Thursday?"

"I run most nights."

"Do you know where the dead man lived?"

He looked down the road. "Back on Forest. The gray house with the ornamental cherry trees out front."

I nodded. His dog, a big, happy black Lab with a wet nose the size of a ripe plum, sniffed my coat. He yanked the leash and the dog sat.

"I jog down all these streets on a regular basis. I try to get in three or four miles a day, so I pretty much know the neighborhood. Who parks in their driveway, who parks in the garage. Stuff like that. One night, a couple weeks ago, there was a strange car in that driveway. I figured they had company."

He didn't even have to describe it. Just as he spoke, I could see it. A dark, full-sized station wagon, with a chrome roof rack. I couldn't tell the make or model, but it looked to be in good shape. Snow lazily drifted to earth in big flakes, covering the driveway. I wondered if the police had noted the tire tracks or if the snow had melted before Claudia Sumner had discovered her husband's body.

"—wagon. It was black, or dark red. Something like that. The funny thing is, it was backed right up to the garage door."

"Did you see anyone?"

He shook his head. "The garage door was down. At the time, I didn't give it much thought."

"What time was this?"

He let out a breath. "I usually start out about eight thirty, so it would've taken me about fifteen minutes to get there. Maybe eight forty-five."

I looked at my watch. "You're late tonight."

"One of the kids is sick. The whole day's been shot."

"Have you talked to the police about this?"

"I didn't think it was important."

"Would you be willing to?"

He shrugged. "I guess. But what good would it do? I didn't see anyone and I didn't see the license plate."

"The cops like to be thorough. Your name, sir?"

"Paul Linski. I live a couple of blocks from here over on Cherry Tree Lane." He gave me his phone number, and I told him the police would be in touch. I patted the dog, and Linski waved as he took off down the road.

I got back in the car.

"You knew," Richard said. "When you were talking to him, you already knew what he was going to say."

"When he said he saw the car, I knew it was a dark-colored station wagon. If I can find some pictures online or at the library, I might be able to pick out the year and model."

Richard put the Lincoln in gear then pulled into a nearby driveway to turn around. "This is too weird. *You* are too weird."

"Thanks. I love you, too." Satisfied with what we'd accomplished, I turned my thoughts to a more important issue.

"So where's a good place to get wings?"

FOURTEEN

MY FIRST CALL SUNDAY morning was to check the central library's recorded message for their hours. The second call was to Maggie.

Nervous as a teenager, I punched her number. The phone rang four times. Didn't she ever pick it up on the first ring?

"Hello?" She sounded breathless again.

"Hi, Maggie. It's—"

"Jeff! Good to hear from you."

"Am I interrupting anything?"

"No. Just rushing around getting ready for Mass at noon. It's Palm Sunday. I'm going to the Basilica in Lackawanna. Want to go? I could come pick you up."

"I haven't been to church in years. I wouldn't know what to do any more." A funny feeling welled inside me. Apprehension? I wasn't sure. "Anyway, I've already made plans to go to the library this afternoon."

"How about next Sunday? It's Easter."

"Let me think about it. I thought you lived in Clarence. Why go to church all the way out in Lackawanna?"

"I grew up there. I love the Basilica; it was my parish. You ever been there?"

"No. A sinner like me probably wouldn't be welcome."

"Don't be silly. Besides, they've been restoring it for years. It's worth it just to see the gorgeous art and stained glass."

"I'll think about it. But I would like to see you again."

"Make me an offer."

We settled for lunch on Tuesday.

RICHARD AND I TURNED Brenda loose in the home decorating section of Buffalo's Central Library; then we attached ourselves to microfilm machines. We were able to backtrack Walker Construction's downfall from articles in the financial section of *The Buffalo News*.

We split up the work. Richard looked into the company's history, while I concentrated on the people.

Watching Richard work, I realized he would've made a damn good investigator. He thrived on digging through minutiae—a necessary evil. No wonder he missed his research job.

We lost track of time. The librarians literally had to bully us off the equipment to get us out. By that time, we were starved. We found Brenda in the main lobby, loaded down with coffee table books. It took no persuasion at all to convince her to go out for an early dinner. We settled on the Red Mill, because Brenda thought its paddlewheel looked quaint.

Richard and I brought along our research to compare notes. His pages were well-organized, and he bucked the old physician's cliché by writing in neat script. Mine looked no different from what I'd done in high school—haphazard. But I could read them, and that's all that mattered.

After ordering drinks, Richard settled a pair of reading glasses on his nose and shuffled through his notes. "Walker Construction's financial problems began after they contracted to build a shopping mall on the outskirts of Cheektowaga," he began. "The land was purchased, but the permits were delayed time and again when environmental studies got bogged down in red tape. They'd already ordered extra equipment and building materials, but every time construction was slated to start, something else would crop up to halt work.

"Another shopping mall was proposed on a site on Walden Avenue," he continued. "Despite the same delaying tactics, Pyramid Construction weathered the bureaucratic storms better than Walker. Walker Construction's loans were called, penalties were levied, and the company was strangled. They ended up laying off fifty percent of their work force under Chapter Eleven bankruptcy. That was the beginning of the end."

"I got the names of five company officers, including acting company president Sharon Walker," I said. "I want to interview as many of them as possible. It might take a few days."

"What did you learn about Sharon?"

"She took control of the firm after her father's fatal heart attack in the midst of the bankruptcy proceedings. I found the others in the city directory or the phone book. Now I have to figure out exactly what I want to ask them."

"Not bad for an afternoon's work," Brenda said.

The waitress arrived, forcing us to consider the menu.

"I was busy, too," Brenda said after we'd ordered. She produced a handful of glossy brochures. "Richard, you never told me there's a ton of great stuff to do in Buffalo. Did you know there's a theater district downtown? And the Albright Knox Gallery. It probably isn't the Huntington, but won't it be fun to find out?"

I remembered Richard's comment days before about broadening his horizons. Instead, he looked like a deer caught in the headlights of a speeding car. I tried not to smirk, but I was glad it was him and not me.

I AWOKE THE NEXT MORNING with the beginning of one of my skull-pounding headaches, and immediately popped two of the little pink tablets. I was getting low. I'd have to get Richard to write me a prescription.

After fortifying myself with a cup of coffee, I got on the phone. Charles Nowak had been Walker Construction's vice-president, so he probably knew just about everything there was to know about the company. When I called his home, his wife gave me his work number and suggested I contact him there. He was now a sales rep with a competing construction company.

But I didn't want to concentrate on only those at the top. While I had her on the phone, I told Mrs. Nowak I was working on a fraud investigation. Did she know of anyone whose actions might've led to the downfall of the company? She tried to be discreet but dropped one name: Ted Schmidt, a former employee who'd been caught stealing and selling heavy equipment. He'd gone to jail for at least a year. That was all she knew.

I called and talked with Nowak, explaining the situation and making an appointment to see him later that afternoon. Next I tried the Orchard Park Police Department. Detective Hayden was out, but expected back at eleven. That gave me a couple of hours to kill.

I knew from experience that cops—and nosy reporters— often believe they know who killers are, but don't have enough proof to make an arrest. Before I visited Detective Hayden, I decided to try and see Sam Nielsen. He had to know more about the case than had appeared in the paper. My problem was getting him to spill it. I might have to dangle a carrot of my own in front of him. But what? No way did I want him to know how I knew what I knew.

Richard didn't seem to mind adding another destination to the day's itinerary. To prepare myself for the meeting, I donned my sling and combed my hair to de-emphasize the shaved areas of my skull. Didn't help: I still looked like a shock therapy patient.

Brenda came in with the mail just as we were about to leave. "There's a letter for you, Jeffy."

I took the envelope from her, opened it, and smiled: my Federal Income Tax refund. The post office had delivered it to my old address, but my landlord had forwarded it to me.

"It ain't much," I told Richard, "but I need to cash this."

"No problem. We'll stop at a bank this morning."

Despite the gray skies, Richard seemed in good spirits. Once we hit the road, I broached a subject that had been on my mind for days.

"Rich, when can I drive again?"

"When you're better."

"Who's going to decide that? You, me, or some other doctor?"

"Right now I think I'm a better judge than you. You're not ready."

"I feel fine," I lied.

"You don't look fine. Have you seen the dark circles under your eyes? And you're paler than snow."

I pulled down the mirror on the passenger side visor and had a look. Okay, so there were circles under my eyes. I hadn't been out in the sun in nearly seven months, was I supposed to look like some tanned and healthy beach bum?

"I have a lunch date tomorrow with Maggie. I'm trying to get to know the woman; I can't have you tagging along forever."

"I don't mind driving you around. I'll drop you off at the restaurant and, when you're ready to leave, you can give me a call and I'll come get you."

I let out a breath. He was being obstinate. Or maybe I was. "Can you give me a timetable? If I was your patient, how long would you make me wait before I could drive?"

"If you were my patient, I'd order bed rest. Unfortunately, I'm only your brother, and you're notorious for ignoring my advice."

"Richard!"

"Another three or four weeks. Jeff, don't be so impatient. You nearly had your head caved in. Give yourself time to heal."

He was probably right, but I was ready to get on with my life. Whatever it ended up being.

Richard dropped me off in front of *The Buffalo News* building, intending to find a parking space. He said he'd hang around the lobby until I came down. I didn't anticipate being inside too long.

I managed to slip by a security guard and found the crowded newsroom bustling with ringing phones, lively conversations, and reporters at their computer terminals hacking away at the news of the day. A tall young woman in a very short skirt told me where to find Nielsen's desk.

I immediately recognized him as the reporter I'd seen at the church. Over the years Sam had lost most of his dark, wavy hair, but he was the same guy I'd known at Amherst Central High. We'd never really hit it off. To him I was just some nerd with a camera, while he'd been Mr. Popular and the editor of the yearbook. My self-esteem, low as it currently was, was still higher than it had been more than eighteen years before. I marched up to his desk and introduced myself.

"Sam Nielsen? I'm Jeff Resnick. I've been reading your stories on the Sumner murder case. I hoped I could have a few moments of your time."

He pointed to the empty chair next to his desk. "Sit down." His face betrayed no hint of recognition. Just as well. "What's your interest in the case?"

"I'm an insurance investigator—currently unemployed. I was recently mugged," I said, hastily explaining my infirmities. "I'm trying to—" I gestured with my right hand, as though I'd forgotten what I wanted to say.

"Polish up your skills?"

"Exactly."

"What have you come up with so far?"

"Not a whole lot. I talked with his neighbors, his wife, some of the people he worked with."

"Guy was a first-class prick, right?"

"He hasn't been portrayed that way in the paper."

"No," he admitted. "He was friends with the editor in chief. That's colored our reports a bit. But you want a relatively prominent murder victim portrayed in a positive light, at least if you want the crime solved. If the public doesn't care, then someone who knows the truth might not come forward."

"And your editor wants the crime solved."

"You got it." He scrutinized my face. "What did you say your name was? You look familiar."

"Jeffrey Resnick."

He shook his head. "Can't place you. But it'll come to me."

"The whole situation reads like something out of the *National Enquirer.*"

"Hey, don't blaspheme in the newsroom," he warned good-naturedly.

"I'm curious. Your stories haven't mentioned what happened to Sumner's wallet and car keys. Were they found in the car?"

"In the glove box."

That in itself was unusual. "Anything missing?"

"Just the cash. About seventy dollars. This case has got to break soon. Somebody knows something. Somebody tipped the cops on where to find the victim's—"

"Guts," I supplied.

"Yeah. It's just a matter of time before the whole thing breaks."

"You obviously have an inside line on what the police know. Are they close?"

He shrugged. "They're too busy arguing jurisdiction. The body was found in Orchard Park, but he was murdered in Holland."

"Have they narrowed down a list of suspects?"

He shook his head. "They keep running into dead ends. But I've got a feeling about this one."

"A hunch?"

"Yeah. You depend on them in this job. Whoever told them about the murder site is going to lead them straight to the killer. Guaranteed."

"Hey, Sam, got a minute?" a voice called.

Nielsen glanced over his shoulder, recognized the speaker, then turned back to me. "Excuse me." He got up, joined the man out in the hall, both turning their backs to me.

I glanced at the reporter's desk. A fat file folder labeled Sumner sat among other clutter.

Nielsen was deep in conversation.

I flipped open the file. Scribbled notes, typed pages—

one askew. A photocopy—the letterhead said Amigone
Funeral Home. I almost laughed, remembering the absurd
name for the local chain of family-owned funeral homes,
not for the first time wondering if their clients asked themselves…am I gone?

Nielson was still talking.

I reached over, slipped it out, set it on top. The list of
funeral attendees. Two columns of neatly typed names—with
one exception. Hand written, wedged between Mr. and Mrs.
Michael Tessier and Clarence Woodward, was the name I'd
hoped to see: Sharon Walker.

She hadn't been included on Claudia Sumner's original list.
Someone had added her name at the last minute. Interesting.

I closed the folder just in time. Nielsen turned back, took
his seat again.

"Sorry about the interruption."

"No problem." I stood. "I won't take up any more of your
time. Thanks for talking to me."

He grabbed a business card from the top drawer of his desk.
"If you come up with something, give me a call."

"I'll do that."

His gaze remained fixed on my face. "You sure we haven't
met before?"

I shrugged. "Thanks again."

WE CROSSED INTO THE village of Orchard Park and found the
Orchard Park PD located in the Municipal Center, a brick
structure with a faux-colonial facade. We parked and headed
inside. Detective Hayden was in. The receptionist first called
him, then ushered us through a series of halls to his office.

Hayden sat behind a big, ugly, steel-and-Formica desk littered
with stacks of case files, papers, and official-looking garbage.
He held a mug of coffee in one hand and a jelly doughnut in the
other. Confectioners' sugar clung to his upper lip.

"You two joined at the hip?" he asked, eyeing Richard.

"Are you really the stereotypical cop who drinks coffee and eats doughnuts?" I shot back.

Richard glared at me. "I have the car," he explained.

Hayden pointed to the two chairs in front of his desk. "Sit. I checked with NYPD. You really were mugged."

"You couldn't tell?" I said, brandishing my broken arm.

Hayden shrugged. "So why'd you want to see me?"

"The Sumner murder."

He leaned back in his chair. "Of course. Dig up any clues?" His sarcasm bugged me.

"Only his guts."

He looked skeptical. "That was you, huh?"

I pulled out my notebook, giving him specifics that hadn't been mentioned in the media. "We called 911 from the Jubilee parking lot on Kenmore Avenue at one forty-seven on Saturday afternoon. The remains were found on Route 14, two-point-three miles south of Vermont Hill Road."

His skepticism dissolved. "Yeah?"

"We left our shovel out in the field. It was made by the Hawking Company."

His expression turned absolutely grim. "How'd you find…them?"

"Then the uh…viscera…matched Sumner's DNA?"

"Yeah. Now answer my question. How'd you know where to look?"

"This is the part you're not going to believe."

FIFTEEN

"WHY COME TO ME?" Hayden demanded, after I'd told him about the dreams and how they'd intensified once I returned to Buffalo.

"You're in charge of the investigation."

"What do you want? Publicity—your name in the newspaper?"

"That's the last thing I want. I want to find out who killed Sumner and bring that person to justice."

Hayden snorted. "Now you sound like the Lone Ranger."

I got up. "Come on, Rich. I don't need this shit."

Hayden leaned back in his chair. "Now let me give you a scenario. Say a doctor, an expert on anatomy, held a grudge against a bank official. And say this doctor had considerable holdings at the bank. Let's say he also had an accomplice, perhaps his younger brother—"

Richard's eyes blazed, but he held his temper in check.

I didn't.

"My brother is not a surgeon, and he's not a butcher. And neither of us could hit the broad side of a barn with a bow. If you're too narrow-minded to listen to what I have to tell you, so you can catch a goddamn murderer, you can just go fuck yourself, Hayden. Let's go, Rich—"

"Wait. Tell him about the jogger."

"What jogger?"

I had to take a breath to quell my anger. "I found a potential witness for you. One who may have seen the killer's car the night of the murder. But, if you're more interested in spinning fantasy—"

Hayden's eyes betrayed his interest. "You got a name?" I gave it to him. He made a note. "Anything else?"

I sat down again. "What do you think of the murderer's profile they printed in the paper last week?"

"We're working on some leads," he said evasively. He turned and rummaged through a cabinet behind his desk, then handed me a black plastic rectangle: a garage door opener. "Okay, Mister Psychic, get any vibes off this?"

"I can't plug into this stuff like tuning a radio, you know."

"Try," he said. "We recovered it with the victim's car."

I clasped the remote, closed my eyes, and waited. What was I supposed to get? A lot of people had probably handled it. How was I supposed to single out the killer?

But I did get something.

An impression.

A figure, dressed in a dark hooded sweatshirt and dark jogging pants. I couldn't see the face. The killer had pressed the button, and the garage door had slowly risen. Then the killer had jumped into the station wagon, pressed the button again, and the door descended. The station wagon roared to life and the remote was tossed onto the empty passenger seat.

I shook my head, handing it back to the detective. "Sorry."

Contempt shadowed his eyes, but I wasn't about to try to qualify my impressions to give him ammunition to shoot me down. He put the remote back in the cabinet.

"Anything else?

I shook my head and Richard and I stood.

"I'll call this Linski guy."

I headed for the door. "You do that, Detective."

"And I'll be sure to call you if I need you. I know where to find you."

The cold air outside seemed fresh and clean next to the overheated clamminess of the station. I breathed deeply.

"Thanks for defending my honor back there," Richard said.

I shrugged it off.

"You okay?"

"Just pissed."

"Why didn't you tell him about Sharon Walker?"

"He doesn't believe me. But, after he talks to Paul Linski, he might cut me some slack. And maybe in a couple of days I'll have something concrete to give him."

"You got something from that remote, didn't you?"

"Yeah, but I couldn't tell if it was Sharon. Maybe after I meet her, I'll know for sure."

"When are you planning that?"

"I don't know. First I want to find out more about her."

He pressed the remote to unlock the car door for me then headed for the driver's side. I looked behind me. Hayden stood at one of the station's windows, staring after us.

WE STOPPED AT A BRANCH of Bison Bank and cashed my check. Having my own money almost made me feel like a contributing member of society. That elation was brief, however, thanks to the headache hovering on my fringe of awareness. It threatened to take center stage until we had chicken sandwiches at a fast-food joint in Niagara Falls. Richard explained the biochemical correlation between head-aches and an empty stomach over a second cup of coffee.

Thanks to my windfall, I was able to pay for our lunch, an extremely small gesture of thanks for all Richard had done for me, but it made me feel better.

Afterwards, we headed for Keystone Construction. We were a couple of minutes early, but Charles, "just call me Charlie," Nowak was waiting. A stocky, balding, good-natured man, he looked every one of his sixty-plus years.

Richard waited in the reception area while I met with the former Walker Construction V.P. Sitting in one of the two chairs facing his desk, I wondered if my tiny cubicle back at Travelers in Manhattan had been so mundane.

"Thanks for taking time to see me," I started after the introductions. "I'm looking into the relationship between Matt Sumner and the demise of Walker Construction, to see if there might be a connection."

"I've been reading about his murder in the paper." He shook his head. "It's terrible. But why do you think the two are connected?"

"I can't go into that right now. But I hoped you could shed some light on his connection with Walker."

"Sorry. I didn't know the man personally. Big Jim Walker dealt with him on a one-to-one basis. He died several years ago."

"That's when his daughter took over the business, wasn't it?" He nodded.

"How long have you known Sharon Walker?"

"Since she was born. Jim and I started the business together. We were friends since we were kids."

"I'm curious. Why didn't you take over when Jim Walker died?"

"Jim had the majority interest in the business. He left everything to Sharon. She felt only she could follow in his footsteps, and she's not one to delegate authority."

"I take it that wasn't in the company's best interests."

"Not when we were hoping to build the Broadway Mall." He shook his head. "Sharon burned a lot of bridges when the company was in trouble. She tried to keep it from falling apart, but she just didn't have the experience. And she wouldn't listen to anyone who did."

"Are you still in touch with her?"

He shook his head. "I don't think she talks to anyone from

the company. She and her son live in that old, rundown house out in East Aurora. It's all she had left after the bankruptcy. She's got enough money to make ends meet, thanks to a trust fund, but that's about all."

East Aurora. That confirmed it. I'd definitely spoken with Sharon on Saturday night.

"Did she have much contact with Matt Sumner at the bank?"

"Yes. Matt worked closely with Jim and our comptroller. I know he felt as bad as the rest of us when the company failed. He did everything in his power to keep us afloat."

"Did you all socialize with Sumner?"

"Not me. But Sharon did for several years. She was engaged to his son."

"Oh?"

"Five or six years ago."

"I understand Rob Sumner married someone else last fall."

"I wouldn't know that. Jim was disappointed when they broke up. He liked Rob. Being an only child, Sharon was used to getting what she wanted, when she wanted it. I don't think that set right with Rob's family—particularly his mother."

"Was Matt Sumner fond of Sharon?"

He shrugged. "I really don't know."

"Would you know if Sumner cheated on his wife?"

Nowak blinked, startled by the question, but answered it anyway. "I don't know for sure. But there were rumors."

"Such as…?"

He shook his head, unwilling to speculate. I tried another question. "I understand Walker Construction had other troubles during the bankruptcy. Do you know where I can find Ted Schmidt?"

"I suppose he's out of jail by now. He cost the company a couple hundred grand. Maybe it wouldn't have saved us, but we wouldn't have gone under as fast, either."

"Getting back to Sharon, was she friendly with anyone in the office?"

"Not really."

I frowned, frustrated. Then it occurred to me; Sharon would never confide her problems to a man she saw as a rival for control of the company. "How about any of the women?"

"She might have talked with Lucy Kaminski. She was Big Jim's secretary for over twenty years."

"And when Sharon took over—?"

"She worked for Sharon."

"Do you know how I could get in touch with her?"

He took out the telephone book, flipped through the pages, jotted down a number and address on a piece of paper, and handed it to me.

"You wouldn't happen to have a photograph of Sharon, would you?"

He looked thoughtful. "As a matter of fact—" He reached behind him into a file drawer. "I used to have this on the shelf over there. Put it away when the glass broke."

He handed me a framed eight-by-ten photo—a group shot. Charlie stood with a woman who matched him in age and size, presumably his wife, next to a tall, rugged man and a teenaged girl.

"Big Jim was my best friend for almost fifty years."

"This is Sharon and her father?"

He nodded. "Maybe ten or twelve years ago."

Sharon had been athletic-looking, with long, mousy brown hair. Dressed casually in jeans and a sweater, she wasn't pretty, but her blue eyes sparkled. In the photo, she looked at her father with love and admiration.

"Were they close?"

Nowak nodded.

I traced my finger over the picture of Sharon. Her face seemed familiar to me. An image flashed in my mind—a woman, jogging. My eyes slid shut and the memory came back to me as clearly as when I'd actually experienced it. A woman had jogged in the cemetery the day Sumner was buried: Sharon. She must've just left the grave as we approached. No wonder the killer's vibrations had been so strong.

I opened my eyes to find Charlie Nowak staring at me. Embarrassed, I handed back the photo, cleared my throat, and asked a few more questions, but I didn't expect any other revelations. He'd already been more cooperative than I could've hoped. Still, I was glad when the secretary interrupted us with an important call. I saw myself out.

"Well?" Richard asked once we were outside.

"Definitely worth the trip." We got in the car and I told him about Sharon's broken engagement and that she lived in East Aurora, just down the road from Holland where Sumner had been killed. "I've got to talk to Sharon's secretary."

"What's next?" Richard asked.

"I'm going to see Maggie for lunch tomorrow. I need to talk with Ron Myers at the bank again, too, if you can help me out with that. I don't think that entry on Sumner's calendar referred to him, but if the police have questioned him about it, I want to know whatever he told Hayden." I rubbed at my temples.

"Still got the headache?"

"Yeah. They haven't been so bad for the past couple of days. But today... God, I feel rotten."

"I told you, you're pushing yourself too hard. You won't be happy until you end up in the hospital again."

I didn't want to argue with him, and sank back against the seat and headrest. But I had one more place to go. "I want to stop at the bakery."

"What bakery?"

I hadn't told him about my friend Sophie. "On Main Street in Snyder. There's someone I want you to meet."

"You sure you're up to it?"

"It's on the way. Just head for home." I hoped I'd doze off, but no such luck. I opened my eyes a few blocks from the storefront, got my bearings. "Just up ahead, on the right. It's the place with the blue sign."

Richard pulled into the half-empty lot. "So who am I going to meet?"

"A cool old lady. She told me to trust this empathic stuff."

Richard didn't roll his eyes, but he looked like he wanted to.

The place looked different in daylight. More modern. And I didn't remember all the wedding cake toppers on display on the shelves behind the glass case that served as a counter. A chunky, middle-aged man stood behind the cash register, ringing up a sale as we entered. My head was pounding. It was an effort to stand, to think. But I needed to connect with my new friend and mentor, so I waited until the customer ahead of me started for the door before I stepped forward.

"Hi. I'm looking for Sophie."

"Who?"

"Sophie Levin. I met her here last week."

He shook his head. "Nobody here by that name."

"Older lady—with a Polish accent."

Again he shook his head. Richard looked at me doubtfully.

"She lives above the shop."

"You must have the wrong place. No one's lived upstairs in years. We don't even rent it out. It's our office space."

That funny feeling was back in the pit of my stomach. "Did she ever live here?"

"No one's lived upstairs—not since the last tenant died some ten years back."

"Was she electrocuted?"

He shrugged. "I dunno. That was before we bought the property. Can I interest you in some fresh bread? We've got a nice rye."

"No, thanks."

Richard nudged me. "Come on. Maybe the place you're looking for is in the next block." He sounded like the placating professional again.

The man behind the counter merely shrugged.

We got back in the car.

I'd met Sophie—spoken with her. She wasn't a figment of my imagination.

So where the hell was she, and why was I so confused?

SIXTEEN

TUESDAY DAWNED GRAY and cold. The headache was still with me. I couldn't even remember if I'd joined Richard and Brenda for dinner the night before. The evening was just a blank.

My breakfast consisted of three pink tablets. For a while it seemed to quell the pounding. What kept me going was the thought of seeing Maggie again.

Richard called Ron Myers and begged a favor—an appointment for me at eleven. Since Myers was actively campaigning for Richard to deposit all his money with Bison Bank, he was more than happy to grant me an interview, hoping to solidify a deal.

Meanwhile, Brenda had scheduled an appointment for her and Richard to look at a clinic downtown. She was hot for them to volunteer their time and skills somewhere, but he didn't seem enthusiastic. I couldn't tell what was going on with him. What he said he wanted and what he really wanted seemed to be two different things.

I was putting on my shoes when Brenda ducked her head inside my door. "Phone call for you."

"Female, I hope," I said, thinking of Maggie.

"No such luck."

Who the hell could be calling me?

I followed her into the kitchen, picked up the extension. "Hello."

"What's going on?" Sam Nielsen's voice. "Suddenly you and your brother are suspects in the Sumner murder case."

My mouth went dry. "How did you get this number?"

"Directory Assistance."

"I'm not listed."

"Your brother is. I remembered your face five minutes after you left my office yesterday. The geeky photographer on our school yearbook. You still play basketball?"

"Yeah. Tell me why we're suspects."

"More your brother. The rumor around Orchard Park PD is that you're some kind of psychic."

Holy Christ. Hayden hadn't promised he wouldn't talk about me. I'd just assumed….

Nielsen was still speaking. "—that it was you who found Sumner's body parts out in Holland. Possibly put them there. Do you want to comment?"

"No."

"How about off the record?"

My hand tightened around the receiver. "Why should I believe you?"

"I protect my sources."

I didn't know what to say. I had to warn Richard. We needed to contact his attorney—cover our asses.

"Hayden seems to think you haven't told him all you know," Nielsen continued.

Maybe I should've told the cop more. Maybe— "What makes you think I'll tell you?"

"Picture this headline: Psychic Finds Sumner Remains. That's not the kind of information you want circulated, now is it?"

The pounding in my head increased. I'd been back in Richard's life a couple of weeks and already I'd ruined it, just when he'd returned to Buffalo, getting ready to resume his career. "What's this going to cost me?"

"Just information."

"Like what?"

"You got a suspect for the murder?"

"Nothing concrete."

"We could help each other." He sounded sleazier than a Vegas lounge lizard.

"I don't have enough facts to make an accusation."

"We could work together to get the evidence. Come on, Jeff—we're old high school buddies."

"I remember you, too. You thought I was a geek, and now you want my cooperation?"

"My editor's on my case. He wants a new angle—now," Nielsen said.

I swallowed. To placate him, I'd have to throw him a tidbit. "Concentrate on Sumner's former lovers."

"You think a woman did that to him?"

"Doing the deed and responsibility for it aren't necessarily the same thing."

"Sounds like a longshot to me. Come on, Jeff—give me a name."

"I can't. Not yet."

Nielsen was quiet for a few moments. "All right. I'll give you a couple of days to think about that headline. How it could change your life. I'll be in touch."

The connection was broken.

I hung up the receiver, stared at the wall phone.

Richard ambled into the kitchen. "You about ready to go?"

I turned to face him, feeling shaky, and leaned against the counter for support.

He frowned. "What's wrong?"

"Hayden told a reporter that we found Sumner's remains. This guy, Nielsen, wants me to tell him what I suspect or he'll go public that I'm a…that I can sense…." I couldn't finish the sentence.

"Jesus," he muttered.

"If we don't leave now, we're going to be late," Brenda said as she entered the kitchen. She stopped, took in both our faces. "What's wrong?"

"Maybe we should consult a lawyer."

Richard nodded.

While he drove, I relayed the story to Brenda. By the time I finished, she looked as grim as I felt.

They dropped me off at the bank at ten fifty-five. Richard said to call him on his cell phone when I was ready to leave. I told him to just meet me outside the bank at one, after I had lunch with Maggie.

Speaking with Nielsen had shaken my confidence. I no longer felt up to talking with Myers, but I had an hour to kill before I was to meet Maggie. I reported in with the reception-ist who'd greeted Richard and me the week before. She ushered me into Myers's office.

I'd arrived right on time, but he was engaged in what turned out to be a lengthy phone call with an important client. He motioned me to sit and I took in his office as I waited. I tried not to think about screaming headlines in seventy-two-point type and studied the objects decorating Myers's work space. Several frames sat on his desk, but I couldn't see the photo-graphs. His office faced east, on the opposite side of the building from Sumner, with a view of more office buildings. Obviously he wasn't as important as Matt Sumner had been.

Finally Myers hung up. "Sorry about that. How can I help you, Jeff?" His smile and enthusiastic handshake didn't conceal his true motivation—to get his hands on more of Richard's millions. He saw me as a means to an end. The feeling was mutual.

"I don't know if my brother explained the situation, but I'm investigating Matt Sumner's death." The muscles along his jaw tightened at the mention of Sumner's name. I'd definitely touched a nerve.

Myers said nothing.

"I understand the police have already spoken with you. Your name was on his calendar the day he died."

"I never even saw him that day." Myers stopped himself, as though afraid to offend me.

"I don't think you had anything to do with his death," I assured him. "I hoped you could tell me more about him."

"Just what are your credentials, Mr. Resnick?"

I met his wary gaze. "I'm an insurance investigator." And please don't ask for proof, I mentally amended.

He didn't, probably figuring a millionaire's brother had no reason to lie.

Myers sat back in his chair, the strain around his eyes visibly relaxing.

"What do you want to know?"

"I'm getting conflicting pictures of him. He was a saint or a sinner, depending on who you talk to."

"He was that. A saint and a sinner."

"How so?"

He eyed me critically. "Look, whatever I tell you is in confidence, right?"

"Absolutely."

He took a steadying breath. "Matt treated some of the staff like dirt. Particularly the women. He could be a real jerk. He had this way of making you feel like you were shit, and grinning all the while. He really turned on the charm with the clients. His smile, his manner with them was worth a million bucks. In fact, it was worth more than that to the bank."

"I'm particularly interested in his relationship with the people at Walker Construction."

"You mean Sharon Walker." It wasn't a question.

I nodded, surprised he knew her by name.

"Matt and I worked closely with the lawyers to pound out a settlement. Sharon and the company comptroller visited often during the bankruptcy proceedings."

"What's your impression of her?"

"Tough. She wore all the right clothes, but something about her didn't fit the image she tried to project."

"Was she overly friendly with Sumner?"

He shrugged. "Matt always had a woman on the side. I

suppose she could've been one of them. I know he talked his
son out of marrying her. If he had a relationship with her,
he never said. He didn't brag about those things, but
everyone knew. Sometimes he'd show up with other women
at company functions. He'd introduce them as clients.
Claudia knew; she didn't care. She had his money. That's all
that mattered."

"What was his relationship with his children?"

"Rocky. The youngest was in rehab a couple of months
ago. An alcoholic at sixteen." He shook his head. "To be a
success in this business, you have to put in one hundred and
ten percent effort. Matt put in more. He sacrificed his family
life for the job. But then my wife divorced me last year for
the same reason. She took the kids and moved to Ohio. Now
I've got nothing but this job." Regret colored his voice.

"What about the charity work Sumner did?"

"Company-directed. I work with a camp for kids with
cancer. Matt had United Way and leukemia. Sometimes we're
given three or four charities and we delegate. Those with the
most seniority get the high-profile charities. The company
looks good and it's a tax write-off."

I thought of Sumner's glowing obituary and frowned; only
P.R. after all.

"I understand Sumner went out of his way to help Walker
Construction during the bankruptcy," I said.

"He originally approved those loans. The deal we cut
netted half the bank's outlay, but we still lost millions. No, he
didn't go out of his way to help them."

That conflicted with what Charlie Nowak said, but it had
a ring of truth. "Did he ever speak of Jackie?"

Myers shook his head. "Was she another girlfriend?"

"I don't know." I remembered something Maggie mentioned to me at the bar. "How about the guy he fired at Christ-
mastime. Don…Don—"

"Don Feddar," he supplied, and shook his head. "It's too bad what happened to him. I'm not at liberty to discuss it, but you might want to speak to him yourself. He's in the phone book."

I nodded. Thanks to the ache in my head, I couldn't think of anything else to ask. "You've been very helpful, Ron."

"Your brother means a lot to this bank. If we could get our hands on all his money—"

I forced a laugh. "You're an honest man. I'll mention it to him, but I can't guarantee anything."

"I can't ask for more." He offered me his hand. "Let me know if I can do anything else for you."

"As a matter of fact, I wouldn't mind having a look at Sumner's office. Just to get a feel for the man."

He hesitated—seemed to weigh the value of pleasing me—then shrugged. "No problem."

He led me down the hall to the office. Except for the furniture, the room was stripped. Maggie had done a good job of removing everything personal.

"I have a lunch meeting in a few minutes. You can just shut the door when you're done," he said.

"Thanks."

"Let me know if I can be of any more help." Myers shook my hand again before leaving.

I took in the bare walls. Although devoid of his possessions, there was still a lot of Matt Sumner left in the room— much more than there'd been in his own home.

Head pounding, I moved to the leather chair, sat down, and closed my eyes.

I wondered if those pills I'd been taking had lost their effectiveness. I reached into my jacket pocket and took out the prescription bottle. Three tablets remained. I took out two, choking them down without water.

A glance at my watch told me I had ten minutes before I was supposed to meet Maggie. I leaned back in the chair and looked out the window. A typical cloudy day in Buffalo. Years ago, the seemingly perpetual gray skies had depressed me;

now they seemed familiar and I realized with some surprise I was starting to feel at home here again. Would I still feel that way if Nielsen made good his threat?

I couldn't afford to waste the time Myers had given me and, straightening in the chair, I began my search. I opened the desk drawers. Empty. I went through the credenza—nothing there either. Yet I couldn't shake the feeling I'd missed something.

I checked under the couch cushions, and down the sides of the chairs. Nothing. I was about to give up when I thought to look under the desk. Bingo! Caught between the center drawer and the desk frame was a mangled envelope. With some careful maneuvering, I managed to extricate it. I sat in Sumner's chair and smoothed the crumpled paper on the desk. The return address on the upper left-hand corner said Roche Biomedical Laboratories. It was empty, and was postmarked two days before the murder.

SEVENTEEN

A SECRETARY GAVE me directions to Maggie's office. She greeted me with a sunny smile that almost made me forget how crappy I felt. She had on a navy suit with a powder blue blouse, and the same gold chain around her neck. It made her look like a high-powered executive. Despite my own office attire, I felt like someone you might avoid on the street.

"Hey, I thought we were going to meet downstairs."

"I'm a few minutes early. I can wait."

"Thanks. Be right with you."

I took one of the chairs in front of her desk and she turned back to her computer. She made a call, switching back and forth between two databases as she spoke. The fact that she was busy gave me the opportunity to think up various topics we might discuss over lunch. Only, with my head about to explode, I didn't feel like talking. I didn't feel like eating or even thinking. At that moment the whole lunch idea seemed like a big mistake.

"Sorry about that," Maggie said at last. "I'm in the middle of organizing a conference and it's turning out to be a bitch."

She grabbed her coat and we headed for the elevator. A minute later, we were waiting for the light to change at the corner outside the bank. A ripple of pleasure shot through me when she grabbed my hand as we crossed the street. Her gloved fingers curled around mine and held on tight.

We ended up at a pizza joint around the corner. I wasn't interested in food, but Maggie ordered us a small pepperoni and mushroom pizza and a couple of Cokes. My broken left arm rested on the table as I rubbed my forehead with my right hand.

She touched my sleeve. "Are you okay? You don't look well."

"Since the mugging, I get these miserable migraines." I braved a smile. "I have to admit you're the bright spot in my day."

She smiled. "How's your case going?"

"I have a few more people to talk to."

"You're really treating this like a job. Have you thought about doing it for a living?"

"I did. I was an insurance investigator, remember?"

"No, I mean being a cop. Or a detective. It's never too late to start over."

"'Fraid not. In fact, I thought about being a bartender. Just until I figure out what I want to do. My brother's been on my back. Says I shouldn't even think about work for another few weeks."

"He's a doctor. He should know."

"He's my big brother and he still thinks of me as a fourteen-year-old kid." That came out sounding a whole lot angrier than I'd meant. "Don't listen to me. I don't know what I'm saying."

She changed the subject. "Have you had a really good fish fry since you got back to Buffalo?"

I shook my head. A mistake.

"You've got to have one on Good Friday and I know the perfect spot."

"I'd like that."

"Great. I'll pick you up at your house about six."

"Good. You can meet Rich and Brenda, too."

Her expression darkened, but amusement flashed in her blue eyes. "Uh-oh. Meeting the family already?"

"Hell, you've met Rich before."

"As a client, not a person."

I had to smile. "And you have to call him Richard. He hates being called Rich."

"You call him that."

"I know."

"Are you sure you're not still fourteen?"

I shrugged, and she grinned.

"Hey, you've got to go to the Broadway Market, too."

"My mother and I used to do that every year when I was a kid." I managed a smile at the pleasant memory. It was one of the few traditions we'd observed.

"I'm taking my mother-in-law on Friday."

"Mother-in-law? I thought you were divorced."

"Yes. I got the house, but Gary's mother, Lily, lives in the downstairs apartment. She takes care of my dog when I'm at work. It's a great arrangement."

Our pizza arrived and Maggie doled out pieces for each of us. The aroma made me feel sick. Maggie dug in with gusto. She wiped her mouth with a napkin. "Mmm. This is great. Aren't you having any?"

"I'd like to…but I don't think it's a good idea right now. Don't let me stop you. Enjoy." I took a tentative sip of my Coke. Much as I wanted to be with her, I was counting the minutes until I could get out of there and go home to my bed. I took out my prescription bottle. The last tablet. I downed it with a swallow of Coke.

She ate slowly and in silence, watching me, looking more and more worried as time went on.

"Sorry I'm not better company."

"Hey, if you don't feel well, you don't feel well. I wish there was something I could do. Want me to call your brother?"

"He'll pick me up at one o'clock." I took another sip of my drink. Coke is supposed to help settle your stomach, but its sweetness sickened me. I pushed the glass aside.

The waitress came by. "Everything okay?"

"Can you wrap this?" Maggie asked.

"Sure thing." She took the leftover pizza away.

"You want to take it home for later?"

I shook my head and winced. The waitress returned with a brown paper bag and the check. I fumbled with my wallet, pulled out a ten-dollar bill. My vision doubled; I couldn't even see the amount on the slip of paper. "Is this enough?"

Maggie took the money and the check from me. "It's fine."

"No doubt about it. I make a great impression. Broke, sick…a real winner."

"It's refreshing to find a man with vulnerabilities. I can't tell you how many macho jerks I've met in the past five years. Come on."

She grabbed my arm, pulled me up, and helped me on with my coat. Then she paid the check and, with her arm wrapped around mine, guided me back across the street. She parked me in one of the chairs in the bank's overheated lobby, then made a quick call to her office from the receptionist's desk. Moments later she took the chair next to me. "I'll wait with you until your brother gets here." She took my hand and squeezed it reassuringly.

Embarrassment doesn't begin to cover what I was feeling…except at that moment I felt so awful I would've accepted help from the devil himself.

When Richard's silver Lincoln pulled up in front of the bank at three minutes past one, Maggie helped me to my feet and steered me toward the door. "Want me to go out with you?"

"No, please. Gotta have some dignity."

"Okay." She squeezed my hand again. "See you Friday night, right?"

"I wouldn't miss it."

The cold air hit me like a left hook, making the ten or so feet from the door to the car seem more like a mile. I practically crawled onto the back seat.

"How'd your lunch go?" Brenda asked as the car took off into traffic.

I sank back into the seat. "Fine."

My voice must have sounded strained, for she turned to look at me. "Are you okay?"

"I've been better."

I could see Richard's eyes glance at me in the rear-view mirror. "I got us an appointment with my lawyer in twenty-five minutes. You up to it?"

No, I was tempted to wail, but he wouldn't need to consult an attorney if it hadn't been for me. "Sure." I closed my eyes and sank back against the leather upholstery, hoping I could survive another hour.

RICHARD'S LATE GRANDFATHER had been a partner in the local attorneys' office that still handled Richard's affairs. Morton, Alpert, Fox, and Jemison had been, and still was, one of the most respected firms in town. That they'd kept the old man's name years after his death reaffirmed the respect he'd commanded.

Daniel Jemison, son of the last of the original partners, was about Richard's age. Dressed in a drab gray suit, white shirt, and dark tie, the trim, sandy-haired lawyer didn't impress me as a man with much imagination. Throughout Richard's narration, Jemison's face remained impassive; only a raised eyebrow now and then betrayed he was even listening. I sat hunched in my chair, massaging my forehead, wishing the steady thumping would stop.

When Richard finished, Jemison swiveled his chair to gaze out the window, which overlooked the HSBC Arena, home of the Buffalo Sabres hockey team. We waited for long moments before he finally spoke.

"My advice is to go home and devote yourself to TV reruns."

I glanced at Richard in the adjacent chair. He looked as baffled as I felt.

"I beg your pardon," Richard said.

"Don't do anything. Don't even leave the house if you can manage it."

I leaned forward in my chair. "But I know—"

"Whatever you 'think' you know is immaterial, Mr. Resnick. There are any number of possible litigants who could drag you into court. The woman you suspect. The police. Any

of the people you've interviewed. It wouldn't hurt for you both
to leave town—lose yourself in a big metropolitan area: New
York, L.A. Let this whole situation blow over."

The pain in my skull flared.

Richard stood. "Thanks, Dan. And thanks for seeing us on
such short notice."

Jemison rose. "Always a pleasure." He shook hands with
Richard, but I turned away before I'd have to.

I shuffled out the door to the reception area.

Brenda put down a magazine, rose from her seat, and
joined me as I headed for the elevator. "You look awful."

"That's just how I feel."

"Did it go badly?"

"You'll have to ask Rich. I just want to go home."

Richard had joined us by the time the elevator arrived. We
rode down in silence with several others. The walk to the
parking garage seemed liked miles. Several times I almost
stumbled on the sidewalk. It was only Brenda's steadying
grasp on my arm that kept me upright. I tried to catch a glimpse
of Richard's expression, but he kept a pace or two ahead of us
until we got to the car. He opened the back door and helped
me in. A minute later, he'd started the car and we headed home.

I shut my eyes, concentrating all my energy on controlling
my gag reflex. I was determined not to throw up on Richard's
beautiful leather upholstery. I heard them conversing quietly,
but couldn't spare the effort to listen.

It seemed a long time before Richard pulled up the
driveway and stopped the car by the back door. Brenda helped
me into the house, and I waved her off as I staggered to my
room. I pulled off my raincoat, the tie came next, then I blindly
fumbled with the belt at my waist. I kicked off my shoes and
walked out of my pants, all the while ripping open the Velcro
fasteners on the brace, and dumped everything into an untidy
pile on the floor. Then I crawled onto my bed, wrapped myself
in the spread, and collapsed.

My pulse pounded through my skull. Sound and light were my enemies as I huddled into a ball of misery, pain, and despair. I hadn't felt this bad since I'd regained consciousness back in the hospital after the mugging.

I heard a faint rustle and cracked an eye open far enough to see Brenda picking up my clothes, hanging them on hangers. "Hon, you really shouldn't take off that brace."

"Not now," I murmured.

"You going to be sick?"

"Maybe."

She bent low by my bedside. "If you can't get to the john, the wastebasket's here. Okay?"

I tried to nod and ground my teeth against the nausea. Then she was gone.

It's scary that a headache can be so thoroughly incapacitating. This was worse than the worst hangover.

I lay there, barely breathing, as even that sound jarred my brains. It seemed like hours before I dozed off. At some point I found myself in the tiny bathroom, worshiping the porcelain god with the dry heaves, but the next thing I knew, it was dark and Brenda was back in my room. The light from the hallway gouged my eyes like knife thrusts.

"Jeffy? You want some dinner?" she asked, her voice gentle.

I groaned. "No."

"How about soup?"

It seemed like she'd asked me to explain a complicated math problem rather than answer with a simple yes or no.

Then Richard crouched beside me, his face only inches from mine. "When was the last time you took your medication?"

I had to think about it, and thinking was an effort. "Lunchtime. I—I ran out."

"Jesus," he swore, then he went away, too.

Sometime later, I came to again and found the bedside lamp blazing. I covered my eyes with my hand, surprised to find my face damp. Sweat? Tears? I wasn't sure.

I barely managed to raise myself from the oblivion of misery. Richard hovered somewhere above me. I heard him talking, but caught only fragments. "Ease the pain…non-narcotic…better by tomorrow…."

A needle pricked the inside of my right arm. He kept on talking, his voice a soothing croon, and I sank back into a fog bank of exquisite pain.

Whatever that magic syringe contained must have done the trick, for although I tossed and turned all night, plagued by dreams of teenagers wielding baseball bats and clubbing me senseless, I did sleep. When I woke the next morning, the pain was bearable.

At some time during the previous day, someone had taken off my dress shirt and the brace was back on my arm. They'd taken good care of me. Now I needed to find out if Richard intended to throw me out on my ass. I couldn't blame him if he did.

I stumbled from bed and found a navy velour robe draped across the top of my dresser. I put it on, awkwardly knotting the belt at my waist.

I must have looked a sight when I staggered out into the kitchen and found Richard and Brenda seated at the table with the breakfast dishes still in front of them. "Any coffee left?" My voice sounded husky as a chain-smoker's.

"Sit down. You really want coffee? How about some hot chocolate?" Brenda asked.

I sat. "I'll take the chocolate." Settling my weight on my good arm, I closed my eyes, breathing shallowly.

"You want something to eat?" Richard asked.

"I'm not ready for food."

"You going to live?"

I squinted up at him. "You tell me."

Instead he got up, grabbed a white paper bag off the counter, and took out a whole pharmacy of new and different drugs, setting them in front of me. His expression was stern, but his voice was gentle. "I'm telling you this as your concerned brother and as a licensed quack. Don't fuck with your health."

I blinked, surprised at his choice of words.

"You ever read the instructions that came with your prescription?"

"Of course. Well, kind of. Only what was on the bottle."

"Do you know what happened yesterday? You overdosed. Every pill you took made the headache ten times worse. You can't pop those things like candy. There's a regimen involved when taking this stuff."

"Well, I didn't know." It sounded lame, even to me. The whole episode should have terrified me, but I'd instinctively known that Richard would be there for me, that he'd take care of me. Exactly what I hadn't wanted only weeks before.

"I can't take care of you," he continued, as though reading my mind. "I'm too emotionally involved. I've arranged for someone at the UB clinic to see you on Monday." He took two of the pills from one of the bottles. "Take these now. We'll go over the rest of the routine when you can think straight."

"Yes, sir," I murmured with respect. He spoke to me like I was a five-year-old, but I was too tired to complain, and ready to do just about anything so as not to endure a repeat of the previous day. Brenda put a small glass of water in front of me and I downed the pills.

"Anything break on the Sumner case yesterday?"

"Jeff!"

"Rich, I gotta know."

"No. Nothing happened. No one was arrested."

Brenda placed a steaming mug before me and took her seat.

I took a sip of chocolate, avoiding both their gazes. "Sorry I crapped out on you yesterday. We should've talked about...." I wasn't sure how to finish the sentence.

"About Dan's advice?" Richard said.

I nodded. "I'm sorry I dragged you into all this, Rich. I—"

He held up a hand to stop me. "I've had a day to think about it. If you want to continue looking into Sumner's murder, I won't stop you. Hell, how could I?"

"But, Jemison said—"

"I know this is important to you. I just want you to consider the consequences if you continue with your—" It cost him to say it. "—investigation."

I thought carefully before answering. "I keep asking myself, what're the consequences if I don't? I *know* what I *know*. I can't explain to you why I feel obligated to keep looking for answers. I just have to do this."

He didn't say anything for a long moment. Then, "Okay, then let's talk about what you're going to do today—which is nothing," Richard said.

"No argument there," I said, glad he'd changed the subject. And I didn't do anything else that day but rest. I managed to drink the whole mug of chocolate before crashing for a three-hour nap. For lunch, I kept down an entire bowl of soup. By Wednesday evening I began to feel almost human again and choked down at least half the dinner Brenda served me. I watched the evening news, glanced at the newspaper to look for anything new on the Sumner investigation, and was in bed and asleep by eight o'clock.

Thursday morning, I was ready to go back to work.

EIGHTEEN

BRENDA HAD SCHEDULED another clinic visit, so the two of them were gone before ten o'clock. Meanwhile, I started the day by checking the newspaper to see if Sam Nielsen had made good his threat to write about me. He hadn't. Yet.

Next I got on the phone, checking with the library, the ever-handy City Directory, a patient library assistant, and the local phone book to find the Walker employee who'd been prose-cuted for theft. I found four Theodore Schmidts. I narrowed the field to two. On the last call I hit pay dirt. The woman who answered said Schmidt was her boyfriend and I could find him at his job any time during the day.

After that, I called Rob Sumner's house. No answer. I'd have to try again later.

I retrieved the piece of paper Charlie Nowak had given me days before, and dialed Big Jim Walker's secretary's home number. It rang several times before an older woman answered. "Lucy Kaminski?"

"Yes."

"My name's Jeffrey Resnick. I'm investigating Matt Sumner's death. Charles Nowak gave me your name and thought you might be able tell me—"

"I'm sorry. I didn't know the man."

"But you did work for Sharon Walker."

"Oh, yes. Sharon was engaged to Mr. Sumner's son. But that was years ago."

"Could I come out and talk to you about—?"

"Oh, I don't think so," she interrupted once again.

"Would you speak to me over the phone?"

I pictured her pursing her lips, trying to decide if she should continue the conversation. "I really don't like discussing such personal matters with strangers."

"Of course, you're right," I admitted, backpedaling. "Mr. Nowak said you worked for Jim Walker for over twenty years."

"Twenty-five years," she said with pride.

"Did you retire when the company went under?"

"Yes. It was very sad," she admitted, and launched into a detailed remembrance—just as I'd hoped she would. I made the appropriate oohs and ahs when necessary, and waited patiently until she was ready to talk about what I wanted to hear.

"Everything must've changed when Mr. Walker died."

"Yes. The company went downhill fast. Sharon just didn't have the feel for the business end of things."

"It must've been hard for her—caring for her son and all."

"I know I'm old-fashioned, but if she'd just left running the company to the men, we'd all still be employed. And that poor child. She left him with a babysitter from early morning until quite late in the evening. A mother really needs to be with her baby when he's that small. Once or twice she brought him to the office when the babysitter was sick."

"Did she neglect the boy?"

"Who am I to judge?"

I took that as a definite yes. "Did she ever speak about his father?"

"Never." Her tone changed. "It was very strange. There were four women in the office. We wanted to give her a baby shower, but she refused. She got very angry about it. I think she was embarrassed because she wasn't married. She knew Big Jim would've been disappointed."

"I take it they were very close."

"Yes." She paused. "Oh, dear. I've said much more than I intended. And I don't see what all this has to do with Mr. Sumner's death."

"At this point, I'm just looking into his business affairs."

"I suppose he helped when the company went through bankruptcy, but that didn't save our jobs."

I could certainly identify with that. I made a few sympathetic remarks and ended the conversation.

My limousine picked me up at eleven-thirty and the three of us took a lunch break at a local family restaurant before Richard and I dropped off Brenda at home and started off again. Brenda had given me a point-by-point comparison of the clinics they'd already visited, but old Rich was quiet during her recitation. I could tell the clinic they'd visited that day had not met with his approval. Not that he talked about it to me.

We found Ted Schmidt at Mount Olivet cemetery, behind the controls of a backhoe, digging a grave. I watched his precision with the scoop as it gouged the partially frozen earth, making a hole the exact size of a casket.

It gave me the creeps.

Schmidt was about my age, dressed in work clothes, a heavy jacket, and a yellow hardhat. I waited until he finished the grave before I approached him.

"Ted Schmidt?"

"Who wants to know?"

I handed him one of my cards through the open window on the cab. "I was hoping you'd speak with me about Walker Construction."

His eyes flashed. "Hey, I did my time. I don't need to be hassled about it any more." He shoved the card back at me.

"I'm not here to hassle you. I'm looking into a possible connection between Walker Construction and the murder of Matt Sumner of Bison Bank."

The anxiety in his face eased. "The guy they found gutted in his garage?"

I nodded.

"Cool," he said with an eager smile. He turned off the

big machine, jumped down from the cab. "What do you want to know?"

"Anything you can tell me."

He took off his work gloves. "I didn't work in the office, but I heard what was going on. We all knew the company was going under. Management was hiding assets, so I figured I'd grab my share before there wasn't anything left to get. Only I got caught."

"Did you know Sharon Walker?"

"Everybody did. She could handle anything on the site. Run a backhoe, drive the trucks, dump a load of gravel as good as me. But she forgot all that when she went into the office."

"So she was kind of a tomboy growing up?"

"She was the son old man Walker never had. He even called her Ronnie. First day of trout season, deer season, those two were gone."

I remembered the reference on Sumner's calendar on the day of his death: Ron. And she was a born hunter, too.

"Was she good to work with?"

"Before she went in the office, yeah. Just like one of the guys. After her father died and she took over, she started wearing high heels and suits with frilly shirts. She became one of those Feminazis. You know, bossing everybody around. Thinking she was hot shit."

"I take it she was the one who had you arrested."

His anger flared anew. "The lousy bitch." He jabbed his finger in my face to emphasize his words. "Other people were doing the same as me—looking out for themselves—but who did they prosecute? Me!"

Schmidt spewed venom against Sharon and Walker Construction for another ten minutes, giving me his personal opinion on each and every member of management, and the company's personnel policies. Obviously time in jail had done nothing to cool his hatred toward the company. I was grateful to finally escape.

"You okay?" Richard asked as I got in the car. His tone betrayed his amusement.

"I don't think I'll need my ears cleaned for a long time. He reamed them out nicely."

"You should've seen yourself, Jeff. He was shouting in your face and you were bending back so far I thought you'd fall over."

"But would you have rescued me if he'd really gotten physical?"

The lines around Richard's eyes crinkled. "I've got the cell phone. The police are as near as 911."

"Thanks for your concern. Hey, can I use this thing to call Rob Sumner's house?"

"Sure."

I dialed. No answer.

"What now?" he asked.

"I haven't talked with the guy Sumner fired. If we could stop over there, I could get that out of the way, too." I took out my notebook and found the address. As it turned out, it was in the neighborhood and minutes later we pulled into the driveway. As usual, Richard had come prepared, and hauled out a bulky medical text to read while I worked.

I rang the doorbell and waited. A rusting Reliant sedan sat in the driveway, so I figured someone had to be home. Finally the door opened. A harried-looking man of about forty stood before me. Dressed in jeans and a flannel shirt with the tails untucked, his bare feet were stuffed into worn slippers. A wet dishtowel adorned his shoulder and a screaming baby straddled his left hip.

"Yeah?" he demanded.

I handed him one of my cards. "Don Feddar? My name's Jeffrey Resnick. I'm looking into Matt Sumner's death, and—"

"Too bad he didn't die sooner. We'd've all been a lot better off!"

I wasn't sure how to reply.

"Can we talk?"

He nodded at the baby. "If you can stand her crying."

He gestured for me to enter. I followed him through the house. Toys were strewn about the place. Dust bunnies thrived in the living room, and the kitchen floor looked like it hadn't been mopped in months. He sat the baby in the high chair and cleared a stack of laundry off a chair for me.

He tossed my card on the table without looking at it. "I'm currently a house husband," he said, shoving a teething biscuit at the baby. She grabbed it in her chubby hand and stuffed it in her mouth. Her cries faded to whining. "I haven't worked since December twenty-third. Wasn't that a nice Christmas present for the wife and kids?"

"I heard. That's why I wanted to talk to you."

"You wanted to know if I murdered him, right? If I was going to do it, I'd have done it months ago. And no, I don't hunt."

"I heard the police already grilled you."

"Grill is right. They had me down at the station in Orchard Park for six hours a couple days after the murder." He shook his head, sat down, and continued folding laundry. "I told them, the night Matt was murdered I was at Tracy's dance recital. She's my oldest. I got over a hundred witnesses. I took the video of all the kids. I'm duping copies for a bunch of the parents. Anyway, it didn't matter to the cops that I have an alibi. They figured I could've had someone else do the deed. Yeah, and how was I supposed to pay for it?"

A little girl about three, dressed in a miniature jogging suit with Sesame Street characters marching across her shirt, came into the kitchen. She latched onto Feddar's leg. "Daddy, I don't feel good." He grabbed another teething biscuit from the box on the table and handed it to her.

"I heard you got fired for approving loans without proper documentation."

Feddar nodded. "Matt disputed that the signatures on the loans to Walker Construction were his."

"He accused you of faking his signature?"

"It was my word against his, and he was a vice president. Lying bastard."

"Was that the first time it happened?"

He shrugged. "Upper management only cares about their own—and the bottom line."

It sounded like run-of-the-mill corporate bashing to me, but I didn't doubt him. I'd seen some pretty ruthless managers in the insurance business, managers who'd denied claims on a whim. It sickened me, but I was a small cog in a big machine. That's why I was sacrificed when others with less experience were saved.

"Could Sumner have had it in for you?"

The little girl dropped her biscuit on the floor and tried to climb onto his lap. Feddar kept pushing her down, but she wasn't easily deterred.

"I don't think so."

"Was he friendly with others in management?"

"Only to the extent that it involved business. I don't know what he did in his spare time, other than—" He broke off, looked at his children. "F-U-C-K-ing any woman desperate to get out of the secretarial pool, although it wasn't so bad the past few years. He was afraid of a sexual harassment lawsuit."

I thought about Maggie having to work under those conditions.

"He'd gone as far as he was going to go in the company," Feddar continued. "I got the feeling he was bored. I know he had a younger woman on the side for several years, but he saw other women, too."

"Did he brag about it?"

"No, but I know she had a child. I heard snatches of conversation. I got the feeling he was fond of the kid. Hard to believe a snake like that could have a heart buried under all that flab. That softness for little kids was one of the reasons he did so much charity work. Katie here is prone to ear infections—she's got one working now. Matt always asked about her."

"How old is she, three?"

"Three and a half."

Jackie was four—only a few months difference.

"I got the impression Sumner didn't get along with his own children."

"That's true. He couldn't accept teenage rebellion. He was a strange man. He did a lot of good—raised a lot of money for good causes, but he could be such a bastard, too."

"Daddy, you said a bad word. I'm gonna tell Mommy," the little girl scolded.

"He did have a certain charm, though," I pressed.

"Oh, yeah. Never forgot a name or a face. It worked well for him in business and in his charity work. He could remember how much a contributor gave from year to year. That was a big part of his success. He could flatter you and make you believe lies were truth."

"Could he have been blackmailed?"

"Matt was too smart for that. He would've found a way to wheedle out of it."

The baby's biscuit was soft and gummy and she methodically smeared it through every inch of her sparse hair. Feddar picked up the child at his knee and draped her over his shoulder. She quieted, wrapping her small fingers around the folds in his shirt.

"Did he drink?" I asked.

Feddar laughed. "He couldn't handle it. I once saw him fall face-first—drunk—into a plate of linguine. That was at a Christmas lunch, and we'd all had a few. Funniest thing I ever saw, but no one dared laugh. One of the women felt sorry for him and drove him home. He came on to her in her car. Needless to say, that was the last time she played Good Samaritan."

"I'm getting an uneven picture of this guy."

"He missed his calling. He should've been an actor. He was

a sleazebag, but it was amazing to see him charm women. He was good with all the clients, and if he wanted to encourage young talent at the bank, he'd do it. If you went to his alma mater, he practically kissed your ass."

"Where was that?"

"Notre Dame."

"You didn't go there?"

"Hell, no. Buff State."

"Daddy, I don't feel good," the little girl murmured.

"I know, sweetie," he said and patted her back. "The only good thing that's come out of all this is that I spend more time with my kids. But I'm not much good at housework. My wife is supporting us now, but when my unemployment runs out, I'll have to find something. We can't live like this and keep the house."

I nodded. If Richard hadn't rescued me, I might've become another statistic on the homeless front.

I thanked Feddar for his time, and made a hasty exit.

The day was winding down, and I was tired. I used Richard's cell phone and finally got hold of Linda Sumner, Rob's wife. When I explained I was looking into her father-in-law's death, she suggested I come over about six-thirty, after Rob came home from his job as assistant manager of a pizza parlor.

With nothing else to do, Richard and I headed for home to kill an hour before going out one last time. It gave me time to write up my interviews with Kaminski, Schmidt, and Feddar. I missed my computer. I had writer's cramp by the time I snagged my chauffeur to leave.

At precisely six-thirty we arrived at the little duplex on the fringes of Kenmore. I pressed the doorbell and waited. Finally Rob Sumner jerked open the door. While I'd seen a picture of him in his father's office, it had obviously been taken several years earlier. He looked about twenty-eight, with a beer gut years in the making. His close-set eyes and sullen expression reminded me of a schoolyard bully.

I introduced myself, but he didn't invite me inside. Despite the cold, he stood in his shirtsleeves—his hands jammed into his jeans pockets.

"My mother warned me you might be by to badger me."

"That's not my intent. I'm looking into your father's death. I hoped you could clarify a few things."

He scowled. "What do you want to know?"

"When did your relationship with Sharon Walker end?"

"What difference does that make?"

"I'm looking into the connection between the Walker Construction firm and your father."

"You think someone at Walker could have murdered Dad?"

"It's possible."

He thought about it for a moment, then answered. "Sharon and I went together for a couple of years. I met her at a party my dad threw for some of his clients. She came with her father. We got to be friends. We went out for about two years."

"When was this?"

"Six, seven years ago."

"Did you have her added to the list of those allowed in the church?"

"Why would you need to know that?"

"Do you know who the father of her child is?"

"No, I don't! And what's more, I don't care. Look, what's this got to do with my father's murder?"

"Do you still have a relationship with her?"

He took a step forward, forcing me back. "Hey, I don't need you coming around here saying things to upset my wife."

I kept my voice level. "I only told your wife I was looking into your father's murder."

His eyes flashed in outrage. "I don't need any more trouble."

So, there was trouble in newlywed paradise.

"What kind of trouble, Rob? Do you know something you haven't told the police? Did someone threaten you?"

"No," he shouted, but his furtive glance convinced me he

was lying. "Look, don't bother us again. Or next time-!" He raised a fist, shook it at me, then stormed into the house.

I stared at the closed door for long seconds before I turned and walked down the driveway and climbed into the car.

"I was ready to call 911 that time," Richard said. "What was he so steamed about?"

"I'm not sure. But you know, I got a funny feeling he was covering up something about his father's death. He knows— or suspects—something. And I swear he lied to me about the timing of his relationship with Sharon Walker." I let out a long breath, leaning back in the seat. My conversation with Rob had shaken me more than I cared to admit.

Richard backed the car out of the driveway. "You look beat."

"I feel beat—like I put in a whole day."

"You did." He headed for home, down streets that, despite the gathering gloom, were beginning to look familiar again.

"Look, tomorrow's Good Friday—a holiday for most of the city. Why don't you take the day off, too?" Richard said. "Relax—have some fun. Is there something you'd like to see or do now that you're home? Niagara Falls? Toronto maybe?"

I thought about it for a moment, remembering Maggie's suggestion. "Well, I would like to go to the Broadway Market."

Richard shrugged. "Sure." He looked puzzled. "Why?"

I looked at him, incredulous. "You mean you've never been there on Good Friday?"

"I don't think I've ever been there."

"I guess I shouldn't be surprised. It is a working-class haven."

"Now let's not get nasty," he said, his amused tone making me smile. "Seriously, Jeff. Take a day off. Will it really make a difference?"

"Probably not. And from everything I've found out, the victim deserved what he got."

"It's not your place to judge."

I made no comment. But if what he said was true, why had God, or the fates, dragged me into this whole mess? Sumner's small act of kindness—buying that crummy vase for my mother's birthday—had indebted me to him. An out-of-proportion debt, but a debt nonetheless. I suppose no cosmic rule said I had to like the truth I uncovered. And deep down I knew this little mystery had kept me going. Without it, I might've given up entirely.

"A day off?" I repeated, the idea beginning to appeal to me. "Okay, Rich. You've got a deal."

NINETEEN

THE MORNING STARTED with sunny skies and warm temperatures, the kind of day that makes you mistakenly think
winter's gone for good. As a kid a trip to the Broadway Market
on Good Friday had been a tradition for me. Though grown,
I was no less delighted.

Richard seemed nervous about taking the Lincoln to that
part of town, so we ended up in Brenda's Taurus. Cars
jammed the side street, waiting to get in the ramp garage.
We circled around, looking for a place to park, and ended
up on the roof.

We walked down three flights of stairs and entered the
Market. Young and old people of all ethnic backgrounds
packed the seedy-looking warehouse space. The market's
worn, concrete floors and walls of peeling paint couldn't
dispel the holiday spirit.

Stalls and kiosks were scattered across the floor and clus-
tered around the edges of the room. Vendors sold wooden
Ukrainian Easter eggs, tacky ashtrays, cigarette lighters and
other trinkets, Lotto tickets, and Easter plants. We passed
meat counters where people lined up four or five deep, waiting
to buy their holiday roasts or fresh Polish sausage.

You don't mess with a woman bent on shopping, and
Brenda had a purpose. Richard and I were soon separated
from her in the crowd. I wandered the place in a pleasant fog,
comparing the present-day Market with the one I remembered. Paranoia struck when I remembered Sophie Levin's
warning about danger in even innocent situations. I found

myself searching the crowd for a woman with a small boy. Not shadows of my past, but Sharon Walker clutching her crossbow, dragging her young son behind her.

Pausing at a candy counter, I studied the offerings. "You getting anything for Brenda?" I asked Richard.

"She doesn't go in for that kind of silliness."

"Well, if you don't buy her something, I will. Then I'll look like a hero on Easter morning."

He frowned, then bought her a two-pound box of assorted chocolates. But he made me carry the bag so she wouldn't suspect anything.

By the time we caught up with Brenda, she was loaded down with grocery bags—more food than the three of us were capable of eating. "That's the beauty of owning a freezer," she quipped. "Now what else do we have to get?"

"A butter lamb," I said.

"Which is?"

"Butter in the shape of a lamb. It's a Polish Easter tradition," Richard explained.

"What are the pussy willows for?" she asked, seeing a woman pass by with an armful of them.

"Dingus Day," Richard said.

"Yeah. You buy them and hit Richard with them on Easter Monday. Then you go to a tavern, drink beer, and have fun."

She looked skeptical. "Why?"

"It's Polish tradition," Richard said.

"But you're not Polish," she said.

"I'm half Polish," I said.

"Well it doesn't show," she teased good-naturedly. "Oh, eggs! We have to get eggs."

"What for?" Richard asked.

"Coloring, of course. And we have to get the dyes, too."

Richard looked at me and frowned.

"You can be such a stuffed shirt, Richard," Brenda said. "But Jeffy and I are determined to have fun."

"I'm not opposed to having fun. I'm just not very artistic."

"You don't need to be, my love." She patted his cheek and he faked a smile. Then she started off in the direction of a poultry stand. "It's all settled—egg coloring after lunch. Wait until you see what I got. We'll have a feast guaranteed to clog your arteries."

We got the eggs, and the dyes, and started for home. And lunch was a feast. Brenda laid the cold cuts on a platter and we made deli-type sandwiches out of ham, tongue, sliced beef, bologna, and liverwurst. She bought Polish rye bread with caraway seeds and set out a jar of horseradish that brought tears to the eyes and cleared our sinuses. For dessert, she bought fresh *placek*—that wonderful, sweet, crumb loaf— and sugar cookies, which tasted terrific with hot, strong coffee. I ate more in one sitting than I'd eaten in months. For the first time in a very long while, I felt happy, and it was the company as much as the good food.

After eating too much, we all felt logy. I volunteered to clean up while Brenda and Richard headed for the bedroom and a nap. I was glad to give them a chance to be alone. I'd been monopolizing too much of Richard's time.

I hit the mattress, too, but sleep didn't come quickly. I kept thinking about Sharon Walker, her crime, and the small boy who'd witnessed it. And wondered what in hell I could do about it.

I MUST'VE DOZED OFF, because the next thing I knew noises from the kitchen woke me.

Brenda sat at the table. The eggs were in a shallow bowl, already boiled and cooled. She measured water into four old-fashioned glasses. "Hey, Jeffy, sit your butt down and let's decorate these eggs."

"Coffee," I rasped. "Got any instant?"

"Not in this house. I'll make some while you fix the colors and start dunking."

I read the directions and dropped dye tablets in the glasses. Then I picked up the transparent wax crayon that came in the package and took an egg in hand.

"What're you going to draw?" she asked.

"An Easter cross."

"Draw flowers, too."

"But all I can make are dumb-looking tulips."

"Just make it pretty."

She brought over two steaming mugs. After two weeks, she knew just how I liked my coffee. We sipped our coffee and dipped eggs like a couple of contented children. I debated spoiling the mood, but something had been nagging me.

"Brenda, why don't you and Richard get married?"

The joy of the moment left her face. She stared at the glass of blue colored dye, taking her time to mull over the question.

"Jeffy, there's a lot of guilt involved when you love a white man," she said, her voice soft. "Some of the worst racists I know are African-Americans. Some in my own family."

"Your mother?"

She nodded. "For most of my life I've worked in the white world. Two—possibly three—other people of color worked at the Foundation in Pasadena, but that's all. I know I was hired as a token black, but that's where it ended. I worked damn hard and I earned every cent of my pay. And I was paid well. I don't need Richard's money. I have my own and I spend it."

"You didn't answer my question."

She frowned. "I was married before. To a man of color. He abused me. He felt emasculated because I had a better-paying job than he did." She stopped, pursed her lips. "It's more a woman thing than a race thing. I'm a person. I won't be a man's property ever again."

"But Rich isn't like that."

"I know. But it's been hard coming to Buffalo. It's a con-

servative, blue-collar town. And this is a very white neighborhood. It would be difficult for Richard to live here with me
as his wife."

"He loves you."

"It's more complicated than just love."

I hesitated, almost afraid to voice my next question. "Are
you going to leave him?"

Her eyes flashed in anger; then she shook her head and picked
up another egg, carefully dipping it into the glass of dye. "You're
braver than your brother. He's afraid to ask that question."

"Don't leave him because of me. I'll go before I let that
happen."

Tears brimmed her eyes. She reached for my hand. "Jeffy,
nothing you could do would come between us. You could be
the glue that ultimately holds Richard and me together." She
smiled at my puzzlement. "It's okay, you don't have to understand. I don't even understand. But, like those visions you
have and hold as truth, I hold this as truth."

I didn't know what the hell she was talking about, but then
we were hugging each other and I felt better.

"What's going on?" Richard asked, entering the kitchen.

Brenda and I pulled back, looked at one another, and smiled.

"Nothing," I said and took another sip of my coffee.
"Nothing at all."

"Sit down and draw a caduceus," Brenda told Richard, the
somber spell broken.

"What on earth is that?" I asked.

"The medical symbol. A snake and staff," he explained,
taking his seat. He turned to her. "And why would I want an
Easter egg with a caduceus on it—if I could even draw one?"

She held up one of the eggs decorated with my artistry.
"Because this is the sorriest example of an Easter egg I've ever
seen. You have to be better at it than your brother."

He shrugged and picked up the wax crayon. "It's blunt."

"So sharpen it." I handed him a paring knife. "Hey, guys,

I'm going out with Maggie tonight. Should I tell her about this psychic stuff?"

"Yes. If it's going to make a difference, you want to know before you get too involved," Brenda advised.

"Just do what feels right," Richard said. He frowned at the crayon. "How am I supposed to draw something as complicated as a caduceus when the crayon is clear wax and I can't see what I've drawn?"

"Draw a tulip. It's easier," I said.

Richard's artistic endeavors were no better than mine, I noted with satisfaction, but the egg-coloring project was a success, if only for the fun we had.

We finished about five, which gave me an hour before Maggie arrived.

I showered and changed and found myself sitting on the stairs by the front door like a dog awaiting its master. I admit it, I was looking forward to my night out. Since I still had cash left from my tax return, the evening would be on me—not her.

With time on my hands, I thought about Rob Sumner. He knew—or suspected—a lot more than he'd let on. I prayed for sudden insight so I'd know what part—if any—he'd played in his father's death. Not that I believed he participated in the murder, but I couldn't shake the feeling he was somehow involved, however indirectly.

And perhaps Sharon's next victim?

Now where did that come from?

I was still pondering different scenarios, with Rob at the center, when the doorbell startled me. I jumped to my feet and opened the door. Maggie stood on the steps, poised to ring the bell again. Her unzipped, iridescent, down jacket seemed to waver between lavender and blue. Dressed in jeans, boots, and an emerald green sweater, she looked terrific.

"Hello!" She took a step forward and gave me a quick peck on the cheek. "Good to see you looking better."

"Glad to be feeling better." I held on longer than absolutely necessary, soaking up that wonderful, peaceful aura she seemed to emit. I stepped back. "Come on in."

"Sorry I'm late. Lily had a crisis. She ran out of whiskey and her boyfriend was coming over. Elderly love."

I suppressed a smile.

She looked around the grand entry hall. "Great house. I could kill for a tour."

"It's not mine, or I'd say yes. But I'll bet Brenda could be talked into it. Come on. They're in the study." I didn't bother to take her coat, as we were going to leave in only a few minutes. Maggie followed me through the long corridor to the opposite end of the house. Richard sat behind his desk; Brenda was on the couch facing the fireplace. "Rich, Brenda, this is my friend Maggie Brennan."

Richard stood. "Hi, Maggie, I think I recognize you from the bank." He held out his hand to shake hers.

Brenda came up behind her.

"This is Brenda."

Maggie turned and blinked, momentarily startled. I may have forgotten to tell her Brenda's black. "Oh. Nice to meet you," she said, extending her hand.

"We've heard a lot about you. I understand interior decoration is a hobby of yours?"

"Yes. You have a lovely home."

"In desperate need of updating. Would you like a tour?"

Smiling, Maggie glanced at me. "I'd love one."

The women disappeared and I scowled at Richard. "Well, I won't be eating dinner for a couple of hours."

"Have a seat," he said, gesturing me into the empty wing chair in front of his desk.

He took his own seat and started flipping through pages of what looked like bank statements. "Counting your millions?"

Richard frowned. "Take my word for it, having a lot of money is a burden."

"I could get used to it."

"I doubt it. I'm forty-seven years old. Brenda doesn't want to get married, and she certainly doesn't want children. So what am I going to do with all that money in one lifetime?"

"Give it away."

"I've been meaning to. Grandmother got burned by a bogus charity. I guess that's why I'm stalling. I haven't even invested the money, much to my accountant's dismay. It just keeps growing, even though most of it just languishes in bank accounts."

"Give it away," I repeated. "Make it a business. Check out every charity. If it's legitimate, send them money."

"I'd have every charity in town kissing my ass."

"Give it anonymously."

He looked thoughtful. "Maybe."

"Just leave me a million or two, okay?"

"I thought you liked your independence?"

"I do. And I'm kidding."

He shrugged, the barest hint of a smile on his lips. "I'll leave you a million anyway."

"Don't hurry and die on my account. I kind of got used to having you around."

"Seriously, Jeff, years ago I offered to send you to college. That offer's still open. Or I'll set you up in business, if that's what you want."

"Look, Rich, you could buy me my own insurance agency, or a McDonald's franchise, but then it wouldn't be mine. It wouldn't be something I'd earned."

"I can lead you to the road to success. You'd have to stay there on your own. You'd do it, too. You have integrity, Jeff. And my offer stands."

"Then how about a compromise? I'm going to need transportation to find a job. Maybe in a couple of weeks we could go look at cars. But I'll pay you back. It's important to me to pay my way. Understand?"

He smiled. "Too well. You're as bad as Brenda." He collected the papers in front of him, put them into a file folder, and deposited them in his desk.

"What about you? What do you want to do?"

He shrugged. "Brenda's got her heart set on volunteering at a women's clinic. But a clinic that also handles abortions is a little too high-profile for me. I want to help people, but I don't want to be a target."

"How about opening your own clinic?"

He shook his head. "All my money wouldn't be enough to fund it. Plus the logistics are beyond comprehension. That's why we've looked into working for an established clinic."

"Do you really want to volunteer your time?"

"I might like to work at UB's clinic. And maybe teach."

"What does Brenda think?"

"I've bored her with it for so long she cringes at the mention of UB. But I always thought of the place as home. I know that sounds silly, but I do."

"No sillier than having visions and trying to solve murders. In fact, it sounds a helluva lot saner to me."

"The problem is nothing can compare with my job at the Foundation. I worked with some of the greatest minds and computer equipment." He shook his head ruefully. "So much of my life was tied up in my work that I didn't have time for anything else—except Brenda, and she shared that work."

"So, you're not a shrink."

"No, but I've done my share of counseling other people."

Including me, I thought. "So what stage of grief are you in now?"

"Acceptance. Thanks to you."

"You mean my pitiful life made you realize how good you've got it?"

He looked stricken, until he realized my sarcasm held no animosity. "Actually, yes."

I shrugged. "I'm glad one of us got something out of this experience."

He leaned back in his chair. "Give yourself time. It's taken me a year to get this far."

"Then talk to Brenda about UB. She's cool."

He smiled. "You're right, she is."

Maggie's boot heels tapped on the parquet floor. Laughter preceded their entrance.

"You ready?" I asked Maggie.

"Sure." She nodded at Richard. "Hope to see you again soon."

Brenda and Richard waved to us as Maggie backed out of the driveway, making me feel a bit like a kid out on a first date. She headed toward Main Street, then turned right, heading away from the city. "Where are we going?" I asked.

She gave me a wry smile. "Nowhere fancy. Just good, cheap food."

TWENTY

"WHAT DO YOU RECOMMEND?" I asked, peering at Maggie over the top of my laminated menu.

"The fish fry, of course."

Mike and Ann's Tavern wasn't fancy. Plastic flowers in plastic vases decorated each table. No one seemed to mind—every seat was taken. But it wasn't only the good food that had attracted Maggie.

"I'm allergic to cigarette smoke," she explained. "This was the first smoke-free bar I came across. That doesn't matter now that the laws have changed. But this is still the best place I know for a fish fry."

"I had a feeling you didn't like being around smoke."

"Who does? If I'm exposed to it for even a few minutes, I suffer for days. I just have bad lungs."

My eyes wandered down the front of her sweater. I wasn't disappointed in what I saw. She cleared her throat and I looked away, pretended to study the daily specials.

The beer-battered haddock, fries, coleslaw, and fresh-baked rye bread were excellent, and the portions generous. Too generous for me. Maggie assured me her dog would do justice to the leftovers.

We talked while we ate. Maggie had so many interests and amusing stories to share. In comparison, I felt like the dullest man on earth. I gave her the rest of my history—how I'd lost my job at Travelers, then used all my savings just to survive. I told her about landing the new job and how life was on the upswing until the mugging.

It seemed like every sentence I uttered began with, "I used to…." I used to play racquetball. I used to dabble in photography. I used to target shoot.

I used to have a life.

"My sister Irene says you're a loser. That I should run away from you as fast as I can."

My stomach tightened. She'd said the words with such lightness that it almost sounded like a joke. But her sister might be right.

"Then why didn't you cancel tonight?"

Maggie's gaze held mine. "Because the day I met you, when you shook my hand, I felt—" She stopped, as though having trouble putting her thoughts into words. "I felt something."

I had, too. I liked it. Wanted more.

She hesitated, then reached across the table and touched my hand, reigniting that same spark of something inside me once again.

We sat there, amidst the dinner crowd bustle, staring at each other. Smiling at each other. Studying each other. Then a shadow darkened her deep blue eyes. She released her hold, reached for her coffee cup, and lowered her gaze. "There's something I should've told you."

I swallowed dryly. "Oh?"

"Matt and I were…together for a while."

Oh shit. And I'd told Nielsen to concentrate on Sumner's ex-lovers. I worked at keeping my voice level. "You had an affair?"

She placed the cup back in its saucer, toyed with her spoon. "It was right after Gary left." Her face seemed to crumple. "When your husband leaves you for another man, you feel like a failure as a woman. Matt and his never-ending string of compliments made me feel desirable again. But it wasn't long before I felt pretty darn cheap."

For a moment I thought she might cry. Then she took a breath and straightened in the booth. "Matt took advantage of me when I was vulnerable. I'm not making excuses for myself.

I should've known better. When I finally realized what I'd allowed to happen, I was angry. I broke it off. Matt took his revenge. Got me transferred back to the secretarial pool, where I started. It took me four years to move up to the top floor again. And he made my life hell once I made it back, too."

Her anger and resolve, stretched across the expanse of table, touched me. "Why didn't you tell me this sooner?"

She wouldn't look at me. "I didn't want you to think less of me."

I studied her troubled face as she tried to distance herself from the hurt.

"I don't think less of you. I think less of him."

Her smile was thin-lipped and embarrassed.

I needed more from her. But how could I get it without seeming as big a jerk as the man who'd used her? "What about Sumner's children? Ron Myers said the youngest son has a drinking problem."

"Michael went to rehab after he showed up drunk at school, toting a loaded gun. I'm the one who made the arrangements to get him into a place near Albany. Matt's daughter, Diane, is the only sane one in the family."

"What's with Rob?" I asked. "When I spoke to him yesterday, he was pretty hostile. I got the impression he really didn't want anyone looking into his father's death. Like he might've known something about it."

"I don't know. Matt was great at damage control. I wondered if Rob got caught stealing or maybe selling drugs a couple of years ago. He was in some kind of trouble, but it all blew over."

"Did Sumner confide in you about such things?"

Maggie shook her head. "He didn't respect me—or any other woman. I once heard him tell one of the guys that women were only walking twats. I know that's vulgar, but that's what he was."

I frowned. The more I learned about Sumner, the more my revulsion grew. But I needed to find out more.

"I'm trying to get in Sumner's head—get a better understanding of him. Does that make sense?"

She nodded.

"Then tell me, where does one have a clandestine affair in Buffalo?"

"We'd meet at his condo. I don't think Claudia knew about it. I don't know if he owned or rented it. It might even belong to the bank. You wouldn't believe the assets they have."

Someone dropped a quarter in the jukebox. Elvis began singing "Suspicious Minds."

Maggie leaned forward, spoke louder. "I found a duplicate key in his desk while cleaning out his office." She patted her purse beside her. "I don't know why, but I took it."

My eyes widened as a whole range of possibilities blossomed in my mind.

She smiled coyly. "Wanna take a drive?"

THE CONDO WAS IN A tract of ubiquitous clones in Tonawanda, off Sheridan Drive. If you came home drunk on a Saturday night, you'd probably never find your own place.

Maggie parked in the short drive, killed the lights and engine. No porch lamp shined at number three twenty-two. It wasn't much to look at. A double garage took up most of the front of the place. The entrance was a white steel door. A round, leaded window was the only source of natural light on the south side of the first floor, although double dormered windows were centered on the story above.

We got out and I looked around. No neighbors peeked out to watch us. Not even a barking dog cut the silence.

Maggie headed for the front door, stuck the key in, and reached for the handle.

A sick feeling welled in my stomach.

"Wait! You have gloves?"

I met her on the steps, could hardly see her eyes in the dark.

"What for?"

"If the cops haven't been through here already, we don't want them finding our fingerprints when they come."

"Good idea," she said, and pulled a pair of knit gloves from her coat pocket. I held the cuff of my right glove between my teeth and pulled it on my hand, as she fumbled with the key in the lock.

The condo was dark. I waited until she shut the door behind us before patting the wall in search of a light switch.

A crystal chandelier illuminated the entry. Stark white walls, tiled entry, carpet and sectional furniture in the room straight ahead: the place reminded me of a hospital. No art or photos decorated the hall. To the right, a staircase led to the loft above. The place felt cold, like no one had been there in weeks.

We wandered into the living room, Maggie flicking on switches as we went. A cathedral ceiling soared some twenty feet above us. Rectangular skylights, like black eye sockets, reflected the glow of track lighting. A black-and-white, modern-art painting decorated the space above the white mantle. A companion piece of corporate art hung near the dining table. The rest of the walls were blank. A natural-looking fake fern filled the cold hearth. A stereo cabinet held audio equipment, but few CDs. The black box of a TV sat on a pedestal across from the couch, its remote the only clutter in the room.

"Not much personality, is there?" Maggie commented. "It hasn't changed a bit since I was here five years ago."

"Apart from the style of furniture, it's not much different from Sumner's house."

I ventured farther into the sterile room, looked over the breakfast bar into the galley kitchen.

"What's through that door? The garage?"

She nodded.

"And upstairs?"

"Two good-sized bedrooms. A terrific bathroom. Double shower, Jacuzzi bath. There's a hot tub on the deck." She walked over to the French doors. Beyond her I could see the lights of the other condos on the next street.

"The basement opens out to the back courtyard. Matt had a wet bar down there. Pool table, too. Wanna see?"

I shook my head, looked around the room once more. Too bad I couldn't touch anything. I just hoped I'd suck up whatever residual essence remained of Sumner by other means.

I closed my eyes, breathed deeply, opening myself up to the place. Tendrils of something nudged at my brain.

Maggie and Sumner had made love here. He'd touched her. Maybe memorized her every curve.

A wave of jealousy washed through me.

Don't think about it.

But I couldn't stop. It ate at me.

I squeezed my eyes shut tighter.

The tendrils grew stronger. I wasn't sure just what it was I was getting—but I was definitely getting something. Fear, maybe, but unlike what I'd felt before. I concentrated and the feeling swelled. Yes, another's stomach-churning fear.

"You okay?" Maggie asked, worried.

I let out a long breath, forced a smile. "Yeah. Let's look upstairs."

Maggie led the way, turning on more lights as we went. It seemed to enhance my newly awakened senses, the fear expanding with each step.

"This is the guest room," she said, adopting a real estate broker's cadence, "but I doubt anyone's ever stayed here."

Like the living room, it was a study in black and white. The headboard and matching dresser were ebony enamel. A white spread covered the mattress, and sheepskin acted as a throw at the left side of the bed, its ivory softness a contrast to the stark white carpet. No night tables with bedside lamps for reading comfort. No books, either. No decorations on the walls. I opened the closet door. Nothing. Not even coat hangers.

"Next is the bathroom. I'd kill for one like this," she said and flipped on a switch.

Chrome and tile sparkled like something out of a builder's brochure. Except for a box of tissues, there was nothing in sight to indicate anyone lived here. I opened the medicine cabinet. An electric razor, toothpaste and single toothbrush, mouthwash, cologne, a can of men's hair spray, and a half-empty box of condoms. Old Matt liked to be prepared. A drawer in the vanity held a dozen new toothbrushes—no doubt for use by Sumner's lady guests—and an unopened box of disposable cups. Freshly laundered white towels sat neatly stacked in the linen closet.

"I take it Matt didn't spend a lot of time here."

"It didn't take him long to climax," she said, sarcasm filling her voice. She cleared her throat. "The master bedroom's got a king-sized bed, a down comforter and—" I felt her tension rise.

I left the bathroom, saw a hand towel on the threshold between the master bedroom and hall. A dark smudge marred its pristine state. "What's wrong?"

She wrinkled her nose. "Do you smell something?"

I did. A flat, coppery odor I recognized.

"Stay here," I told her and headed down the hall.

I hit the light switch. Blood—like paint on a blank canvas—splattered the walls by the right side of the bed.

"What is it?" Maggie called.

I moved to the far side of the bed, careful not to tread on the footprint stains that ruined the carpet.

Claudia Sumner lay huddled on her side, naked, the top of her head blown clear away.

"Jeff?" Maggie cried, fear threading her voice.

No gun was visible. Where were Claudia's clothes? Her car? In the garage?

My gaze drifted to her face as phantom images of Shelley's murder exploded in my mind. But it was Claudia's blood, brains, and bone sprayed across the walls, floor, and bed.

The room was suddenly too hot, making it hard to breathe. I backed away, hoped to hang onto my stomach contents long enough to reach the bathroom.

I brushed past Maggie, threw up in the sink. Coughing and gasping, I ran the water until I could catch my breath.

"What did you see?" she cried. "What's in there?"

I wiped my mouth on my sleeve.

"Claudia."

Maggie's eyes went wide with fear. "She's...dead?"

I nodded. "Hours ago. Maybe even yesterday."

She took a ragged breath, eyes wild, and backed away, crashing into the wall, then bolted for the stairs.

"Wait!"

I caught her at the landing, grabbed her sleeve.

"We've got to get out of here!" she wailed, and tried to pull away.

I pushed her against the wall, pinning her with my body.

"Listen to me. We can't panic. You hear me?" She shook her head, terrified. "Maggie, listen to me." I clasped her chin. "We've got to turn off the lights. Make it look like we were never here."

"I'm going to lose my job. My God, we could go to jail!"

"No one has to know we were here. We wore gloves. It's going to be okay."

But she covered her face with her hands, weeping. I pulled her close, let her cry on my shoulder. I smoothed her hair in rhythm with her sobs. "It's okay, Maggie. It'll be okay. I promise."

"How? How can it ever be right?"

I had to come up with something. Some answer. She was depending on me.

I drew back, looked her in the eye.

"You ever do any acting?"

Since I'd already reported one find to the cops via 911, I figured I'd be pushing my luck to try it again. In the parking

lot of a drugstore, I wrote Maggie a script. She practiced it
three times, speaking lower, slower, sounding sexy as hell.

We stood under the glare of a mercury vapor lamp, clutching the phone between us, Maggie transmitting her fear like
carrier waves. She pressed the touch-tone pad. It rang twice.

"Please listen," she said calmly. "I'll only say this once.
There's a body at three twenty-two Maiden Lane. Claudia
Sumner, wife of Matthew J. Sumner. She was shot. Today,
possibly yesterday. Please send someone."

I pressed the switch-hook and our eyes locked. "You did
great, Maggie."

A tear rolled down her cheek. "Let's get the hell out of here."

MAGGIE EASED THE SHIFTER into park and turned off the
engine. We hadn't spoken in the ten or so minutes it had taken
for her to drive me back to Richard's house. The silence continued to lengthen.

Finally Maggie let out a sigh. "I feel like a criminal and
I'm not guilty of anything."

"Technically, we're guilty of breaking and entering."

"Oh, shit." She sank back against her bucket seat.

"The question is, who else knew about the condo? And
what was Sumner's wife doing there—naked and dead?"

"Waiting for a lover?" Maggie suggested. She, too, had
seen through Claudia's facade of the faithful wife. "But who'd
kill her and why?"

"Probably the same person who killed Matt. Maybe for the
same reason." I wasn't ready to tell her what I thought about
Sharon Walker.

Her gaze was fixed on nothing, her brows furrowed with
worry.

"Don't think about it," I said.

"How can I stop?"

"You just have to."

We both had to.

"What if someone saw us? What if—"

"If the neighbors saw or heard anything, the cops would've been swarming the place. We did them a favor. It could've been days—maybe a week—before some poor cleaning lady found her."

"I'm glad I didn't look. Have you ever seen anything like that before?"

The memory of my trip to the morgue to identify Shelley's body would be with me until I died.

"My ex-wife was killed the same way. But I didn't see her until the coroner cleaned her up. This was a lot worse." I'd have nightmares for weeks.

"I wish I'd never found that damn key," Maggie said and turned her face away. "I'm sorry. This isn't how I'd planned to end the evening."

"Me, either."

"I like you, Jeff, a lot. But after what happened tonight, I—"

She didn't have to say the words. I already knew. "You don't want to see me."

"I'm not saying it's forever. Give me a few weeks and maybe we can try again. It's just…."

I cupped her chin, turned her face toward me, and leaned across the shifter, pressing my lips against hers. There was no passion in her response; neither was there revulsion. Maybe we *could* try again in another couple of weeks. Maybe.

TWENTY-ONE

CLAUDIA SUMNER'S UNTIDY death kept me awake and staring at the ceiling for a long time. She must've known all about little Jackie. Otherwise why was she so interested in finding out the beneficiary of the fictional insurance policy I'd mentioned when I'd met her? Did she wonder if her husband had changed his policies—maybe even his will—to include his lover and bastard child?

Ron Myers said Claudia loved money. She also loved her children. How far was she willing to go to protect them and their inheritance? If Sharon confronted her—demanding Jackie's share of Matt's estate—Claudia could've been foolish enough to argue with her about it, not knowing she was Matt's killer.

Sumner's tryst with Maggie had happened at the condo five years before. Little Jackie was now four years old. Had Sumner bedded Sharon immediately after Maggie had broken it off? If so, Sharon would've known about the condo. It fit the time line. Had she lured Claudia there? Her death fit the pattern of humiliation, too. Sharon had taken Sumner's clothes before killing him. That she'd do the same to his wife made sense, as well. And killing Claudia at the condo, where Matt had slept with all his side-dishes, was the ultimate degradation.

I got up late and found Richard and Brenda at the kitchen table still reading the paper. "Morning," I called, shuffling toward the coffee pot.

They looked at me over the tops of their respective newspaper sections. "Good morning," Richard said. Did I detect a sliver of ice in his tone?

"Did you have a good time last night?" Brenda asked.

"Uh…yes and no." I grabbed a cup from the cupboard and poured myself some coffee.

"There's been a development in the Sumner case," Richard said, folding the front page of the paper to show me the banner headline. "They found his wife murdered."

I gulped my coffee. "Yeah. I know."

He studied my face. "How do you know?"

I considered lying. Decided against it. "Who do you think found her?"

"Jeffy!" Brenda cried.

"Christ, now what kind of trouble are you in?" Richard asked.

"Nobody knows it was us."

"Us?" Brenda said.

"Maggie was with me." I explained how she'd found the duplicate key to the condo in Sumner's office. I left out the part about Maggie's affair with the dead man.

"I don't see how they can connect either one of us."

"Oh no?" Richard turned, grabbed a Post-It note from the counter. "That reporter called three times last night. You snuck off to bed before I could give you the messages."

"Uh…thanks. I guess. I'll call him later."

They gave each other worried looks, but Richard shook his head, and they both found places other than me to look at. Finally Brenda refolded her section of newspaper. "Tomorrow's Easter Sunday; we really should go to church."

"Church?" Richard echoed. "But we never go."

Brenda shoved the Life & Arts section's color spread in front of him. "The paper says there's a Basilica in Lacka-wanna. Look at these pictures; the statues and stained glass look terrific. Its design is supposed to be based on St. Peter's in Rome. And it sure wouldn't hurt you couple of sinners to go." With that, Brenda got up from the table, clearing away some of the dishes.

"But you're not Catholic."

"The two of you are. Maybe it'll rub off on me."

Richard scowled. "What time?"

"Noon." Brenda looked at me. "Want to come?"

I shrugged. "Sure." Besides, Maggie had said the Basilica was her parish. Maybe I'd see her there.

The phone rang. Richard's scowl deepened. "I'm not answering it."

"Me, either," Brenda said.

I got up, picked up the receiver. "Hello."

"Jeff." Sam Nielsen, sounding insufferably pleased. "You've been avoiding me."

"No I haven't. I just wasn't home when you called last night. Why have you been annoying my family?"

"Me, annoy anyone? Ha! I was just wondering if you heard about Claudia Sumner?"

I didn't answer.

"A woman called 911. You know who?"

No way was I going to implicate Maggie. Some part of me still hoped I had a chance of being with her. "I read about it in the paper."

"That's not what I asked."

Damn him. He was going to hound me until I gave him something more. "Look, I've just moved back to Buffalo and I don't have any wheels. I need to make a few more inquiries. You available this morning?"

"Name the time and place."

We agreed to meet in an hour. I hung up the phone to find Richard and Brenda staring at me. "Do you think that's a wise move?"

"I gotta get him off my back. If nothing else, I'll bore him to death."

Brenda let out a sigh but said nothing.

"And I'd like to go to East Aurora this afternoon, if you don't mind driving, Rich."

"Why?"

"To meet Sharon Walker."

Brenda sat down at the table again, her eyes flashing. "No, Jeffy. Don't do it."

"Why not?"

"Because from what you've told us, she's a vicious murderer. Maybe she killed Sumner's wife, too. I don't want you to be next."

"She's not going to kill me. I'm not stupid enough to accuse her."

"What will you say to her?" Richard asked.

"I'm not sure. I figured I'd just wing it."

"Wing it?" Brenda asked.

"Then what?"

"Then I'll go to Detective Hayden with everything I've got on her. It's up to him to decide if he wants to pursue it. I'll wash my hands of the whole thing once I talk to him."

Brenda crossed her arms over her chest. "Amen!"

A SHINY BLACK SUV WITH the license plate HOTNEWS pulled up the driveway exactly on time. I headed for it, slammed the door after I got in.

"Where're we going?" Nielsen asked.

"You like pizza for breakfast?"

"Not since college. Why?"

"We're going to the joint where Rob Sumner works."

"What for?"

"To talk." I gave him the address. "Put this sucker in gear and let's go."

"You don't expect him to show for work the morning after his mother was murdered."

"Of course not. But that doesn't mean I can't talk to his co-workers."

Nielsen shrugged and backed out of the driveway and headed for Main Street. "Why the interest in the son? You think he's involved?"

"I don't know. Something in his attitude makes me suspicious."

"Is this a psychic insight?" he asked, with more than a hint of contempt.

"It's a gut reaction. I've got years of investigative experience behind me. I've worked in the field for the last fourteen years."

"I did some digging on you. You had a pretty good career going."

"And it would've continued, if I hadn't been mugged."

"As of yesterday, NYPD hadn't made any headway on that."

He had done his homework. "I didn't think they would."

Nielsen palmed the wheel as he turned onto Transit Road. "You want to tell me how this psychic stuff works?"

"No."

"Aw, come on, Jeff. We're old school pals."

"I've forgotten a lot since I had my brains scrambled, but I know for a fact we were never friends."

"That could change."

"Why?"

Nielsen braked for a red light. "Because if you've got genuine psychic abilities—"

"Less than a minute ago you were sneering at the idea."

"I admit I'm a skeptic."

"And I can't put on a show for you. This stuff is hit or miss."

"So you were scamming Hayden?"

"No. Sometimes—and only sometimes—I seem to tune into people's emotions. The rest of it just kind of happens."

"And this only started after the mugging?"

"Yeah, and I hope like hell it goes as fast as it came."

Nielsen pulled into the pizza parlor's nearly empty parking lot. The Open sign was still dark, but lights burned inside the building. "How are we handling this?" I asked.

"I'll just watch you in action."

I glared at him for a moment and got out of the car. He tagged behind me. The shop's door was unlocked and we stepped inside.

"We don't open for another half hour," said a teenaged girl mopping the entryway.

"I'd like to speak to the manager."

"That's me," said a harassed-looking man of about forty, coming up from behind the girl. His nametag read Dennis Sloan. "You interested in the assistant manager's job?"

"No." I introduced myself, ignoring Nielsen, and pulled out one of my business cards. "I'm here about an employee, Rob Sumner."

"Ex-employee."

Interesting that Linda Sumner wasn't aware of her husband's current employment status. Just where had he been going every day, when he should've been working?

"I'm looking into Matt and Claudia Sumner's deaths. Can you give me some insight into Rob's character?"

He scrutinized my card. "I can't tell you why he was let go—corporate policy."

"What can you tell me about him?"

Sloan took a half-step back, crossed his arms over his chest, his expression stony.

"When was he fired?"

"Two weeks ago."

Just about the time of his father's death.

"I understand he's not very responsible—or reliable," I said. "And maybe he drinks a little too much. Expects other people to clean up his messes." I thought about Rob's parents, and wondered if Claudia had slipped her son money to keep him afloat until he found another job. "He's also got a violent streak."

Sloan's eyes flashed, and his mouth went tight. "No comment."

He didn't need to say a word. "Thanks for your help." I couldn't keep the sarcasm out of my voice.

We went back outside, and headed for Nielsen's car. "That went well," he said.

I could've decked him. He opened the driver's door as a

rusty Ford Escort pulled into the lot, parking in the spot farthest from the entrance. A tall, skinny kid dressed in the franchise's standard uniform got out. On an impulse, I jogged over to meet him.

"Can I talk to you for a minute?"

He looked at me suspiciously. "What about?"

"Rob Sumner." I handed him my card as Nielsen joined us. "I'm investigating his parents' deaths. What can you tell me about Rob?"

"He's an asshole," the kid answered without hesitation.

"Why'd he get fired?"

"He was balling one of the waitresses in the storeroom after hours."

Good old Rob—following right in his old man's footsteps.

"He was already on probation for beating up my buddy, Gene," the kid continued. Reticence wasn't his problem.

"Gene was another employee?"

"Yeah, until that bastard Sumner got him fired last month."

"What happened?"

"Rob said Gene was stealing money from the girls' tip jars. But it was Rob who took the money—Gene saw him. After Mr. Sloan fired him, Gene came back to have it out with Rob. He didn't know the guy's a psycho. He broke Gene's nose—really messed up his face."

Sloan watched us from the restaurant's plate glass door. I nodded in his direction. "Don't let him give you a hard time for talking to me. The First Amendment says you're entitled to an opinion, kid. Thanks for the information."

I headed back to the SUV with Nielsen trotting to keep up. "You got some good stuff. Why don't you don't look happy?" he asked.

I waited until we were inside the car and he started the engine before answering. "Rob Sumner threatened me the other day. At the time I didn't take it seriously." I looked down at the sling surrounding my broken arm and thought about the throbbing in my skull that never really went away. "Maybe I should."

"It's a tough game you're playing," Sam said. "Or maybe I should remind you that it isn't a game. Just keep in mind how Sumner was killed and what happened to his body afterwards."

I turned to stare at him. He didn't have a clue what I knew—what I'd seen. And I wasn't about to tell him.

TWENTY-TWO

RICHARD CUT OVER FROM the Thruway to Route 400, heading southeast. The ride so far had been silent, and though I couldn't pick up on anything Richard felt, I could tell by his body language that he was nearing the boiling point.

"What if you're wrong? What if it wasn't her?" he blurted at last. His fingers, wrapped around the steering wheel, were white. I held onto the envelope of evidence I'd brought along nearly as tightly.

I glanced across the seat. "I'm not wrong."

"You haven't even considered the possibility that someone else could've killed Sumner."

"I don't have to."

He kept his gaze fixed on the road. "I don't like this. I don't like it one bit."

As I gazed out at the colorless countryside, doubt crept into my thoughts. A week before, Richard had suggested I might be twisting the facts to support a delusion. That accusation still haunted me.

"Okay, Rich, say Sharon wasn't the murderer. There's only three other possible suspects."

"That you know of," he shot back.

I ignored him. "Claudia Sumner, for one. With her husband conveniently out of the way, she was eager to get on with her life. She liked money and seemed to know about every one of his insurance policies. She knew of his affairs, and she was conveniently out of town at the time of the murder. Nice little alibi. I got the impression that her life would improve with

Sumner out of the way. No doubt she'd planned to find someone else who could maintain the lifestyle she obviously enjoyed. That is, if he wasn't already waiting in the wings."

"Of course, the fact that she's been killed, too, eliminates her from the running."

"You got that," I agreed. "How about her son? Rob Sumner and his father didn't get along. Rob had been in some kind of trouble several years before. Maggie thought it might be drugs. She wasn't sure."

"What else?" Richard asked, giving me a quick glance across the seat before turning his gaze back to the road.

"Rob's former girlfriend had been screwing his father. Not pretty, but that would've been ancient history—hardly worth killing his father for years later. Rob lost his job around the time his father was killed—but that was no motive for murder, either."

"Strike two," Richard said. "Although, from the looks of his house, Rob wasn't living the good life."

"No," I agreed, "and he cheated on his wife only months after their marriage. A chip off the old block. He stole tips from waitresses who made less than minimum wage, and he's got a violent streak that's easily aroused. He may not have killed his father, but once the will's read, he'll probably profit from his father's death."

"Who else?"

"Don Feddar, the guy Sumner fired before Christmas. He might've had a motive for murder, but he also had an undisputed alibi for the evening of the killing. And he certainly couldn't afford to pay anyone to do it for him. Strike three and out."

We were silent for a minute or two. Richard finally broke the quiet. "Everything you've said to count out the other suspects sounds totally logical. But have you used logic to support your theory that Sharon killed Sumner?"

"I *know* what I *know*," I said, but he was too intent on driving to notice the glare I gave him. "However jumbled the original vision was, I'd known about the murder before it happened. I knew the murderer had stood at the grave on the day of the funeral. Something directed me to the murder site and the victim's last remains. The same thing compelled me to go to Sumner's neighborhood, where I found the jogger who'd seen the killer's car. I also knew the killer had handled the garage door opener."

"All intangibles," Richard muttered, waving a dismissive hand at me.

"Hey, I sensed the killer at the funeral and at the cemetery; that's why I was so sure that the killer had sent Sumner the invitation to the child's birthday party. That was the first real evidence that led me to Sharon Walker. Her son was born on January tenth—same as the invitation. Sharon Walker was engaged to Rob Sumner before her child was born. Sharon Walker had business dealings with the murdered man. Sharon Walker was a skilled hunter. A skilled hunter killed Matt Sumner."

"There're lots of skilled hunters around here."

"Oh, come on, Rich. A good investigator relies on his instincts. And, damn it, I know Sharon Walker murdered Matt Sumner."

"Your belief in her guilt isn't hard evidence. In the eyes of the law, she's innocent until proven guilty. Have you found enough to take to the police?"

I sank back in my seat. "I don't know." I studied the scenery flashing past the window, caught sight of a house number. "Should be close now."

Richard braked, pulling over to the shoulder of the road.

Sharon lived on the outskirts of town, but I knew the place before I saw the numbers tacked around the front door. The gloomy skies added to the air of neglect that hung around the old farmhouse. Ancient forest-green paint was sun-blistered and peeling, half the shutters were gone from the windows, and the gutters around the front hung precariously from the edge of the roof. Four steps led to a rickety porch. A good gust of wind would probably knock it down. The detached garage looked forlorn at the end of the long, rutted drive. Sticks and bits of trash covered the matted lawn. In the driveway sat a maroon Chevy Caprice station wagon with a chrome roof rack. Richard pulled his car up behind it and shut off the engine.

We got out and I headed straight for the wagon. The driver's door had been painted over in a slightly different color, probably covering an advertisement for Walker Construction. I touched the tailgate and a shudder of revulsion ran through me as conflicting visions of Sumner lying in the back of the car seemed to explode behind my eyes. I had it: She'd driven the barely conscious man to Holland. After she'd killed him, she'd loaded the body into the back of the car once more and taken it to his home. And all the while she'd felt powerful and dangerous. It had excited her.

"Well?" Richard asked.

I nodded, letting out a ragged breath, needing to clear my head of the remaining web of strong emotions. "He was in there all right. After he was dead, she…covered him with a dark blanket."

To the right of the car, away from the house, sat a dilapidated barbecue. Bricks had fallen from it in a waterfall of debris.

The muddy ash pit beckoned. I picked up a stick and poked at the grayish goo, turning up swatches of scorched fabric. "She must've burned his clothes here." I dislodged scraps of different materials from out of the muck.

Richard held out a clean handkerchief and let me settle the fabric evidence onto it, one at a time; then he carefully folded it and put it into his coat pocket. He glanced over his shoulder at the house.

"Someone was just at the window."

"Was it her?"

"I only saw the curtains move."

I looked back down at the ash pit, suddenly afraid—and not just for myself. This woman had already committed one— probably two—terrible crimes.

"Maybe you should wait in the car. Two of us could be intimidating. I don't want to push her into doing something stupid."

Richard didn't look happy. "Whatever you do, don't provoke her."

"That's the last thing I intend to do."

He nodded and turned, heading back to the Lincoln.

I crossed the twenty yards of brown lawn to the house, climbed the porch steps, knocked on the door, and wondered what the hell I'd say to the woman. I waited about thirty seconds before knocking again.

Time dragged.

It would be smarter to just forget the whole thing.

What if she remembered my voice from that prank call the week before?

I was about to try one last time when the door was wrenched open.

"Yeah, what do you want?"

Dressed in stained gray jogging pants, sweatshirt, and sneakers, her bleached hair cropped short, Sharon Walker was overweight and unattractive, her expression haunted. Not at all like the photo of the young girl I'd seen only days before.

She wasn't what I would've expected of Matt Sumner's lover—or Rob's.

"Ms. Walker? My name's Jeffrey Resnick and—"

"I know who you are."

"Did Rob Sumner call you?"

She crossed her arms across her chest. "Yes. What right have you got to say that Matt was killed by somebody at Walker Construction? What right?"

"I didn't say that. I told him I was looking into his father's dealings with Walker Construction."

"Why?"

I chose my words carefully. "There seems to be a question of impropriety."

"Even if it was true, which it isn't, what difference could

it possibly make now? He's dead. My father's dead. Walker Construction is dead. It doesn't matter any more."

A small boy, about four years old, pushed forward, attaching himself to her leg. He looked like a miniature version of Matt Sumner.

"Is that Jackie?" I asked.

"His name's Jimmy. He was named after my father."

"Was he once called Jackie?"

"What were you doing poking around my car and my yard? You're trespassing on my property. I have every right to call the cops and have you arrested. Now get out of here." She turned to go back inside and I grabbed her arm.

"Wait—!"

A second became an eternity as the vision of what she'd done—all the triumph, the horror, and the fear—hit me as hard as being clobbered with that baseball bat.

I saw them—standing by the barbecue, arguing—Sumner waving a letter at her. She screamed at him while the little boy cowered in terror behind her. My hand tightened around her forearm, but I couldn't move as the vision shifted.

Claudia Sumner had pleaded for her life—but Sharon made her kneel on the condo's virginal white carpet, held the snub-nosed revolver to the base of her skull, and pulled the trigger.

"Let go!" Sharon yelled.

Overlapping images of Sharon and Sumner—Sharon and Claudia—assaulted me, squeezing the breath from my lungs. Feelings of fear, anger, and triumph bombarded me.

The boy leaped forward, punching me on the thighs. "Leave my mommy alone, you bad man."

Face twisted in fury, Sharon wrenched away from me, shoved me, sent me tumbling backward down the steps—only the rickety rail saved me. She grabbed the boy, slammed the door. The deadbolt clicked in place.

Muscles quivering with shock, I pulled myself upright. Gasping for breath, I forced myself to move.

To get the hell out of there.

Headed for the car, breaking into a jog for the last ten yards.

Yanked open the passenger side door.

Scrambled in.

"What happened?" Richard demanded.

"Go! Now!"

The tires spun in the gravel as he gunned the engine. The Lincoln jerked down the drive and onto the highway heading west. Numb, I sat there, staring at nothing, the fingers of my right hand clamped around the door's handgrip just to keep from trembling.

"Jeff!" Richard's voice was stern.

"She killed him, all right," I blurted. "He showed her a copy of the lab report. The one that told him the hair sample he'd provided did not match his DNA exactly. And he knew. He knew! So he came out to her house to confront her. Told her she wouldn't get another dime out of him. If she wanted money, she could go to the boy's father. She could go to Rob for money."

"Good grief," Richard muttered.

The images began to sort themselves out in my head.

"She bent down, grabbed—" I had to concentrate to understand. "Grabbed a brick from the barbecue, slammed it into his skull. The kid went berserk. She thought she'd killed Sumner. When he wasn't dead, she flipped out—decided to have some fun with him. She's strong. She dumped him in the back of the station wagon, took him out to Holland, cut off his clothes with her deer-skinning knife, let him squirm in the snow, all the time taunting him. He didn't believe she'd actually do it. He begged her to stop, but she only laughed. The kid got out of the car, ran across the snow—shrieking, crying. She screamed at him to get back in the car. The kid was terrified. She crouched down, cut Sumner free, told him to run. Then she took aim with the bow."

"Jesus. You got all that from just touching her?"

"More." I shuddered again, frozen to my toes. "I have to assimilate it."

He pulled into the parking lot of a diner along the road. By then my initial panic had subsided. I grabbed my envelope and followed him inside. At nearly three in the afternoon, the place was deserted. Richard pointed to a booth near the front, and a waitress in a white uniform and black apron came to the table. "Coffee and apple pie for both of us," Richard said.

"A la mode?" she asked hopefully.

"Plain."

She frowned, but hustled off.

"I don't want anything," I said.

"Shut up and do as I tell you for once."

I shut up.

The pie was typical diner fare. The filling oozed out of the crushed crust, making it look as though someone sat on it. Stale, too. The coffee was bitter.

"What else?" Richard prompted.

"Sharon was screwing both of them. Rob because she thought she loved him, Matt because she wanted to save her father's construction company."

"Did Rob know at the time?"

"I don't know. But his father paid her, supported the boy. Something must've happened." I thought about it for a moment and realized what I'd seen for myself. "Sumner noticed the boy had his wife's nose. To confirm his suspicions, he had the kid's hair DNA tested, comparing it with some of Claudia's as well as his own. Because it matched factors from both of them, the test proved it was Rob, not Matt, who fathered Sharon's son."

"How do you know that?"

I pulled out the wrinkled envelope. "I found this in his desk the other day."

Richard studied it. "This doesn't prove anything." He handed it back.

"Not by itself. But it wouldn't be hard for the cops to get a copy of the letter. Our Ms. Walker had strung Sumner along for over four years and, with the gravy train about to end, she wasn't about to let him have the last word."

"What about Sumner's wife?"

"Sharon went after his estate. No way was Claudia going to let her have any of the money. But she'd underestimated Sharon. Thought she could reason with her."

I sipped my coffee. "It bothers me that Rob Sumner called her. Told her I might be out to visit her. Why would he do that?"

"Maybe he's afraid of her," Richard suggested. "He, of all people, knows what she's like. He may suspect she killed his father—and his mother."

"He knows something," I agreed. I thought about it for a moment. "Maybe he wants her to get caught. She's practically living in poverty. She could go after him for child support now that his father isn't paying her. Maybe he wants her out of the way. So he called her to make her angry—"

"At you," Richard finished. "He may have deliberately set you up as a target."

"How? Sharon only knows my name. The cops and Sumner's family know I don't work for the insurance company. But only Detective Hayden and Sam Nielsen know where I live. I haven't left much of a paper trail here in Buffalo…yet." That last word seemed to hover over the table like a prophetic curse.

We sat in silence for long minutes. Dishes clattered in the kitchen. Static-laced Muzak came from a speaker in the ceiling.

Richard indicated the plate in front of me. "Eat up."

I did my best, but neither of us could finish.

"Where to?" Richard asked once we were in the car.

"Let's get this envelope of stuff to Detective Hayden. After that, I don't want anything more to do with Sharon Walker."

IT WAS HAYDEN'S DAY OFF. I tried his home phone number and found him in. He wasn't exactly happy to hear from me, but told me to come over anyway. He lived in one of the older neighborhoods in Orchard Park.

Two boys' bicycles, covered in fresh mud, were clashed on the soggy ground in the front yard. The basketball hoop over the garage door had no net. It started to rain as I knocked on the side entrance door. Richard looked morose and huddled into his jacket. I knocked again, and a matronly woman answered. "Mr. Resnick? Won't you come in? My husband is in the den."

The tidy, dated kitchen reminded me of a set from a sixties sitcom. The aroma of meat loaf and boiled potatoes filled the air. An unfrosted chocolate cake, cooling on wire racks on the counter by the sink, added to the sense of unreality. We followed her through the orderly house to the den. She ushered us inside and closed the door behind us.

This was obviously Hayden's domain. Family photos were scattered over the walls, including a large color portrait of Hayden, his wife, and two preteen boys. Bowling trophies shared shelf space with a clutter of books, magazines, and other memorabilia.

"Still joined at the hip, I see. Sit," Hayden commanded. "I don't like my weekend interrupted," he warned without preamble.

"With any luck, you'll never see me again after today." I handed him the envelope.

"What's this?" He lifted the flap and dumped the contents on his desk.

"My case against Sharon Walker."

"Who?"

"The woman who killed Matt and Claudia Sumner. It's kind of a long story. I hope your meat loaf will keep."

I repeated what I'd told him at the police station earlier that week, catching him up with the events that had occurred within the past few days—leaving out the part where Maggie and I found the second victim. While I spoke, he pawed through the envelope's contents. He didn't ask where I got the copy of Sumner's calendar, and I wouldn't have told him. Richard handed over his handkerchief with the fabric swatches.

Hayden leaned back in his Naugahyde swivel chair. "All circumstantial. You haven't got a thing I can go to the D.A. with."

"I know that. But once you subpoena the lab report, that alone should give you a new angle to investigate."

He picked up the envelope. "Where'd you get this?"

"Sumner's office. It was jammed behind one of the drawers in his desk."

"And what were you doing there?"

"I had permission. Ron Myers can vouch for me." I waited, and when he said nothing, "Well?"

"Well, what? There's nothing here. No case."

"Will you at least look into it?"

"Yeah. But it won't come to anything. Guaranteed. Sumner slept with a number of women, but he was usually discreet. He was being blackmailed. He withdrew fifteen hundred dollars from his savings account every month for the past four years. That is, until this past month. He didn't pay and was killed for it."

"It wasn't blackmail. He considered it child support."

"Whatever," the detective said.

"And you don't think a woman could've killed him?"

"Arranged to have him killed? Certainly. Doing it herself? That's another matter, especially considering how it was done."

"Don't be such a chauvinist, Hayden. This isn't the turn of

the century, and Sharon Walker is no dainty little female. She can probably bench-press more than all three of us put together."

"That doesn't prove a thing."

"Then what about her car? It matches the one Paul Linski saw."

"By his own admission, he doesn't know for sure if he saw it on the night the body was dumped."

"What about the carpet fibers? She carted Sumner from Holland to Orchard Park in the back of her station wagon. There had to be fibers on his wounds, in his lungs, or under his fingernails."

Hayden continued to glare at me.

I let out a long, quavering breath, trying to hold my anger in check. I'd wasted my time and his.

"Well, you keep all that stuff, Detective. It isn't doing me any good." I stood. "And if the case is still open in a year or two, maybe you'll be willing to take it under consideration. Come on, Rich, let's go." I paused at the door. "And thanks for telling Nielsen about me. My tax dollars at work."

I opened the door and started back through the house. Mrs. Hayden stood at the counter, assembling her layer cake. I walked past but heard Richard murmur, "Nice to meet you," on his way out. He always did have good manners.

The door closed behind him, and he followed me to the car. The drizzle had turned into a steady downpour. We got in the Lincoln and sat.

Richard turned to me. "I'm sorry, Jeff."

"What for? I didn't really believe he'd go for it. To tell you the truth, I'm surprised he didn't throw us out." I took a breath to steady my shaky nerves. "I've done my civic duty. I reported what I know about a crime. If Hayden chooses to do nothing about it, it's out of my hands."

"I just hope you haven't set yourself up as a target."

Me, too, I thought.

Richard silently fumed for most of the ride back to

Amherst, more depressed about the situation than I was. Time to lighten the mood.

"Did you see the basketball hoop on Hayden's garage?" I asked.

"Yes."

"Whatever happened to ours?"

He frowned. "Grandmother had it taken down the day you left for the Army."

"But you put it up."

"I did it for you. She never bothered to ask me if I'd like to keep it. Shortsighted of her."

"Why?"

"It made it easier for me to take the job in Pasadena. That stupid basketball hoop was the tenuous connection I had with you. She wouldn't understand that you could mean something to me. When it came down, it was the first step toward my freedom."

"I don't get it."

"I was just a possession to Grandmother. She'd won me from Betty. She saw your leaving as another victory. The job in California was my way out, but not without a lot of guilt. I wasn't there when Grandfather died, and I wasn't there when she died two years later, alone. Curtis found her in her bed."

"Did you come back to Buffalo?"

He shook his head. "What was the point? There was no one to come home to. I made all the arrangements by phone. I've never even been to her grave," he finished quietly, his gaze locked on the road ahead, his expression unreadable.

I remembered then what Brenda had said to me the day I'd returned to Buffalo: *It means a lot to him that you're here.*

"You think we could get another one?" I asked.

"Another what?"

"Backboard. I won't be in this brace forever. It might be fun to play some one-on-one again."

He risked a glance at me, his smile tentative. "Sounds like a great idea."

I think we both knew then that I wasn't ever going back to Manhattan.

TWENTY-THREE

THAT EVENING, I SPENT over an hour out in the garage, rummaging through my boxes. The cold and damp seeped through my jacket. I was ready to give up my search when I finally found what I wanted. I scrounged some tissue used in packing my stuff, and wrapped the small object. I hoped Richard would like it.

I also tramped through the loft apartment again, and decided I'd wait until my arm was completely healed before asking Richard if I could live up there. Once I got a job, we could work out some kind of rental agreement. I wanted my own space, needed a place of my own. But I didn't want to go too far, at least not yet.

That wasn't the end of my evening, however. I had one more little mystery to solve. Without a word to Richard or Brenda, I set out on foot, headed down the neighborhood's backstreets for Snyder. The brisk wind was at my back, the clouds overhead heavy and threatening. I needed to talk—but not to Richard, or any other physician or academician at his old stomping grounds of UB. There were still so many things I didn't understand about this crazy new ability I seemed to have acquired—like why had I been blessed with it? Only one other person understood my predicament.

I crossed the parking lot to the darkened bakery and pressed the buzzer at the side of the door, held it for long seconds at a time. After a minute or so, a light came on in the back of the shop, then a large silhouette shuffled toward the door.

"Stop already!" came Sophie's muffled voice through the

glass as she flipped open the lock. "Come in before you let in all the cold."

"Where've you been? I came to see you the other day and they never heard of you."

"You didn't come at night. Alone." Her tone was belligerent. Then she shrugged theatrically, as if that was explanation enough. "So, why'd you come now?"

"I need to talk to you."

She nodded, and motioned me to follow her into the back room once again. "Instant coffee all right?"

I nodded, taking my seat at the card table. She filled the same saucepan with water, set it on the hot plate above the sink. I remembered that, days earlier, the baker had sidestepped my question about electrocution.

"Don't you think that's a dangerous arrangement?"

She gestured. "This? I'm always careful." She measured the coffee into cups. "So, you found the killer. I knew you would." We'd never even discussed my case. How did she know? "How can I help you now?" she asked.

"What do I do next?"

"It's in God's hands now."

"That's not the answer I was looking for."

"Who says I have answers?"

"I guess you don't, because you seem to answer most of my questions with questions."

Her eyes crinkled as her lips drew into a self-satisfied smile. Then she shrugged. "Tell me all about it."

She listened patiently, serving the coffee as I told her about Sharon, Sumner's and Claudia's grisly deaths, and all the other prominent players in this little drama.

"You know who did it—you told the police. So what's the problem?"

"The problem is Sharon should be punished for what she's done and nobody seems to care!"

Sophie frowned. "You don't think she's being punished every time she looks at that child?"

"What if she takes her anger out on the kid?"

"That could happen. Jeffrey," she said reasonably. "As long as one person knows the truth, she hasn't gotten away with anything."

"But I don't want to be the sole guardian of that truth."

She smiled tolerantly, patted my hand. "Trust."

"That's your advice? Trust?"

"Things have a way of working out the way they are meant to."

"Unfortunately, too often these days people literally get away with murder."

She shook her head sadly. "That's not all you wanted to ask me, is it?"

"No."

"Now that you believe, you want to know why, eh?"

"Yes."

She shrugged. "Maybe you're just lucky."

"You call this lucky?" With a gesture, I reminded her of my partially shaved head.

"Aren't you doing what you always wanted to do?"

I blinked in confusion. What the hell was she talking about?

"You always wanted to help people," she said. "You just never knew how."

"How will finding Sumner's killer help anyone? It doesn't even help him—he's dead."

"Maybe you'll help that little boy. The one you were worried about just now."

"I don't even like children."

She shook her head. "Everybody loves children. Even you."

I wasn't going to argue.

"What does it matter why you have it? You have it. Now you have to learn to live with it," she said.

"You sound just like my brother."

"He's a doctor—he should know."

"Now you sound like my—" Girlfriend, I'd wanted to say, but that wasn't going to happen now.

Sophie smiled. "I told you, things have a way of working out the way they were meant to." She glanced at the clock on the wall. "Time for you to go."

I got up and followed her through the shop, feeling like a child who'd just been scolded. "Will you be here the next time I come by?"

"Maybe. Maybe not. Here, take a *placek* home for Easter breakfast."

I hefted the loaf. It felt real enough. "Thank you."

She drew me into a hug, kissed my cheek, then pulled back, held my face in her warm hands. "Good things will come of this. They will," she insisted. "Now, take care walking home. Stay on the sidewalk where there's lots of light. I'm too old to have to worry about you."

She radiated a sense of peace and deep affection. I recognized it, understood it. But again I wondered: why me?

"I'll be careful," I promised, and kissed her goodbye.

The lock clicked into place and she waved before turning and heading for the back room once more. I watched as first that light went out, and a minute later the light above the shop burned.

The bakery sign over the door looked shabby, in need of repainting. Was it the same one I'd seen the other day? I couldn't be sure. Maybe I didn't want to know. Tucking the *placek* under my arm like a football, I turned and started for home.

I followed Sophie's instructions and stayed on the sidewalk under the intermittent flare of the street lamps. The long walk home gave me plenty of time to think. Maybe that was my problem—I was thinking too much.

A car whizzed past, splashing dirty water my way. I checked traffic before cutting across Main Street, anxious to get off the busy road and leave behind the stench of exhaust fumes. I headed down a quiet side street, pausing at the corner to pull up my jacket collar against the damp night.

Turning left, I picked up my pace, in a hurry to get back to the warmth of my room, where I could lie awake for endless hours, thanks to my jumbled nerves. Frustration nagged at me. The fact that Detective Hayden wouldn't consider my evidence against Sharon Walker reinforced the reality that I had virtually no control over any portion of my life, and probably wouldn't for weeks, possibly months.

I refused to take the thought any further. Frustration could also be a byproduct of my present physical condition. Before the mugging, impatience had never been a problem. I knew that damned feeling of impotence would eventually pass, but it couldn't come soon enough for me.

Richard's driveway was in sight when I heard the roar of an engine, saw blinding high beams as the car barreled toward me. It fishtailed on the wet pavement, jumped the curb. I leaped into the privet hedge, out of its path, an instant before it would've nailed me.

Heart pounding, I rolled onto my knees, watched the speeding car recede into the night, its taillights glowing. Some trained investigator I was—I couldn't tell the make or even the color.

I brushed uselessly at my muddy jeans. The adrenaline surge that had coursed through me seconds before was already waning. Probably a drunken teenager out joyriding, trying to scare pedestrians.

Or it could've been Rob Sumner.

Or worse, Sharon Walker.

No! They couldn't know where I lived. And how would they have known it was me on the street at eleven o'clock at night? Dressed in dark clothes, I could've been anybody out for a walk.

Okay, maybe the sling on my arm was a dead giveaway.

Maybe.

I groped in the blackness, found the *placek*. One end was crushed, but still salvageable. I stormed off across the lawn for the house. No point in even mentioning this little mishap to Richard and Brenda, yet I couldn't dismiss it entirely.

I hated feeling afraid.

EASTER SUNDAY I AWOKE to the sound of rain pelting against my bedroom window and strained to reach my watch on the bedside table. Eight thirty, lots of time to get ready to go to the Basilica. Best of all, no headache, so despite the gray start, it looked like it might turn out to be a good day.

I showered and dressed, and smelled bacon and fresh brewed coffee as I headed for the kitchen.

"Happy Easter," Brenda called and leaned her cheek in my direction for a kiss.

"Happy Easter," I said. "Where's Rich?"

"Straggling."

"Good. I have something to give him. Just a little thank you. You think I need to wrap it?"

"A present?" she asked, her eyes widening in delight.

"It's not much."

When I didn't offer any other information, she said, "I'm sure it'll be just fine without it." I could tell she wanted to know more, but she didn't ask and I didn't volunteer.

The *placek* still sat on the counter and I grabbed a knife from the drawer, cut a slice from the undamaged end, and plopped it on a plate.

"Where'd that come from?" Brenda asked.

"Just something I picked up."

I sat at the table, grabbing the front section of the newspaper. No headline screamed of Sharon's arrest. Stupid, really. I'd only told Hayden about her the afternoon before. Warrants and such take time. In the unlikely event he had gone after her, it wouldn't have gotten in the paper yet anyway. Nielsen hadn't written about me either. Again, yet.

Despite Sophie's advice to trust that Sharon would be nailed by the cops, I thought about Sam Nielsen's offer. If Hayden didn't act on my evidence within a week, I'd call the newspaper and tell the reporter everything. He promised he protected his sources, and my revelations might force Detective Hayden to take Sharon Walker seriously.

That decided, I studied the national headlines. I couldn't get excited about the latest threat to peace in the Middle East and grabbed the comics instead. Richard came in about the time I finished *Hagar the Horrible*.

"I see you're stimulating your mind," he said in greeting, brushed past me to Brenda, giving her a perfunctory kiss, then stood back, his chest puffed out. "Coffee, woman!"

Hands on her hips, she gazed at him speculatively. "You know where the cups are."

I tried to stifle a smile—impossible—turning my attention back to the paper. In a moment, a steaming cup of coffee appeared in front of me. Richard brought out the sugar bowl and creamer.

"Thanks."

"You're looking chipper this morning," he said, doctoring his own coffee. "And dare I say it, you even look healthier?"

"It's because my heart is true." I poured milk into my cup, stirred it, and took a sip. "Good coffee. You could be in a commercial, Brenda."

"They couldn't pay me enough," she said, and started breaking eggs into a bowl. "Fried or scrambled?"

"I'm just going to have this *placek*," I said.

"You don't eat enough to keep a bird alive," Brenda said, but I knew she wouldn't force feed me, either.

"Scrambled, please," Richard said, grabbing a piece of the paper.

"How come we're not eating those hardboiled eggs we did Friday?" I asked.

"They're just to look at," Brenda said.

"It's a waste not to eat them. I could make deviled eggs after Mass."

"Okay, but I want to take a picture of them first. Richard, where's our camera?"

Richard's nose was buried in the newspaper. "It's around here somewhere. I'll find it later."

Brenda nodded toward Richard, her eyes nearly bulging. I frowned, not comprehending. "The present," she mouthed.

I nodded. "Uh, Rich. You got a minute?"

I waited for him to put the paper down—at least ten seconds. He seemed impatient.

"Now that all this stuff about the murder is more or less over, I wanted to thank you for helping me out, carting me around, being patient, and a good brother, and all that crap."

Okay, so I'm not much of a speechmaker. I took the tissue-wrapped packet from my pocket, handed it to him.

He blinked at me. "You shouldn't have," he said automatically.

"It's not much. Just something I thought you might like."

Puzzled, he studied my face for a long moment. Brenda came up behind him, watching. He fumbled with the wrapping and pulled the beaded chain from the tissue.

"Ivory's not politically correct any more, but what the hell."

"It's a rosary, isn't it?" Brenda said.

"It belonged to our mother. Your father gave it to her. It meant a lot to her."

He stared at it for a long time, his expression unreadable. He ran his thumb over the beads. "I never had anything of hers. I don't even have a photo of her."

I reached over, clapped him on the shoulder. "Well, now you've got something. I think I can dig up a picture, too."

"It's beautiful," he managed, voice husky.

"I should've given it to you years ago. I mean, it came from your father, not mine. For whatever it's worth, I know she loved him a lot. She loved you a lot, too."

"Thank you." He cleared his throat, his watery eyes still fixed on the rosary.

"Happy Easter, Rich."

WE WERE LATE. THE HAM was in the oven and I already had my coat on, when Richard remembered the candy he'd bought Brenda two days before. I didn't mind the delay. If we missed the beginning of the Mass, it wouldn't be a tragedy.

Richard had the Lincoln waiting in the driveway when Brenda and I came out of the house. As usual, I got in the back seat. A funny feeling crept through me as I fastened my seat belt and the car started down the drive.

"Wait a minute, Rich."

He braked. "You forget something?"

"Something's not right." I looked up and down the street, but I didn't know what to look for. Tire tracks gouged the lawn in front of the hedge. Was my unease tied to the car that nearly hit me—could've killed me—the night before?

"We're already late," Brenda reminded us.

Something lurked nearby. Something....

"Okay," I said. "Let's go."

He started off toward Main Street. I couldn't shake the feeling that I should be wary, but I didn't know why and tried to ignore it.

"Did you read the newspaper article on the Basilica, Jeffy?" Brenda asked.

"Nope. Don't know a thing about it."

"It's called Our Lady of Victory Basilica," Richard said. "Only a few cities in the U.S. are so graced by a basilica."

"So how did one end up in Lackawanna?" I asked.

"It was built with the pennies of Polish immigrants back in the nineteen twenties," Richard lectured, "and was the dream of Father Nelson H. Baker, who headed the Homes of Charity. An orphanage, home for unwed mothers—that kind of stuff. He wanted to build a shrine to the Blessed Virgin."

"Kinda snowballed, huh?" I said.

"A basilica is one step up from a cathedral," he agreed. "Anyway, since building a big church isn't a miracle, the Vatican couldn't make him a saint, which is what the locals wanted, so he was posthumously given the title of Apostle of Charity. Decades after his death, he's still revered."

"Did you make all that up?" Brenda asked, giving him the fish-eye.

"No. I went online and read it."

Brenda scowled. "Sounds more like you memorized it for a sixth-grade oral report."

"She's just astounded at your phenomenal memory, Rich."

"Naturally," he agreed as we stopped for a red light. Traffic was light, but I looked around anyway, searching for…I don't know what. I still had that uneasy feeling in my gut. Probably the *placek*.

We arrived at the Basilica about fifteen minutes late for the Mass. The church's large parking area was full on Christianity's number one holy day, so we left the car on the street. The rain had ended, but the skies were still threatening. Braving the gloom, we walked the block or so and entered the main entrance.

The Basilica was packed. The fire marshals would've had a field day if they made a spot inspection. The pews, and every square inch of floor space, were jammed. To sit, we should've arrived an hour or more before the Mass.

I felt dwarfed by the soaring ceiling overhead, awed by the church's grandeur and sense of holiness. The newspaper hadn't exaggerated the amount of gilding, frescoes, and stained glass that seemed to decorate every square inch of walls and ceiling. Life-sized marble statues representing the stations of the cross lined the right and left aisles. The choir was situated somewhere high above us, at the back of the church, sounding like the proverbial heavenly host, and accompanied by a magnificent pipe organ. An usher bustled us down the left aisle, directing us to stop under the station of the cross titled: "Jesus Meets His Afflicted Mother."

"Wow, this place is gorgeous," Brenda whispered, and received a stern shush from Richard.

The singing stopped and the priest began to speak. I studied the altar and the oversized statue of Our Lady of Victory, her arm wrapped protectively around Jesus, depicted as a small boy. It reminded me of little Jackie…or Jimmy. No one had protected him from the terrors of life.

The priest droned on. It would take a long time just to get through Communion. Coming here had not been a good idea.

The air was close. I started to feel claustrophobic. As the choir broke into song, the woman beside me dropped her umbrella. I stooped to pick it up when a sharp ping sent marble shards flying from the mantle only inches from my head. I whirled to see Sharon Walker sixty feet from me across the church. Still dressed in the grubby jogging suit and a lavender ski jacket, her arms were extended in front of her, clasping a handgun, her eyes feral.

The muzzle flashed and Richard shoved me, knocking me into the woman beside me.

The choir still sang as bedlam erupted. Worshipers screamed, crashing into each other, struggling to escape. Sharon shouldered her way through the panicked crowd, heading for the back exit.

Stunned, I looked around. Richard was on his back, his beige raincoat stained scarlet. Brenda jerked with his tie, fumbling to open his shirt. "Call 911," she screamed. "Call 911!"

I fell to my knees. "Rich?"

"She must've followed us—" he gasped, already deathly pale. "Don't let her…get away."

Torn, I didn't know what to do. The singing had stopped, replaced by terrified screams reverberating around the vaulted ceiling.

"Brenda'll take care of me. Go!" Richard said.

His fingers clutched our mother's rosary. I gave his hand a squeeze and pulled away.

Then I was on my feet—smashing into people, pushing past them, heading for where I'd last seen Sharon, relying entirely on my newly awakened sixth sense.

She hadn't gotten away. People jammed the exit to the parking lot, but I turned left, away from the crowd, heading down the stairs and into the church basement.

Sharon had bypassed the bottleneck upstairs, planning to cut through the warren of rooms under the main floor and get out the Basilica's front entrance. I had to stop her. Not because the police wouldn't eventually catch up with her—but because she'd shot my brother. If he died, I'd kill her myself—my own brand of justice.

I had nothing left to lose. I was tired of being a victim.

Dodging into the open doorway, I took in the rows of pews that faced a lectern in the large white empty space.

No Sharon.

I ducked to the right into the ladies' room.

No one.

I didn't check the stalls—I'd lived with her aura for weeks. I could almost smell her.

The door at the far end of the long corridor was closed—locked? She was trapped.

What about her gun? In westerns, a handgun held six rounds. What make did she have? How much ammo did it carry? She'd fired twice. Was it a semi-automatic? Did she have a full clip?

A sign over the open doorway read: Father Baker's Rooms. I crossed the threshold, the floor changing from white ceramic tiles to dated green-and-yellow asphalt squares. The bedlam upstairs masked my movements. I was close—the hairs on the back of my neck acting like radar.

"Give it up, Sharon! I've already been to the police. They know you were blackmailing Matt. They know about the lab report. They know Jackie is Rob's son, not Matt's."

"Liar!"

Bang!

I ducked behind the wall. Now all I had to do was keep her talking until the police arrived. For all I cared, they could take her out with a SWAT team.

"You told Matt you named your son John Matthew after him because he promised to help you with expenses. In return, you said you wouldn't tell his wife. But something went wrong. He told you he wouldn't give you any more money."

"He owed us—he was Jackie's father."

"Grandfather!" I corrected.

Bang. Another shot slammed the mahogany woodwork.

"You're bluffing! You have no proof!"

"I know about the letter from the lab that tested Jackie's hair. The cops know, too."

Bang!

"And they know about Claudia. You figured with her out of the way, Jackie would get his fair share of Matt's estate. You wanted Matt's money."

"He owed it to us. He ruined our business."

"You ruined it with bad management."

Silence.

I tried another tack. "You followed me here."

"Damn right!"

"How'd you find me?"

"Rob's brother-in-law is a cop. He tapped into the DMV files for your address."

Bastard.

"You did everything right until today. I knew you killed Sumner, so you came after me. But you were stupid to try it in such a public place."

"Shut up!"

Bang.

Five down. What if she had another clip? Dumb move. If I was smart, I'd just wait her out—I had all the time in the world.

But Richard didn't.

All that blood....

My anger flared. "You shot my brother, you stupid bitch."

"Like I care. I've got nothing to lose."

"What about your son?"

No answer. She hadn't considered the boy. Maybe she never had. She'd killed Sumner in front of little Jackie.

Realization hit: the woman was crazy. Not temporarily deranged, as defense attorneys love to claim, but certifiably insane. I'd touched her madness the day before and never even recognized it.

"You tried to run me down last night, didn't you?"

No answer.

"You played right into Rob's hands. Did he tell you to come after me?"

"What're you talking about?"

"Rob told you about me, knowing you'd try some asshole stunt. He wanted you to get caught."

"Rob cares about me—he loves me."

"Then why'd he marry Linda? Why didn't he tell Matt that Jackie was his son? How come he's never helped you raise the boy? Because he doesn't give a shit about you or his kid!"

Silence.

Then it hit me: Sharon had only ever loved one person. Someone who'd loved her in return.

"What would your father say about all you've done?"

Her anger rose—I could feel it.

"He was so proud of you. But you let his company fail. Then you tried to save it by sleeping with your fiancé's father. You got knocked up by Rob, and told his father the child was his. When he found out the truth, he cut off the money. So you murdered him—right in front of Jackie!"

"Shut up!"

"Then when I found out, you tried to kill me, but you botched it by missing me and shooting someone else—in front of hundreds of witnesses. Now you're trying for thirds. Stupid, stupid, stupid!"

"Shut the fuck up!"

"It's a good thing Jim Walker's already dead, because this would've killed him!"

She fired six times.

The hammer clicked onto an empty chamber.

I flew into the side corridor, tackling her, slamming her onto the spotless floor as she struggled to reload.

The gun went skittering.

She dived for it, dragging me with her.

Though shorter than me, she was stronger, with two good arms. I grappled to hang on, but her legs flailed and she clipped me on the jaw. Stars exploded before my eyes. I couldn't let her get that gun, but I was tiring. She kicked me loose and scrambled for the gun.

Sirens wailed. Police or ambulance?

On my knees, I dove for her back as she scooped up the gun. Grabbing a fistful of her short hair, I body slammed her—smashed her face-first into the floor. Blood spattered the gaudy tiles and she wailed, struggling to buck me loose.

I rammed her skull against the floor again and again, running on autopilot until her struggles subsided. She lay still, panting, as blood puddled around her battered face. I grabbed her gun, checked the clip.

Reloaded.

I staggered to my feet, wiping sweat from my eyes. My broken arm ached and I swayed, afraid I'd pass out.

Running footsteps thundered. A uniformed cop popped into the open doorway, his service revolver aimed right at my face.

"Freeze! Put the gun on the floor. Now!"

With exaggerated care, I did as he said.

"Flat on the ground!" he ordered.

It took no persuasion—my knees buckled. Seconds later, he had me spread-eagled on the floor, patting me down. He wrenched my arm.

"Watch it, it's broken! I'm wearing a brace. She shot my brother upstairs. She killed Matt Sumner."

"Shut up!"

More running footsteps—the rest of the troops had arrived. I closed my eyes.

TWENTY-FOUR

BY THE TIME THE uniforms had taken me back upstairs, my hands were bound with the heavy plastic strips cops now use instead of handcuffs. The ambulance bearing my brother had already left. A beefy patrolman shoved me into the first pew.

No one knew anything about Richard. No one would tell me anything. Hayden was on his way. The church had been cleared, with witnesses being interviewed elsewhere. Another team of paramedics had arrived and departed, carting Sharon away, accompanied by a police escort.

I hadn't been in a fight since my high school days. I'd never hit a woman. I'd been determined to prevent her from ever hurting anyone else—so why did I now feel so ashamed?

Sharon's bloodied face, twisted with anger, was such a contrast to that of the statue of Our Lady of Victory, which towered above the church's gilded, ornate altar. Some unknown sculptor had captured in stone the embodiment of true compassion. I prayed to the Virgin in an endless litany, *Don't let Rich die. Please don't let Rich die.*

"Strange to see you without your other half," Hayden said from behind me.

I turned and glared at him. "She shot him. Now are you convinced I was right?"

Hayden had the decency to look embarrassed.

I steeled myself to ask the next question. "Is my brother still alive?"

Hayden looked grim. "He was when they left here."

"Thanks," I said. At least he was being straight with me.

"Can you take these off? I only beat up the bitch, I'm not planning to hurt anyone else."

"Did a number on her, too, I hear. Thompson!" Hayden called, and the uniformed cop came over and removed the restraints. Hayden sat beside me on the pew. "Tell me about it."

I did.

"Well, the witnesses confirm she shot your brother. After they finish with her at the hospital, she'll be booked. Then we'll look into the rest of it. Here," he handed me a set of keys. "One of the patrolmen gave them to me. The black lady with your brother asked him to see that you got them."

I stared at Brenda's ring with keys to the house and both cars. Richard's Lincoln was still parked on one of the side streets.

"Thanks."

"They took him to ECMC," Hayden said.

"Where?"

"Erie County Medical Center. Used to be called Meyer Memorial."

I nodded. "I know the place."

"You can give us a detailed statement tomorrow." He clapped me on the back, a gesture that almost resembled friendship. "I know where to find you, right?"

"Yeah, right."

Hugging my broken arm, I got up and headed for the back entrance.

A block from the church, I found Sharon's station wagon. The little boy was asleep on the back seat, his tear-streaked face at peace. He didn't know his mother would never come for him.

The driver's side door was unlocked. I opened it, poked my head inside. "Hey, partner."

The boy blinked awake, unafraid of me. "Go away."

"Remember me, sport?"

"You're the bad man who wants to hurt my Mommy."

"That was a misunderstanding. Do you know any policemen?"

He shook his head.

"I know a cop who'd love to meet you. He's got a shiny badge. Want to see it?"

He shrugged.

I offered him my hand.

The boy looked at the empty driver's seat. "My Mommy's not coming back. Is she?"

"Not right now."

The boy looked back at my outstretched hand. His eyes had a dull cast to them. He'd seen more of life than a kid his age should. Reluctantly he took my hand.

We walked in silence to the Basilica. One of the uniformed officers recognized me and let me cross the police line again. We entered the cavernous church. The detective spoke with the priest in front of the main altar.

The kid held my hand tightly while I spoke to Hayden, cowed by the building's size and grandeur. The pitch of his fear was familiar—I'd been living with it for weeks.

I crouched down in front of him. "Jimmy, Detective Hayden will take you downtown. You'll be okay."

"Where's my Mommy?"

I looked up at Hayden, who towered over us. "Don't worry, kid," the burly man said, "we're taking care of her. Did the Easter Bunny visit your house today?"

The boy shook his head.

"Well, he came to the police station, and I think he left something there for you."

With Sharon's son in good hands, I once again headed for the exit. It was then I saw the rack of row upon row of dancing candlelight. I turned for it and thought of Richard. I'm not religious, but right then I needed God on my side.

My throat tightened as I stuffed money into the slot in the brass box. My hand trembled as I lit the candle. I watched it flicker and steady before I turned and started for the car without a backward glance.

I retrieved Richard's Lincoln and struggled to remember the way to ECMC. I got lost and had to stop at a mini-mart to ask directions. Once there, I parked the car in the hospital lot. I'd been eager to drive, but not under these circumstances. I yanked the keys from the ignition, pocketed them, and sat with my fingers wrapped around the steering wheel. Would Richard ever drive it again? I'd only just found my brother. What would I do without him?

I was wasting time, yet fear kept me from moving. Brenda was alone. She probably needed me…I knew I needed her.

I hadn't needed anyone for years.

I got out, locked the door, and went in search of her.

The emergency room wasn't crowded—major mayhem seemed to be taking a holiday on this most holy day. I found Brenda sitting alone in the far corner of the waiting room, my mother's rosary beads wrapped around her fingers. She saw me and stood. After a quick embrace, she pulled back.

"How's Rich?"

"They had a hard time stabilizing him—he lost a lot of blood. There was a closer hospital, but they said it was better to bring him here. They're more experienced with gunshot injuries." Her voice was so quiet, so lost.

I motioned for her to sit, and she took her seat once more. She bit her lip. "I'm scared, Jeffy. I'm a nurse and I know everything that can go wrong."

I reached for her hand. "You know they'll do everything they can." I was quiet for a moment. "He's going to make it."

"You know this for sure?" she asked.

I couldn't lie to her. "No."

She fingered the rosary beads. "I'll have to seriously rethink this marriage business. I've lived with your brother for seven years. I know him as well as I know myself. But when he came in here, I was nothing more than a friend. I'm a nurse, and they won't tell me anything. His blood is under my fingernails, and they won't tell me anything."

"Well, they'd better tell me."

I got up, headed for the information desk, with Brenda tagging along behind me.

The receptionist wasn't helpful. Having a different last name than the patient was not an asset. I'm surprised she didn't ask for a blood sample for DNA analysis before one of the nurses took pity on us. She made a phone call and found out Richard had been taken to surgery only minutes earlier. Being short-staffed because of the holiday, the surgeon hadn't had time to come out and speak with us. The bullet had ripped through Richard's right lung, causing vascular damage.

"Why don't you go upstairs to the surgical waiting room?"

A TV crew barged through the emergency room entrance. Brenda's eyes widened in panic.

"Is there a way—?"

"They know the drill," the nurse said, eyeing the cameraman. "They're not allowed anywhere near the surgical unit."

Brenda and I followed her directions to the third floor, which was even more quiet than the emergency room. The two of us had the small room to ourselves and settled in for a long wait.

We took turns sitting, pacing, sitting. We didn't talk much. The TV bolted on the wall was tuned to CNN, the newscaster's voice an annoying monotone. I couldn't turn it off, so I hit the mute button and occasionally glanced at the news in mime.

Over and over I relived those terrible seconds at the church. Sharon Walker's skill with a handgun equaled her skill with a bow. If I hadn't stooped to pick up that stupid umbrella, she would've nailed me with the first shot. At least then Richard wouldn't have had to suffer for my…what? Stupidity? Stubbornness?

Please don't die on me, Rich.

Time dragged.

After the first hour, the numbness around my brain cells wore thin. I hunched over on the uncomfortable couch, my thoughts going in circles.

Exactly four weeks ago it had been me in a hospital emergency room. For four days I was a comatose John Doe. No one had worried about me. No one had known. No one had cared.

Four scant weeks ago, my brother had been a stranger. Now I could only grieve for the wasted years when I'd rebuffed his gestures of friendship.

You can't die on me, Rich. You just can't.

I never believed in fate, but the random pattern of my life didn't seem so random any more. Was it preordained that I return to Buffalo? Was it inevitable that crime should continue to touch my life? Shelley murdered by a drug dealer; me beaten and left for dead by a couple of crackheads; Richard shot by a murderer I was chasing. My life's path seemed to follow a downward spiral. If the pattern continued, then Richard was as good as dead.

No!

I looked across the small room at Brenda. Lost in her own thoughts, her gaze was vacant, her eyes haunted. She and Richard had shown me such generosity. Richard had shoved me aside—taking the bullet meant for me. I swallowed a pang of grief. It took me thirty-five years and this tragedy to make me realize how much I needed—loved—my brother.

Anger raged through me. Why hadn't I been warned about this? What good was this psychic crap if it didn't work for me? Sophie said good would come of it. Yeah, then why was Richard being punished?

Some cosmic force had brought me back home, had shown me Sumner's death, compelled me to find the murderer, and I never had a clue or a vision or even a funny feeling that Richard could be in any danger because of it. Sumner was a liar and a cheat. Why was it so important that I find his killer, risking my brother in the process?

Brenda got up, wandered over to the window. She peeked through the slats in the narrow blinds, her expression placid. "You know," she said, breaking the quiet. "Richard wouldn't volunteer at a women's clinic because of the potential for violence. Instead, he gets shot in church. Does that make any sense?"

I let out a shaky breath. "It's all my fault. If I'd never come back here, this wouldn't have happened."

Her eyes flashed. "Jeffy, don't do this to yourself. You made Richard happy. He hasn't been happy for a long time."

"You could've fooled me. He's been preoccupied, depressed—"

"He was worse before you came home. Now he wants to go back to work. He's talking to lawyers about unloading some of that money. He's getting back to being his old self— the man I fell in love with. It's because of you. Can't you see how special you are? What you mean to him—to us?"

No. I couldn't.

The minutes dragged.

Four o'clock.

Five o'clock.

I was about to swear that time had absolutely stood still when an Amazon of a nurse, dressed in surgical scrubs, approached. Her expression was sour, no-nonsense, and short on compassion. Brenda and I were instantly on our feet.

"We had another gunshot emergency," the nurse said succinctly. "Doctor Elliott had to go directly back into surgery. He asked me to speak with you. Mr. Alpert came through the surgery well. His vital signs are good and he's in recovery now."

"Can we see him?" I asked.

She looked directly at me. "Next of kin only."

Brenda's gaze shifted. "That would be you."

"No." I grabbed her hand. "We're family. We're going in together and no one's going to stop us."

The nurse straightened to her full height. "You want to tell that to security?"

Brenda shook her head, her eyes filling with tears. "You're wasting time, Jeffy. Just go!"

I clutched her hand, experienced the conflicting emotions roiling through her.

The nurse heaved an exaggerated sigh, and I realized her gruffness was only a facade. "Okay, both of you. But only for a minute." She pointed her finger right in my face. "One. Minute." She turned on her heel.

Hand in hand, Brenda and I jogged to catch up with her.

I'd never been in a recovery room before, never seen anyone fresh out of surgery. Swathed in a sea of white sheets, Richard looked ghastly, his skin tinged an odd green. Startled, I paused. Brenda's grip on my hand tightened—she pulled me closer to the gurney. A cardiac monitor beeped in rhythm with his heart. IV bags hung overhead.

My stomach tightened. This was me, four weeks before.

As though sensing our approach, a groggy Richard opened his eyes.

"My two favorite people," he rasped. We both reached for his hand. He captured one or two fingers from each of us.

"How do you feel?" Brenda whispered.

"Horrible."

"You'll be okay," I said, trying to keep my voice from cracking. "The shoe's on the other foot. When you get home, I can bully you around."

"Don't even think about it."

My throat tightened. Sorrow and remorse threatened to choke me. "Why'd you do it, Rich? Why'd you shove me aside and make yourself a target?"

He squeezed my fingers ever so slightly. "You're my kid brother…I couldn't let her hurt you." His eyes closed and he was asleep.

Brenda and I hung around the hospital for another three hours until Richard was taken to his room—the best in the hospital—and sleeping peacefully.

We took the elevator downstairs, exited, and walked straight into a mob of reporters with video and still cameras.

"Give us a quote!"

"What's your relationship with Sharon Walker?"

"No comment," I said, pushing Brenda through the crowd.

I thought we'd successfully left them behind when a voice called out, "Jeff Resnick!"

I turned: Sam Nielsen, his eyes bright with anticipation, waited.

Though I might regret it, I made my decision. "Give me an hour to shower and eat, Sam. I'll call you at your office."

"Exclusive," he demanded.

"Yeah." I turned, took Brenda's arm, and guided her away.

The clouds were gone, the crescent moon a slash of pure white light in the cold, dark sky. We pulled up our collars against the cold and, hand-in-hand, headed for Richard's car.